C000089194

Only You

A Standalone Romance

K.T. Quinn

CONTEMPORARY ROMANCE

Copyright © 2021 K.T. Quinn

All rights reserved. No part of this publication may be reproduced, distributed, or transmitted in any form without prior consent of the author.

Edited by Robin Morris and Gail Gentry

Follow me on social media to stay up-to-date on new releases, announcements, and prize giveaways!

www.ktquinn.com

Books By
K.T. Quinn

Only You

Make You Mine

Yours Forever

1

Molly

The Day It All Started

"Where the hell is the tour guide?" I muttered to myself.

I'd been pacing around the hotel lobby for twenty minutes. The tour guide was supposed to meet me *here*, inside the lobby. Part of me was afraid I had missed him, but I had come down early just to avoid that possibility. He was late.

After an eight-hour flight to Italy, I was anxious to get out there and see the city. I didn't want to wait anymore!

I walked by the concierge desk, but nobody was there. I could hear him in the back room, fervently discussing something in Italian with the other hotel employees. There was some new flu strain here in Europe, apparently. I saw a news bulletin about it while waiting for my luggage in the airport, but of course it was in Italian so I could barely understand what was going on.

I paced across the lobby, turned around, then paced back. The whole point of me flying to Rome a day before my girlfriends was to do some sight-seeing alone. The Colosseum, the Roman Forum, the Trevi Fountain, and the Spanish Steps.

Don't get me wrong: my girlfriends were great. I loved them.

But they were a lot to handle. They wanted to guzzle wine and flirt with every sexy Italian man they came across. To them, the ancient history of Rome was just that: ancient history.

But me? I actually *liked* history. I wanted to go on tours and listen to what the tour guide explained! If I could do that once by myself, then I would be fine with letting loose with the girls when they arrived.

If my tour guide ever showed up...

I scanned the lobby. The Residencia Al Gladiatore hotel was older than most American cities. The lobby had marble floors and white columns, with a fountain in the middle of the room that gently poured water from a Roman statue. The ceiling was domed, with plenty of glass to let in natural light. It was beautiful and ornate, and most importantly: it was just two blocks from the Colosseum itself.

There were only three other people in the lobby. An older couple was standing by the entrance with their luggage, waiting on a taxi to take them to the airport. Then there was a guy sitting in a chair by the front door. He looked like your stereotypical Italian hunk: olive skin, thick black hair, the right amount of scruff along his jaw. A chest that was broad enough to eat dinner on.

Too sexy to be my tour guide, I thought. Tour guides were always nerdy, or perky, or nerdy *and* perky. This guy had a dark, brooding look about him.

The man's shoulder and arm muscles pressed tightly against his polo shirt as he glanced at his watch. Then he saw me looking at him. He smiled briefly before returning to whatever he was reading on his phone.

Nope. Definitely not the guide.

I looked at my watch and tried to relax. Maybe the tour was running late. It was a walking tour, after all, and they probably had to stop at every hotel along the way to pick up the other tour members.

After a few more minutes of pacing, I rang the bell at the concierge desk. He emerged from the back room looking flustered.

"Yes, miss?" he asked in a thick Italian accent.

"Have you seen my tour guide? He was supposed to meet me in the lobby half an hour ago."

He gave me an apologetic look. "I am so sorry, we do not have any contact with the guides. Please call them directly if you have any concerns."

He hurried into the back room, then began shouting at someone in Italian. There was a lot of commotion, with several voices chiming in, the tones tense and sentences short. They sounded afraid.

I pulled out my phone and went through my contacts, then stopped myself. Even now, it was as automatic as breathing: when something was wrong, I called my mom. But I couldn't call her now, no matter how much I wanted to.

Instead, I did as the concierge suggested: I looked up the tour phone number and called them. A woman answered in Italian.

"Parla inglese?" I asked. "Do you speak English?"

"*No,*" the woman replied. Hold music took over the line.

I tapped my foot while listening. I was tired. I was jet-lagged from the overnight flight. I hadn't showered or fixed my hair, because I didn't think I had enough time before the tour.

I wanted to see the city, damnit!

"*Hi, hello?*" a man answered. "*I am to speak the English with you now?*"

"Yes! Hi!" I replied. "My name's Molly Carter, and I'm waiting at the Residencia Al Gladiatore hotel for my tour guide. He was supposed to be here thirty minutes ago."

"*Yes, I am so sorry, yes, please wait. I am looking the records now. Ah. Yes! Your guide is there now! He is waiting for you!*"

I gazed around the lobby. "I'm standing in the lobby. I don't see anyone with a tour guide uniform."

"*Uniform? Ah, no, there is no uniform,*" the man replied. "*He is, ah, normal dressed, yes? Blue shirt. Jeans pants."*

I glanced at the guy sitting by the front door. "Blue shirt? Black hair?"

"Yes! Black hair! And, ah, hair on his face."

"A beard?"

"A beard! Yes!"

"You have got to be kidding me," I said.

"No, I am quite serious! Do you see him? He is there..."

I hung up and strode across the lobby to the guy. Blue polo. Jeans. Black hair, and short-cropped beard. This was the guy all right. I stopped in front of him and crossed my arms.

"Do you speak English?" I asked.

Despite his dark features, his eyes were steel-grey, like storm clouds above a restless ocean. He blinked them at me and said, "Uh, yes?"

I hesitated. This was the kind of guy my girlfriends wanted to meet on the trip. Tall, dark, and handsome. Maybe thirty years old. Broad shoulders, wide chest, muscles that were *strong* but not too bulky.

He gazed up at me with curiosity, with the tiniest hint of a smile on his lips. There was a tour pamphlet on his lap. The same tour I was taking. That confirmed it for me.

"I've been waiting here for thirty minutes," I said.

"So have I," he replied in a deep voice. He didn't have any trace of an accent.

I gritted my teeth with annoyance. "I've been pacing back and forth. I even made eye contact with you earlier, but you didn't come up to me."

He tilted his head slightly. "You didn't come up to me, either."

"This is unbelievable." I took a deep breath. "Well? Are you just

7

going to sit there?"

"Honestly? I'm not sure what else to do," he replied. His English was *very* good. He sounded American. That infuriated me even more.

I let out an annoyed groan.

And how did this guy react? He *laughed* at me.

He chuckled like it was all a joke to him.

I knew this kind of guy. A guy who had skated through life thanks to his handsome face and the sexy stubble on his jaw. The kind of guy who expected women to melt into a puddle the moment he flashed his sizzling smile, the same one he was giving me now. It *almost* worked on me.

Almost.

I pointed a finger down at his face. "Listen. I didn't fly around the world just to get laughed at by a cut-rate tour guide."

"Tour guide?"

"Yes, tour guide! I just called the office. I came here to get away from my problems, and all I wanted was to tour the city before my friends arrived, and you're sitting around like it's my fault..."

I trailed off as someone tapped me on the shoulder. He was a portly middle-aged man, with a light-blue shirt and jeans. He had a black beard that ran halfway down his chest.

"Buongiorno!" he said in an Italian accent. "You must be Miss Carter, yes? I am sorry for the lateness, but I have had to give an explanation to every member of the tour. We will not be touring the city today, I am afraid. The Colosseo is closed, as well as many of the other public sites. The mayor is preparing to issue a curfew order. Of course you will receive a full refund for the tour, do not worry."

I glanced back at the guy sitting in the chair. He was smiling smugly at me. And he managed to look sexy doing it, which made it worse. My stomach turned to liquid as I realized my mistake.

This is embarrassing.

2

Donovan

The Day I Got Yelled At

This is hilarious, I thought while the girl went off on me. *She's pissed about something.*

I listened to her and answered her interrogation with honest answers, yet it didn't appease her.

"I've been pacing back and forth," she went on. "I even made eye-contact with you earlier, but you didn't come up to me."

Wait a minute. Was she upset that I didn't hit on her? This woman expected me to walk up and flirt with her just because we made eye-contact?

I knew girls like this. Girls who expected to get *whatever* they wanted by showing a little bit of cleavage and smiling at whoever was in their way. And when they *didn't* get their way, they pouted or threw a temper tantrum.

Don't get me wrong. She was a sexy little thing. An oval face, silky black hair, and as many curves underneath her sun dress as a Roman aqueduct. But I had better things to do with my last few hours in Rome before I flew home.

She stood there, waiting for some sort of answer with her hands on her hips. I didn't know what else to do except defend myself by telling her she didn't come up to me either.

It was the truth, but it seemed to infuriate her. She let out a sound like an annoyed cat, which made me chuckle.

Which was the *wrong* response to give this girl.

She aimed a pink fingernail at my face and said, "Listen. I didn't fly around the world just to get laughed at by a cut-rate tour guide."

I blinked. "Tour guide?" Suddenly it started to make a little more sense. She thought I was someone else. Probably the same tour I was waiting for.

I tried to quickly explain the misunderstanding, but she kept going off on me. All I could do was sit there and suffer her tirade while trying not to set her off by smiling again.

The *actual* tour guide picked that moment to come through the lobby doors and tap her on the shoulder. He spoke to her, calling her Miss Carter, but I was barely listening because I was trying to hold my laughter in.

She turned back to me, her plump lips parted slightly with an embarrassed look on her face.

"Do you yell at every guy minding their own business in the hotel lobby?" I asked.

"Only you," she said curtly. Then, without another word, she stormed away from us and disappeared into the elevator.

The tour guide sighed, then turned to me. "Buongiorno, Mr. Russo?"

I stood and held up the tour pamphlet. "That's me. Did you say the tour has been canceled?"

He gave me a sad smile. "I am afraid so. Everything in the city is closing early today, by order of the mayor. Of course you will be given a full refund, or a chance to rebook with us at a later date."

"Today's my last day in Rome, so I'll take the refund." I glanced at my watch. "Is it that serious? The virus, or whatever?"

"It appears so. I am terribly sorry for the inconvenience, sir..."

I shrugged. "Not your fault."

After he left, I made a phone call to the airline. There was a long hold line, but then I got through to a customer service representative. My flight was delayed until further notice.

Well, shit.

Not only that, but it looked like all flights were being grounded. The Italian Prime Minister was speaking that evening, and everyone expected him to announce a full lockdown. It was getting *bad*.

I'd heard stories about the virus. It had made its way across Asia and was springing up in Northern Italy. I'd been too busy in the last week to pay much attention to it, though. I assumed it would blow over, like SARS or the bird flu or all the other scares over the past decade. But if flights were being grounded...

A shiver went up my spine.

I wasn't much of a long-term planner. I grew up moving from army base to army base every two years, so I never had a *chance* to think ahead. By the time I made plans, dad would uproot us and I'd have to start all over from scratch.

But when it came to the short-term, I was a man of action. Building a shed? I could sit down and create a building plan in minutes. Road trip? Give me a map and I'd plan the perfect route.

Stuck in Italy during a pandemic? Better load up on supplies before shit *really* hit the fan.

I checked my wallet. I still had plenty of Euros. There were several markets within walking distance of the hotel, and a big grocery store two miles away. Good thing I had splurged on a hotel room with a stove. I could cook my own food if need be.

I went outside, forgetting all about the pissed off girl who had been berating me just minutes before.

3

Molly

The Day The Lockdown Began

I forgot all about the guy I had mistakenly berated when my friend Sara called me.

"What do you mean, your flight is canceled?" I asked.

"*It's not just our flight,*" she replied. "*It's all flights! Everything going in and out of Rome is canceled. It's the same for most of Italy, I think. It has to do with that new virus.*"

"I thought it was isolated to that area by the Swiss border," I replied. "My travel agent told me it wouldn't affect my trip!"

"*Why did you leave a day early?*" Sara complained. "*If you had been on our flight this wouldn't have happened...*"

"I don't know." My throat tightened. "What am I supposed to do without you? I was really looking forward to this trip."

"*I know. This sucks. We're going to be checking in to see if our flight gets rescheduled. I have to go. I'll let you know if anything changes. I miss you, Molls!*"

"Miss you too."

I sat on the bed and sighed. The urge to feel sorry for myself was overwhelming. It had been one bad thing after another this year. No matter how hard I tried, I just couldn't win. Not even on my vacation.

"Forget that," I said out loud. "I'm here. I'm the lucky one who got to arrive before everyone else! I'm going to enjoy the city by myself."

Even though the Colosseum was closed, I could still walk to it and admire it from the outside. Not to mention exploring the rest of the city. It was close to lunchtime now, so getting some delicious Italian food sounded like a great way to brighten my mood. I put my shoes back on and took the elevator back down to the lobby. Thankfully, the sexy guy I had yelled at was gone.

The concierge was behind the desk. I walked up to him and asked, "The man who was in the lobby earlier. Is he a guest at the hotel?"

"Mr. Russo? Yes, he has been a guest for the past week. I believe he is departing this evening."

I breathed a sigh of relief. At least I wouldn't run into him again. No matter *how* gorgeous he was, I dealt poorly with embarrassment. A second run-in might have literally killed me with awkwardness. Even just the thought of it made me cringe.

I shook it off and asked the concierge, "Can you recommend a good restaurant for lunch? Something within walking distance."

He winced. "I am sorry, but you are not allowed to leave the building."

The words were nonsense to me. "I'm not allowed to *what?*"

"The mayor has instituted a stay-at-home order," he said. "No one is allowed in public, unless they have urgent business."

"You have got to be kidding me. Because of the virus thing?"

"I am afraid so. When we have additional information, we will let you know. The Residencia Al Gladiatore is sorry for the inconvenience."

I looked around helplessly. "I was going to get lunch. What am I supposed to do now?"

He gestured to his right. "The hotel restaurant is one of the best in the city, I assure you."

I was too tired to argue, so I walked over to the restaurant. Nobody was inside except for a single host behind the bar. "Buongiorno," he said. "Unfortunately, our dining room is closed until further notice."

"But the concierge said this was where I could get food."

"Our kitchen is indeed open, but only for meals to-go. We can bring your order directly to your room."

I ordered the carbonara and went up to my room. When the food arrived it was room-temperature and tasted like it was reheated in the microwave.

I had a dozen bottles of wine on the spare bed, purchased in the duty-free section of the airport. I had expected them to only last a couple of nights with the girls, but since my friends were no longer coming I had them all to myself.

"Better get started," I said as I opened a bottle of red. "I'm on vacation, after all."

I turned on the TV and found a channel with English closed-captioning. Sure enough, all flights were grounded nationwide. The lockdowns weren't just isolated to Rome: the Italian Prime Minister was announcing a full quarantine beginning that evening across the country. The borders with France, Switzerland, Austria, and Slovenia were closed. Nobody was allowed in or out of the country.

"Holy crap..."

I listened numbly as they talked about strain variants and spread rates. I didn't understand a word, even with the English subtitles. It all went over my head. What I did understand was that they recommended everyone wash their hands with soap and water.

"Two happy birthdays?" I muttered while looking at my hands.

The longer I watched, a feeling of dread crept into my chest. This wasn't just a mild inconvenience to my vacation. This was *serious.*

The door to the adjacent room opened, then closed with a *thud.* I heard my hotel neighbor walk through the hotel room, thumping across the floor. Classical Italian music began playing from a speaker, drifting through the wall into my room. A few minutes later I smelled the delicious aroma of food being cooked. Tomato sauce, spices, and pork filled my hotel room through our conjoining door.

"At least someone's enjoying their stay," I muttered.

I watched TV for a few hours, then drifted off to sleep. The combination of jet lag and good red wine must have knocked me out, because the next thing I knew, fresh sunlight was streaming through the door to the balcony. It was morning, and I had slept for thirteen straight hours.

"Woo, vacation," I mumbled out loud.

I turned off the TV and decided to treat myself to a bubble bath. As soon as I sank into the scalding water, all the stress oozed out of my body. After a few minutes, I started feeling more like myself.

I found a news stream on my phone and let that play while I soaked. More information about the virus was getting out. It was respiratory, meaning it spread through the air. There was also a risk of transmitting it through items, like doorknobs or other objects handed back and forth, although experts didn't know how great the risk was. Everyone was urged to wear a mask when going out in public.

The phrase *global pandemic* was being used. It felt like the beginning of a horror movie.

And the symptoms of the virus itself... Let's just say I didn't want to get it, even though I was a healthy twenty-nine year old.

Ten minutes of listening to that made me glad I was holed up. It was safer to be here than walking around outside, potentially getting infected.

I called room service for breakfast. The bellhop who brought it to me was a skinny teenager wearing a scarf across his mouth. I quickly pulled my shirt up to cover my mouth too.

"I sorry for the food," he said in pretty good, although muffled, English. "The chef did not come in. The hotel is doing its best."

"If the chef isn't here, then who made the food?" I asked.

"The concierge. He is very good, I promise! I helped as well."

I tipped the boy and brought the food inside. I squirted a little bit of liquid soap into my hand and then rubbed it all over the outside of the metal room service dish. Then I removed the lid on the plate.

"Well, at least it's *something*," I muttered. I had come to Italy to eat delicious food. Instead I was making do with cold bread and jam, runny eggs, and lukewarm instant coffee.

My neighbor was making breakfast. Bacon or sausage, based on the smell wafting over to my room. Whoever they were, maybe they should go downstairs to run the restaurant.

I carried my food out onto the balcony so that I wouldn't have to smell my neighbor's food. It was also a beautiful day, and my balcony had a gorgeous view of the city. I could just see the top level of the Colosseum over the building to the right, and the plaza outside the hotel was spread out below me. When I had arrived yesterday, the plaza was crammed with people and street performers. Now it was completely empty.

Rome was one of the most visited tourist locations in the world, but now it was a ghost town. The emptiness gave the beautiful view an eerie pallor.

The loneliness of the city seeped into my mood and I felt very alone. It would have been better if my friends were here, because at least then we could go through it *together*. But by myself...

I reached for my phone, then stopped myself. I would have given anything to be able to text mom just then. She would have known what to say to make me feel better. She always did.

18

I ate my breakfast and tried to enjoy the strange, deserted view.

4

Molly

The Day We Traded

After breakfast, I called the airline to check on flights. I don't know what I expected, but everything was grounded until further notice. The man on the line was friendly and helpful, but he didn't know when that would change.

I brought a book with me for the flight, so I sat on the balcony in the sunshine while reading. I was able to enjoy that for a while, until dark clouds drifted across the sky in the afternoon along with a chilly wind that brought goosebumps to my skin, forcing me back inside.

At three, there was a noise outside in the hall. A shadow passed across the door, and then a note slid underneath into my room. I jumped out of bed and grabbed it. The words were hand-written on a piece of Residencia Al Gladiatore stationary:

Due to insufficient staffing, all hotel amenities are halted until further notice. Emergency supplies will be

provided every afternoon.

Flabbergasted by what I was reading, I threw open the door. The concierge was bending down to slide another note under the door next to mine.

"What does this mean?" I asked, waving the note.

He stood up stiffly and covered his mouth with a handkerchief. "I am quite sorry, but we do not have the staff available to provide even the most basic of services. The maids to clean the rooms, the cooks to run the restaurant... Everyone is obeying the stay-at-home order."

"Then what?" I demanded. "We're being abandoned here?"

"A box of supplies will be delivered to you every afternoon." He pointed to a small cardboard box on the ground next to my door. Another was sitting in front of my neighbor's door.

I picked up my box and opened the lid. Inside was half a sandwich wrapped in cellophane, a bag of potato chips, a biscotti cookie, a single-serving bottle of wine, and a plastic bottle of sparkling water. It looked like the kind of package you bought on an airplane for twenty dollars.

"This is it?" I asked. "I don't mean to sound demanding but... This is all I get to eat every day?"

The concierge looked around helplessly. His eyes settled on the vending machine next to the elevator. He rushed over to it, then used the keys on his belt to unlock the front panel. He gestured at the open machine.

"Please help yourself to anything in here as well." He turned to leave.

"Isn't there anywhere we can go?" I asked. "A bigger hotel that is staffed properly? *Somewhere?*"

The concierge hurried into the elevator. "I am sorry, but this is

21

all we can do for you. Please remain inside your room as much as possible! It is for your safety."

I groaned as I carried my box of supplies into the hotel room. There was a look in the concierge's eyes: genuine fear. The fact that *he* was afraid scared me more than anything else I had seen.

In the face of a global pandemic, my hierarchy of needs narrowed quickly. Forget the relaxing vacation with my friends, and forget eating delicious food at expensive restaurants. I had shelter. I had fresh water. I had food, as pitiful as it was. As long as they kept bringing these boxes, I would be okay. Even without them, I could live on the junk food in the vending machine for days. Maybe weeks.

Not a pleasant thought, but it was *something*.

"And most importantly, I have plenty of wine!" I said out loud, just to hear someone's voice.

I ate my meal even though it wasn't time for dinner yet. The sandwich was comprised of a thin slice of turkey and an even thinner slice of cheese. The bread was dry and tasteless, and the chips were stale.

Delicious smells drifted from next door. What were they making today? The same classical Italian music was playing, too. It felt romantic. It was probably a couple on their honeymoon.

I hope I don't have to hear them having sex.

The smell of pasta filled my room, making a mockery of the crappy lunch I'd had. My mouth watered and my stomach growled angrily.

To get away from the smell, I tied a T-shirt around my face as a mask and walked out to the vending machine. It had a good variety of chips and candy, but I was hungry for a *meal*.

With nothing else to do, I kept walking around. The gym was on our floor. Three treadmills and a rack of dumbbells. Taped to the door was a sign that said "CLOSED" in five different languages.

I didn't see any sign of life anywhere else on our floor. In fact, when I returned to my room I noticed there was a yellow sticky-note taped to the door with "OSPITE" written on it. According to Google, that means *guest* in Italian. They were probably marking the rooms that were occupied, so the boxes of food could be delivered. My room and the room next to mine were the only ones with sticky-notes on our floor.

Content that I had explored my surroundings, I went back into my room and celebrated by opening another bottle of wine.

I had experienced boredom before, but never like this. I was in Rome, damnit! Staying inside was torture. It felt like driving all the way to Disney World and then being told to stay in the car.

After two glasses of wine, my mind went to a dark place and I started playing the "I should have" game.

I should have flown out on the same flight as my friends, rather than a day early. Then I wouldn't be alone.

I should have stayed at a bigger resort hotel, rather than one so close to the Colosseum. Then I would have plenty of amenities.

I should have come years ago, with my parents.

After watching two hours of Seinfeld episodes dubbed in Italian, I finally worked up the courage to open the door connecting me to my neighbor's room. I was greeted with another door that only they could open from their end. There was about a foot of space in between.

I wanted to say hello to the neighbors. To experience all of this with someone else, rather than alone. And most of all I wanted to see if they would share their food.

I raised my hand to knock, then hesitated. The warnings I had seen on TV flashed in my head: stay at least six feet away from other people. Being in an enclosed space with other people was dangerous. They could spread the virus to me.

I went to the desk and scribbled a note on a piece of paper:

It's a ghost town on our floor. Have you seen any other guests up here?

I slid it under the door and waited. A few moments later, the music paused. I heard footsteps. Minutes passed, and then a reply note came back.

Only you.

Great. Thanks for the long, friendly reply, neighbor.

I almost left it at that, but the rumbling in my stomach was getting worse, and I didn't want to fill it with vending machine food. So I wrote another note.

I'll level with you. I'm starving, and the smell of food coming from your place is torture. Do you have a hot plate or something over there?

The reply came back quicker than before.

My room has a kitchenette. I bought supplies at the market right before the lockdown. You want some pasta? I have enough to share.

"Oh thank God," I whispered, before sending my reply.

Yes please! I'll trade you a bottle of wine!

After sending the note, I placed a bottle of wine in the partition space and closed the door. A few minutes later I heard the other door open. A note slipped underneath the door and I heard the door close again.

Come and get it.

Waiting for me inside the partition was a white bowl filled with pasta. I intended to send a thank-you note immediately, but the smell and sight of the pasta overwhelmed my senses, and I immediately sat on the carpet in front of the door and chowed down like a pig. The pasta was angel hair, with a cream sauce and bits of white chicken. Salty, peppery, savory, and creamy.

It tasted better than any pasta I'd ever had in my life, though I knew it was probably because I was hungry.

I read the notes while I ate. It looked like a man's handwriting, and based on the phrasing he was alone.

I wonder what my lockdown-neighbor looks like.

I sent him a thank-you note. His response came back within seconds.

Food for wine? I think I won this trade.

Happy and full, I suddenly didn't feel so alone anymore.

5

Molly

The Day I Made A Friend

I spent the next morning exploring the hotel. It was five stories, and we were on the third floor. The ground floor was deserted. Nobody was behind the desk. All the lights in the lobby were on, though, which made it *feel* like everything was normal. If I tried hard, I could pretend that the staff was having a meeting and would return at any moment.

The front doors which exited into the plaza were locked, and there was no way to unlock them from the inside without a key. I could have easily broken a window, but I decided I wasn't that stir-crazy.

Not yet, at least.

The restaurant was closed. I walked around inside, but the doors to the kitchen were locked. That was disappointing—I was hoping to find some *real* food to eat inside.

Adjacent to the restaurant was the hotel pool. It was an Olympic-length swimming pool, with five lanes and a diving board. Next to the pool were two big hot tubs. The bubbles came on when I flipped a switch. Too bad I didn't bring a swimsuit.

The second floor boasted a lounge with two billiard tables and a pull-down screen for a projection TV. There was also a fully-stocked bar, though the bottles were behind locked cabinets.

"Now *that's* a glass window I'm tempted to break," I said out loud. "When I run out of wine."

When I got back in the elevator, I noticed a phrase engraved in Italian next to the floor buttons. I translated them on my phone: *Rooftop access - fifth floor.*

I exited onto the fifth floor and walked around. I didn't see any rooms marked with sticky-notes to indicate they were occupied by guests. There hadn't been any on the other floors, either. That meant me and my neighbor were the only ones in the hotel. We had the whole place to ourselves.

I kind of felt like Kevin McCallister in *Home Alone,* except I couldn't order a cheese pizza.

The rooftop access was in the stairwell. A ladder extended to a square metal hatch in the ceiling. But there was a padlock on the hatch, preventing me from opening it.

I returned to my hotel room and found a note waiting for me on the floor next to the dividing door.

Want some breakfast? I'm making omelets.

I wrote a reply and sent it over:

I thought you'd never ask! Trade you a bottle of breakfast wine?

I smelled cooked eggs before his reply came.

This food's on the house. I'm Donovan, by the way.

Donovan. Sexy name alert. I wrote a reply:

I'm Molly. Sorry about the notes. I don't think it's safe to chat in person. I'm washing my hands after every note, too. Hope you're doing the same.

A knock came on the door soon after. When I opened it, a plate was waiting in the partition containing a perfectly-shaped omelet. A delicious yellow half-circle of goodness.

The omelet had bits of bacon and onion inside, with a gooey, cheesy interior. When the plate was empty I wondered how I had wolfed it down so fast.

Another note appeared:

Texting is probably safer than passing notes. Here's my number.

With nothing else to do, I crawled into bed and texted him.

Molly: Thanks for the omelet! It was delicious.

Donovan: I hope you're not Jewish

Donovan: Wow, that sounds super anti-Semitic doesn't it? I'm asking because of the bacon in the omelet. I forgot to ask if you had any food restrictions.

I grinned as I typed a reply:

Molly: Actually, I'm an Israeli vegan. I ate the onions and threw the rest in the garbage.

Donovan: Next time I'll send over the whole onion by itself, and save us both some time.

Donovan: Do you accept food from every stranger you meet?

Molly: So far, only you.

Donovan: It could be poisoned.

Molly: Worth the risk. The smell of the food you were cooking was literally torturing me.

Donovan: You know, Hannibal Lecter lured his victims with food.

Donovan: He lived in Italy too!

Molly: Let's talk about a more cheerful topic. This pandemic is crazy, right?

Donovan: It kind of feels like the beginning of a zombie apocalypse movie.

Molly: Did you just get here, like I did?

Donovan: I'm at the tail end of my trip. My flight home was grounded.

Molly: At least you got to see the city before the world ended! So far I've only seen the view from my balcony. Hopefully the lockdown ends in a few more days and things can get back to normal.

Donovan: I don't mind it too much. I'm not in a rush to get back home.

Molly: You don't have to get back for work?

Donovan: I'm kind of between jobs right now.

The talk of work reminded me that I should probably check in with my shop. I did the time change in my head, then called.

"*Nellie's Boutique, how can I help you?*"

"Hey Andrea, it's me."

"*Molly! Are you okay? I heard about the lockdown in Italy.*"

"I'm fine, they have me staying in the hotel room. I'm sure everything will settle down in a few days. How's the shop?"

"*Oh, it's fine. Same old, same old.*"

"Busy?"

She hesitated before answering. "*About as busy as it normally is.*"

That meant it wasn't busy at all.

"*Do you think they'll impose a lockdown here?*" Andrea asked. "*There haven't been any cases in Indiana yet, but what if it spreads?*"

"I'm sure it will be fine," I said. "Just focus on the shop and email me if you need anything. I don't know when I'll be home, but I'll let you know if I find out."

"*Be safe! You'll be in my prayers.*"

I hung up. Business should have been booming right now as

people bought new spring clothes. We had even increased our ad spend over the last two weeks. But if business was still slow...

We'll be okay, I told myself. Mom always said the shop would be fine, even when things looked grim. I just needed to adopt her positive attitude.

Easier said than done while I was trapped in a hotel room on the other side of the world.

I read the text messages I had been swapping with Donovan. After a few days alone, it was so *comforting* to communicate with someone going through the same experience as me. I was picturing him as someone my own age. Maybe a blond with piercing blue eyes. But I hadn't met him, and I had no idea what he looked like.

I wrote a few draft messages, deleted them, and re-wrote them. Finally I hit send.

Molly: Do you think it's safe to have dinner on our balconies tonight?

Donovan: As long as we're six feet apart, I think so. Everyone seems to agree outdoors is safer than indoors. Meet you out there at six?

Molly: I'll bring the wine!

I dressed up like I was going out for a night on the town. A comfortable summer dress, with my good bra. The one that made my boobs look extra perky. I straightened my hair and spent half an hour putting makeup on in front of the mirror.

That's when I realized what this felt like: a date. I was dressing up like I was going out with someone. But I didn't know much about Donovan. For all I knew, he could be in his seventies. He did say he was between jobs. Maybe that was code for *retired*.

I put on heels, examined myself in the mirror, then kicked

them off. Heels would be too much. We were eating on the hotel balcony, not the balcony of a fancy restaurant.

At five minutes to six, I carried a bottle of wine and two glasses outside. Our two balconies were separated by a three-foot gap, but it looked like we could pass food and wine back and forth. Plenty of space, and no mask required. I leaned over the balcony toward his side. His curtains were open, but I couldn't see deep into his room because of the glare from the sun.

I rested my elbows on the railing and gazed out at the city. The plaza below us was still deserted. A stray newspaper blew across the cobblestones, disappearing down an alley next to a chocolate shop that was closed. Above that building was the top rim of the Colosseum, with the sun beginning to set behind it.

The door slid open on the balcony next to mine.

Donovan wasn't in his seventies. He was about my age, with olive skin and dark features. He was tall, with broad shoulders beneath a polo shirt that accentuated his V-shaped torso and tapered waist. He had big hands, big enough to hold two bowls of pasta in one while he used the free hand to close the door behind him. He was wearing a blue medical mask, but above it his steel-grey eyes were sharp. I couldn't see his mouth, but his eyes tightened in a smile.

Donovan is an absolute snack. We should have eaten outside before now. My heart fluttered at the sight of him.

Thanks to the mask, it took me a moment to recognize him.

When I did, my heart skipped a beat for a totally different reason.

Oh no, I thought. *It's him.*

33

6

Donovan

The Day I Scared Her Off

It's her, I thought with a chuckle. *Of course it's her.*

I should have known. It's not like there were a lot of people in our hotel right now. The chaos from the lockdowns had made me forget all about her tirade in the lobby the other day.

It was just the other day, wasn't it? It felt like much longer than that. Like the entire world had changed in the past forty-eight hours. Getting mistakenly yelled at seemed so *quaint* compared to the problems we were all dealing with now. It was actually kind of funny.

But Molly, the girl I'd been texting with for the past day, looked mortified. Her mouth hung open, and she blinked rapidly like she couldn't believe what she was seeing.

So I decided to break the ice with a joke. "If I give you food, do you promise not to yell at me again?"

The joke had the opposite effect. All the color drained from her oval face. "I... I was..."

She looked at the door like she wanted to flee back inside. She took a step in that direction while staring at me like I really *was*

Hannibal Lecter.

"I think I'm going to go..."

"Wait!" I said. My voice was muffled through my mask. "Don't you want your food?" I hefted one of the bowls enticingly.

Molly looked at the door, then looked back at the bowl of food. The hunger in her eyes was obvious. I approached the railing and held the bowl across. I felt like a bird-watcher trying to convince a scared hummingbird to perch on my finger.

She leaned across the gap to take the bowl. But her hands were trembling, and the bowl slipped from her fingers. We both gazed down and watched it smash onto the ground three stories below, scattering pieces of porcelain and red pasta in all directions.

"Damn, I'm so sorry," she said in a rush. "I'm such a mess right now, and I'm embarrassed..."

"Don't sweat it," I said. "I made a big batch. Take this bowl. But *don't* drop it."

I leaned the other bowl across the railing. She reached out and carefully took it with both hands. Only when the bowl was safely over her balcony did she breathe a sigh of relief.

"Let's start over," I began.

Before I could say anything more, she blurted out, "I don't think it's safe to eat outside after all. Sorry."

She opened her balcony door and disappeared inside. The bottle of wine was still sitting on the table, unopened.

"That went well," I muttered to myself as I went back into my room. I retrieved a fresh bowl, filled it with pasta from the pot on the stove, and then went back out on the balcony to eat. Maybe she would change her mind and join me. She did forget about her wine, after all.

While eating my spinach farfalle with red sauce, I noticed Molly peeking through the curtains next door. Whenever I looked over, the curtains quickly swayed back into place. After this happened three times, I pulled out my phone.

Donovan: What happened in the lobby the other day isn't a big deal. Come enjoy the food with me.

Donovan: Unlike the real Hannibal, I promise I don't bite.

She didn't respond, and she didn't come back out. I lingered long enough to watch the sun set beneath the Colosseum to the west, then carried my bowl back inside.

I put the leftovers in the fridge and cleaned up. My kitchenette had a single stove burner, but I really wished it had an oven so I could bake. In the last week at cooking school I'd learned how to make perfect garlic bread, but I didn't have a way to practice.

I'll practice when I get back to Boston, I thought. *Whenever that is.*

Since I couldn't bake my own desserts, I had to improvise. Restrictions were the mother of creativity, after all. I went to the vending machine in the hallway and took three milk chocolate bars and a bag of shortbread cookies. I broke the chocolate up into small pieces and put them in a glass bowl, which I suspended over a pot of boiling water. I mixed the chocolate with a spoon until it was evenly melted and smooth, then I dipped each individual cookie inside. I didn't have any parchment paper, so I cleaned off the counter next to the stove and put the cookies there. Once the chocolate had cooled and hardened, I placed four of the cookies on a paper towel and placed them in the partition between our two rooms.

Donovan: Dessert is served. Compliments of the vending machine and a lot of creativity.

Donovan: Unlike the pasta, I can guarantee the cookies are not poisoned.

36

Molly: Thank you. Sorry for the lobby thing.

Donovan: Seriously, don't sweat it. Want to eat the cookies outside? It's a beautiful night.

She didn't respond, which meant the answer was no. I chewed on the inside of my lip while thinking about it. What more could I do to convince her that the lobby misunderstanding wasn't a big deal? After all, we had much bigger problems to worry about.

I was running low on eggs, so I couldn't make her breakfast in the morning. But maybe I could win her over with some sort of grilled sandwich...

I shook my head. Why was I trying so hard to make this girl feel comfortable? If she wanted to be embarrassed about the lobby thing forevermore, then that was her business. It didn't affect me at all.

It wasn't because I was lonely. I liked being alone. I'd been that way my entire life, since my family moved around so much. Lots of army brats learned to make new friends easily because of the frequent reassignments, but I went in the opposite direction and learned to enjoy solitude. I liked it when things were quiet. It meant I could be alone with my thoughts.

I know why I'm trying so hard.

I bit into one of the cookies and thought about how Molly had looked on the balcony. She was wearing a summer dress that hugged her curves nicely, with a plunging neckline that showed a *lot* of cleavage. Cleavage which she had plenty of. Her hair ran down her back like a waterfall of dark silk. Those plump lips that hung open with shock, then pursed tightly with embarrassment when she dropped the bowl of pasta. Molly looked like she had dressed up for a date.

She looked so good that my cock pulsed with the mere memory of her.

Okay, I thought. *I'm trying hard because I have a hotel crush.*

I decided not to worry about her. If she wanted to be

standoffish, she could go right ahead for all I cared. As soon as this lockdown ended in a few days, we would never see each other again.

But as I stripped down to my boxer-briefs and went to sleep, I couldn't get the image of Molly out of my head.

7

Molly

The Day He Asked Me Out

I couldn't get the image of Donovan out of my head. Standing on the balcony, holding the pasta like my own personal Prince Charming.

I didn't handle embarrassment well. One time when I was a teenager, I accidentally called my calculus teacher "mom" in front of the whole class. For a week after that, I pretended to have the flu so I could stay home from school. It wasn't a big deal, and nobody else remembered it now. But *I* was mortified, and I still thought about the memory to this day.

As far as embarrassing moments went, yelling at Donovan in the lobby was probably in my Top Five. I had quickly forgotten about it because of the pandemic and the hotel locking down, but now that I knew he was my neighbor, all the embarrassment came rushing back tenfold. It was even worse now because he had been giving me food!

And then, when he found out it was me, he didn't get upset. He did the opposite: he made me *cookies!*

What kind of guy did that?

He invited me out to the balcony again, but I didn't dare

accept. I couldn't even respond. Just the thought of going out there and facing him made me cringe. I was too scared to even go out and retrieve my bottle of wine. All I wanted to do was crawl in bed and disappear.

It was made worse by the overwhelming urge to call my mom. She would have listened to the story, laughed with me about it, and then made me feel better.

I just want to go home, I thought.

I was bored the next day. I took another luxurious bath to kill some time in the morning, and when I got out, I had a text waiting on my phone.

Donovan: Sorry, no breakfast today. I'm running low on supplies. But I have leftover pasta from last night if you're hungry.

I ignored the text because I was still too embarrassed to reply.

By the afternoon I was going stir-crazy, so I decided to venture out of my room. I tied a T-shirt around my face again as a makeshift mask. It made me feel like a bank robber.

The hotel tower was shaped like a square, with four hallways making up the sides. If I walked down the hall, after four left turns I would end up back where I began.

The first hallway had a few rooms, the elevator, and the vending machine.

The next hall was full of hotel rooms, all of which were empty.

The next hall had more empty hotel rooms, plus the gym with the big "CLOSED" sign taped to the door in five languages. The wall between the hallway and the gym was all glass, giving me a view of the interior for seven or eight steps.

The last hall was like the second one, filled only with empty rooms. Then I was back to the hall with my room.

I circled my floor like a power-walker at the mall. After a few minutes I started getting into a rhythm.

My hall.

Empty hall.

Gym hall.

Empty hall.

I wondered how long the loop was, so on the next lap I counted my steps. It was about fifty steps per length, or two hundred total. How many were in a mile? About two thousand? That sounded right.

With nothing else to do, I decided to walk at least two miles. Twenty laps.

I put in my earbuds and listened to a news podcast. Normally they covered a wide variety of subjects, but today they were only talking about the pandemic. So far, the United States hadn't implemented any containment measures. There were several more cases in Washington and Oregon, and rumors of two cases down in California. The CDC said they were monitoring the situation and would present guidelines if things got worse.

In Europe, the only countries to institute travel bans were Italy, Spain, and the United Kingdom. International travel was still permitted everywhere else. On my twelfth lap, a brilliant idea came to me: I could travel to a neighboring country like Austria and fly home from there!

But of course that was out of the question. Travel was restricted. I wouldn't even be able to reach the border, let alone cross it. Nobody in or out.

Could I contact the American Embassy in Rome? Maybe they would find a way to send me home. That would be something to consider in a few more days. Maybe things would end naturally before then.

On my next lap, I saw a man bending down in front of my door. It wasn't Donovan or the concierge: it was an older man dropping off our supply boxes for the day.

"Hello! Buongiorno!" I said excitedly. "Do you speak English? Do you have any new information about the hotel? Are they opening things back up soon?"

The man took a step back. "No parlo ingles," he said. He was holding two objects in his hand. It took me a moment to recognize them.

Two single-serving bottles of wine. The ones that came in our care packages.

"Hey..." I said.

He smiled and waved goodbye, then turned to walk away.

"Did you take that from the box? You're stealing our wine!"

The man took off in a dead sprint down the hall, then disappeared through the door to the stairwell. I didn't bother chasing him, both because I doubted I could catch him and because I had plenty of wine in my room.

"At least he left the food," I thought while opening the box.

I continued walking laps while eating my pitiful sandwich. Today was ham and swiss. On the third bite I thought I tasted a drop of mustard. I considered that a win.

But after eating Donovan's pasta a couple of times, this tasted awful by comparison.

Lap number fourteen. Almost a mile done. Empty hallway, then the hall with the gym...

As I passed the gym, I did a double-take. There was movement inside. At first I suspected the delivery-man-slash-wine-thief, but then I realized it was Donovan. He was running on one of the treadmills, facing away from me. He was wearing only a pair of shorts.

I slowed down my pace to get a better look. Donovan pumped

his chiseled arms as he ran. His back was covered with tan muscles which flexed and contracted with every stride.

This would be easier if he didn't look like a snack, I thought.

I reached the end of the glass, and the view was gone.

I continued walking around my loop. I was tempted to go back to my room to avoid the awkwardness of potentially running into him, but I wanted to complete my walking goal, too. I was bored, and I only had five more to go.

Plus, deep down, I wanted to get another look at Donovan.

I slowed down when I passed the gym on the next lap. There was absolutely no denying it: Donovan was sexy as hell. I had pictured him as being muscular underneath his polo shirt, but the real thing was even better than I imagined. And I wasn't just thinking that because I was starved for social interaction from my seclusion. If my girlfriends saw him in a Roman club, they definitely would have hit on him.

On the third pass, Donovan was glistening with sweat. It made his muscles stand out even more than before, if that was even possible. He wasn't too bulky, either—he was chiseled. Just the right proportion to make my stomach tingle every time I laid eyes on him.

I walked faster around the other three hallways so I could get back to him quicker.

He was sprinting on the treadmill now, taking long strides and pumping his arms furiously. I could hear the thumping of his feet on the treadmill as he tried to maintain his speed. His shorts were tight enough that they left nothing to the imagination. His ass looked absolutely wonderful.

When he was out of view, I picked up my pace again. I knew it was wrong to objectify a guy. If the roles were reversed, I wouldn't want some guy ogling me while I exercised at the gym. But I couldn't help but feel excited about seeing him again.

I rounded the corner. The gym was just ahead. Before I reached it, I slowed down so that it would look like I was maintaining a normal pace...

But Donovan wasn't on the treadmill anymore. He was standing in the doorway of the gym, two feet away from me.

I jumped back, then raised my T-shirt mask over my mouth. "You scared me!"

He leaned on the door frame and smiled at me. His chest was an oil painting of muscles, from his pecs down to a six-pack of abs. He casually used a towel to dry the back of his neck. His chest and arms were covered in a sheen of sweat, which made every nook and cranny of his breathtaking body stand out in glorious contrast.

"Getting an eyeful?" he asked in a deep, confident voice.

I blinked. *Nice going, Molly.* Looks like there was a new moment to add to my Top Five list.

"I was walking around on the floor," I said defensively. "I was doing that before you started working out. Which, by the way, you're not allowed to do. The gym is closed."

He kept on smiling at me, like this was all some joke. "It is?"

"Yes. There's a sign on the door."

"I don't read Italian."

"It's in English," I pointed out. "And French, and German, and another language I don't recognize."

"Maybe I don't read any of those. Did you consider I might be illiterate?"

"You're not illiterate," I said curtly. "You were passing notes with me."

Donovan just shrugged. "The door was unlocked. Who's going to stop me? There's nobody else in the hotel to use the gym. The other floors are deserted, I checked. Unless you want to use the gym..."

"I'm fine walking around the hall," I said. "I hate running on treadmills. I prefer to feel like I'm *actually* moving."

44

He toweled off one arm, then the other. I struggled to keep my eyes on his face.

"Want to get dinner on the balcony tonight?" he asked. "Without all the awkwardness this time."

"Oh." I blinked. "I don't... I don't think I want..."

I tried to think of an excuse, but nothing came to me. It felt like my brain had shut off. It probably had to do with the chiseled, shirtless guy smiling at me. I felt my cheeks grow hot.

"Stop trying to think of an excuse," Donovan said. "What else are you going to do tonight? Sit in your room? Come on. It's going to be a beautiful night. You're in Rome. The least you could do is enjoy the sunset. Besides, you owe me a bottle of wine for last night's dinner. See you on the balcony at six."

He returned to the gym, allowing the door to close automatically behind him. He sat down on the weight-lifting bench and began curling a dumbbell. His bicep flexed, and a vein bulged along his olive skin. His dark hair hung across his face as he leaned forward, focusing on the movement...

Eighteen laps is close enough, I thought as I hurried back to my room.

8

Molly
The Day We Had Dinner

I thought about his invitation the rest of the day. He never even gave me a chance to reply. He just assumed I would say yes. But I didn't have to accept it. I could stay in my room and watch more episodes of Italian-dubbed Seinfeld.

The problem was that I was hungry. The half-sandwich hadn't done much to fill the pit in my stomach, and the growling had only gotten worse after my eighteen laps around the building. After a lot of internal struggling, I decided I could handle a little bit of awkwardness.

It's just about the food, I told myself.

I took a shower and washed my hair. When it eventually dried, I straightened it, then found another dress to wear. Despite the informal balcony setting, it *did* feel good to put on makeup and get dressed like I was going out for a night on the town. It helped make things seem a little more normal.

At six, I carried a bottle of wine out to the balcony. Like last night, the sun was falling toward the Colosseum. The city looked older in the dying light, long shadows accentuating the imperfections in the architecture. If I squinted I could pretend I was back in ancient Rome, watching the same sunset as Roman senators and emperors.

I glanced down at the plaza below. The shattered bowl of pasta was still there, and two cats were gently licking up the remains of the sauce.

The balcony door opened and Donovan walked out holding two plates of food. The way he looked in the gym flashed in my head like an intrusive thought: muscles and sweat and bulging veins. Knowing what was underneath his shirt made him just a little bit sexier than before, if such a thing was possible.

"I was afraid you wouldn't come," he said through his mask.

I pulled my T-shirt-converted-into-a-mask up over my mouth. "Like you said, I don't have any other plans. What's on the menu tonight?"

I still felt awkward, like the unpopular kid who was pretending to be aloof to hang out with the cool kids. But Donovan only smiled behind his mask.

"Eggplant parmesan. Since you're an Israeli vegan and all."

It took me a moment to realize he was referring to the joke I made via text message the other day. "Is parmesan cheese vegan?" I asked.

He shrugged. "Guess not. If you don't want it then..."

"I was joking!" I quickly said. "I'm not even close to vegan. I'll eat anything."

I'll eat anything? I winced. *What a stupid thing to say.*

He held a plate across the railing. "Be careful with this one. My room only came with six dishes, and one of them is shattered on the ground below."

Ugh, did he have to mention that again?

"Sorry," I said while taking the plate. It felt like a hostage exchange. Fortunately I didn't drop this one.

"How about some of that wine?" he asked.

"Oh, right." I opened the bottle while he retrieved a glass from his room. He held the glass across the balcony while I poured. One or two droplets fell to the ground below, but those were the only casualties of the transaction.

We sat at our separate tables and began eating. The eggplant Parmesan was *phenomenal,* crunchy on the outside and soft on the inside. Everything was quiet except for the scraping sound of forks and knives on plates as we enjoyed our meal together.

I eyed him across the balcony. When I had seen him earlier, his thick hair was damp with sweat and messy, but now it was combed down the side. He had the perfect amount of dark stubble along his jaw.

I'm having dinner with a ridiculously-sexy guy and I can't think of two words to say to him.

"Where did you get the mask?" I asked.

"I always travel with a mask," he replied. "A habit my dad gave me. He was stationed in Korea, and over there everyone wears a mask while traveling. Guess they had the right idea long before all of *this.*" His fork gesture encompassed our balcony, the city of Rome, and the entire pandemic.

"Guess so," I replied.

Another silence stretched, both because I didn't know what to say and because I was busy wolfing down the food. The cheese covering the eggplant was gooey and fresh.

Finally Donovan put down his fork and fixed me with his steel-grey gaze. "This is dumb. What happened in the lobby was a misunderstanding. Hell, it's *funny* looking back on it. If I can laugh about it, so can you. In case you didn't notice, we have more important things to worry about. So stop being embarrassed, all right?"

He was firm and said it with a disarming smile. Not like a stranger scolding me—but like a friend nudging me away from my destructive thoughts. It was easy to believe him.

"You're right about having more important things to worry about," I said. "Did you see there are six new cases in Washington?"

He nodded. "Wonder how long before it spreads. You from there? Washington?"

"I'm from Indiana," I replied. "No cases there so far."

He took a bite of eggplant and said, "That's because nobody wants to visit Indiana."

"Hey!" I said. "We're not *that* boring. I live in Elkhart, just two hours from Chicago."

"Two hours is a long way. Where I'm from, if you go two hours in any direction you cross through a bunch of states."

"And where might that be?" I asked.

"Boston."

"You don't have an accent."

Donovan shook his head. "My dad was in the Army. We moved around a lot. California, Texas, South Korea. Never stayed long enough for an accent to stick."

"Is that why you're in Italy?" I asked. "The Army brought you here?"

He chuckled. "Nah. I didn't follow in my dad's footsteps. Don't laugh, but I came here to go to cooking school."

"I should have known!"

Donovan shrugged. "It's dumb."

The more we talked, the less I felt embarrassed. We were just two neighbors sitting on their balconies, chatting during dinner. And he *was* easy to talk to, so long as I stared out at the view and not at his chiseled, charming profile.

"I don't think it's dumb." I put down my fork. "You're good at it. And I'm not just saying that because anything is better than the supply package sandwiches they've been giving us."

"Thanks."

"So you want to be a chef? When did you know that's what you wanted to pursue?"

He chewed his food, swallowed, and took a long pull of wine. "It took me a while to figure it out. The problem with moving a lot is that everything changes too much. I had a really good history teacher in San Diego, but then we moved and my new history teacher sucked. So I got into astronomy at my new school."

"*You* were an astronomy geek?" I asked skeptically.

He frowned over at me. "Why do you say that?"

Because you look like a cologne model.

"No reason."

"I wasn't one for very long," he said in a voice that was deep and smooth. "Just when I was getting the hang of it we moved to South Korea. Always jumping from one place to the next before we could put down roots. I couldn't keep a part-time job like that, either. My resume looked thin. When I was old enough I did handyman work, or construction. Manual labor. The kind of thing you didn't need a lot of experience for."

"So how did you get into cooking?" I asked.

"Well," he said, "no matter where I went, the one consistent thing was food. Everyone eats. Restaurants have the same *feel* no matter where you go. People eating, drinking, smiling. So, I took a job as a line cook. The only shift I could get was working at night at a diner by the freeway, which was good because it meant I could keep my day job in construction. Bacon, eggs, pancakes. Not a lot of variety, but that just meant it was a good place for me to learn. When you cook the same eight dishes over and over again, you get pretty good at it.

"I loved it," he went on. "Creating something from scratch and then watching hungry people eat... It felt like I was accomplishing something." He gestured with his hand. "People come in hungry, and they walk out happy. Simple, but satisfying. I looked for jobs at other restaurants so I could learn more and expand my repertoire, but nobody was hiring. That's when I heard about this big cooking school here in Rome. So I saved up my money for a few years and finally flew out here. Guess I got lucky that my classes ended the day before everything shut down."

He's chasing his dream, I realized. I found it endearing. He knew what he wanted to do and was going for it. Knowing his story also made it easier to forget about the lobby incident.

"It paid off," I said, flashing him my empty plate. "That was delicious. *Everything* you've made has been really good."

He shrugged. "The stuff I learned is still fresh in my head."

"What's next?" I asked.

He pulled his mask over his face and carried his glass over to the railing. "Now I'm going to enjoy more wine while waiting out the pandemic."

I filled his glass and said, "I mean, what's next for your career? What are you going to do when you get home?"

He leaned his elbows on the railing and looked out over the city. "I don't know. I'm not good with long-term planning."

"Saving up to go to cooking school in Rome seems awfully long-term," I pointed out.

"Trust me: that's the exception to the rule," he replied. "I guess my next step is trying to find a better job. There are a couple of *really* nice restaurants around Boston I've had my eye on. They're picky with who they hire, but with something like this on my resume? Maybe I can finally get my foot in the door."

He glanced at me and shrugged like it was no big deal, or was embarrassed that he had revealed so much to a total stranger.

Him? Embarrassed? I almost laughed at the idea. He seemed so much more confident than me.

"The other day, you said you were between jobs," I said.

"Yeah, my boss at the diner is kind of a dick. I told him about the trip months ago, but he pretended like he forgot. He wouldn't approve the time off. So I quit."

"That sucks," I said.

"Eh, whatever," he said with a smirk. "I wasn't going to let him get in the way of my trip. What about you? Why'd you come to Rome by yourself?"

"I wasn't supposed to be alone," I said while refilling my own wine glass. "It was a trip I had planned with all my girlfriends. I flew in a day early, because I wanted to do some sightseeing by myself. Turns out that was a mistake. They got stuck at home." I shook my head. "Well, I guess actually I'm the one who's stuck, not them."

"I'm sure they'll open up flights in another day or two," Donovan said. "What do you do for a living?"

"I own a small clothing store."

"You're an entrepreneur?" He nodded approvingly. "Nice."

I sipped my wine. I didn't want to tell him the truth about the store. That I didn't care about it, that it had fallen into my lap and I was keeping it running out of guilt.

"It's okay," I said. "It feels good to get away. At least, it *would* feel good if things weren't..." I gestured at the empty plaza. "It's so weird being here. It feels like... like..."

"Like what?" he asked softly.

"A few days ago, you were cooking dinner next door," I explained. "I could smell everything you were doing. It smelled incredible! My mouth watered, but I couldn't have any. That's what this whole trip feels like. I'm next door to something amazing. I can see it, hear it, smell it." I swung my arm out toward the west. "The Colosseum is *right freaking there,* with the sun setting behind it! But I can't actually enjoy any of it because I'm stuck in the hotel."

Donovan grinned over at me. "What I just heard is that my cooking is as breathtaking as the Roman Colosseum."

"Ha ha," I fake-laughed. "I'm jealous you spent a week here before me. I bet you got to see everything."

"Not really."

"Come on. I'm sure you saw more than I did."

"I had cooking classes every day," he explained. "Then I came back to my hotel room every night and practiced what I learned. I didn't have time to see the city."

I put my wine glass down and crossed my arms over my chest. "You flew all the way to Rome, spent a week here, and didn't see *anything?*"

"What can I say? I'm good with short-term goals," he replied. "I was actually signed up for the same walking tour as you. That's why I was waiting in the lobby that day."

I groaned. "You had to bring that up, didn't you?"

"It wasn't that bad!"

"I was a total bitch."

"You were *feisty,*" he insisted. "There's a difference."

"Kittens are feisty," I replied. "When women are jerks they're—"

"Don't call yourself a bitch," he replied firmly. "If that's what you were, I wouldn't be giving you food."

"Unless the food's poisoned."

He fixed me with a calming gaze. "I promise it's not."

"I still feel bad about the lobby," I mumbled.

He flashed a perfectly white smile. "One more glass of wine and I promise we're even, *Feisty.*"

We put on our masks and leaned across the railing toward each other. The wind shifted, and I caught a whiff of his cologne through my mask. He smelled masculine, like leather and oil. It sent a tingling shiver through my body.

I'm just lonely, I thought. *I barely know this guy.*

53

But did that really matter?

He grinned behind his mask like he knew what I was thinking, his grey eyes piercing into my soul.

"Thanks for the wine, and the good company. I'll leave you in peace now."

You don't have to leave, I wanted to say. *You can stay with me and share more wine and keep me company.*

But I couldn't muster the words before he took my plate and left.

9

Molly

The Day We Had Dinner, Again

I thought about Donovan while trying to fall asleep. He was a lot friendlier than I expected. Most guys who looked like *that* were jerks, because they didn't need to be nice. They could skate through life on their good looks and nothing else. But Donovan didn't fit the mold.

I also replayed the entire night from start to finish in my head, analyzing and over-analyzing everything I said. Our balcony dinner felt like a first date. We shared a bottle of wine and got to know each other. We traded friendly banter and teased each other.

Was he sitting in his bed, on the other side of that wall, doing the same thing? Thinking about me?

The next day dragged on while I waited for us to have another dinner together. I downloaded the New York Times Crossword app, which killed a few hours. When the hour drew close I took a shower, did my hair, and put on a *little* more makeup than last night.

When I went out to the balcony, Donovan was already there. He wore a grey T-shirt instead of a polo tonight, which hugged his frame and accentuated the broad muscles of his shoulders.

"Food's gonna take another thirty minutes," he said. "But we can get started on the wine early, right?"

I unscrewed the bottle. "I don't see why not! I hope you like white. We're drinking pinot grigio tonight."

"I'm partial to reds," he said, "but beggars can't be choosers."

We shared a bottle of wine and talked about anything and everything. The lockdown, grounded flights, the weather back home in America. Once I had a glass of wine—or two!—in me, I didn't feel awkward around Donovan at all.

It helped that he was so damn *charming*. He treated me like we had been lifelong friends, reacquainting after a long absence.

Dinner was spiral pasta in a tangy red sauce. After bringing the food out, Donovan pressed a button on his phone and classical Italian music began playing from a portable speaker on his table.

"What is that, opera music?" I asked.

"There's a phrase for this sort of thing," he pointed out. "When in Italy... No, that's not it. When in the Mediterranean..."

"When in *Rome*, ha ha. I was just joking. I like the music."

"The best part is that we don't have to worry about bothering anyone. I could blast Metallica at the highest volume and nobody would care."

"I heard you listening to it in your room the other day," I said while finishing up my food. "It sounded so romantic, I assumed there was a couple on their honeymoon next door."

"Nothing that exciting," he said.

"Forget exciting, I'm glad it's you instead!"

He looked sideways at me.

Crap. I didn't mean to be that forward.

"I mean, if it was a couple next door," I said in a rush, "I'd have to listen to their loud, passionate honeymoon sex. Plus the food is a plus. With you, I feel like I have my own private chef next door. I don't know what I would do without you feeding me."

"I knew what you meant. I'm glad you're next to me too."

I gave a start. "You are?"

"Yeah," he replied in that deep voice of his. "Because you have wine."

"Oh yeah, right. The wine."

"Plus, if a newlywed couple was next door to me, I would have to share my food with *two* people. With just us, it lasts much longer."

"It would last longer if you weren't sharing it with me," I said. "If you start to run low on supplies and can't share anymore..."

I was giving him an out in case things got bad. But he shook his head and fixed me with one of those charming, heart-melting smiles.

"No way, Feisty. The way I see it, we're in this together now. My food is your food. Until I run out."

"And then what?"

"Then I'll *really* go all Hannibal Lecter on your ass."

I laughed and said, "I've never had someone threaten cannibalism on a date before."

As soon as the words were out of my mouth, I winced.

"What I mean is, this *feels* like a date. On some weird reality TV show."

"It kind of does," he said. "Cannibalism is off the table. Noted. What do you *normally* do on a second date, then?"

"It's been so long I don't even know! Usually just dinner I guess, although I think the last guy I dated took me to the movies on our second date..."

I trailed off as he began chuckling. That's when I realized what he really meant. Donovan was talking about *sex*. He was casually asking how far I went on a second date with a guy.

57

"Oh," I said.

He waved it off. "Wasn't trying to get too personal. Just making a joke."

"I don't like to move too fast, I guess," I said awkwardly. "I think it's better to get to know a guy first, you know? I don't like to sleep with a guy until, um, a while."

"Sure. Totally," he said.

Damnit. I didn't mean for that to sound so prudish. I wasn't opposed to moving fast with someone, if they were the right guy. It's just that I'd never had the opportunity. Out of the three serious boyfriends in my life, I had only slept with two of them. Donovan probably thought I was one of those save-it-for-marriage types, which was *not* the impression I wanted to give.

Not that it mattered, anyway. Regardless of whether or not this was a date, we couldn't get close to each other. Not with everything going on.

Which was too bad, because if things *were* normal I could see myself moving awfully fast with Donovan, if he took the initiative...

Donovan leaned on the railing and gazed out at the sunset to the west. I did the same. The sun had dropped below the top rim of the Colosseum, scattering orange and pink rays through the multitude of Roman arches. It was breathtaking.

"Okay, be honest with me," Donovan suddenly said. "Yesterday, you kept walking by the gym to check me out, didn't you?"

The question caught me off guard, and I sputtered for a moment. "I was walking around the floor. That's all."

He raised a skeptical eyebrow. "Five times in a row?"

"I was doing laps around the building!" I protested. "For exercise. Because unlike *some people*, I respect the fact that the gym is closed."

He looked back out at the plaza. "You walked awfully slow every time you passed the gym. I could see you in the mirror."

"I was tired. From walking so much," I said curtly.

He laughed, and I laughed with him. I didn't feel embarrassed anymore, even though getting called out like that normally would have sent me fleeing into my room. Like he had said: the pandemic seemed to make all other problems and awkwardness shrink away. That and the three glasses of wine I'd had.

"What would you be doing right now?" Donovan asked, changing the subject. "If things weren't, you know, apocalyptic."

"Right now? Probably going to a night club in the city. Dressing up, dancing with my girlfriends, maybe flirting with exotic Italian men. Then walking back to the hotel through Rome, drunk and happy."

Donovan nodded along, then glanced over at me. "If it's any consolation, you look beautiful. Even if we don't have anywhere to go."

I sipped my wine to hide my blush. "Do you flirt with a lot of women during global pandemics?"

"So far, only you," he said with another white smile. "But this is my first pandemic, so..."

The music changed to something a little more upbeat. Brass instruments and a pounding drum. Donovan pushed away from the railing and swayed back and forth, like he was dancing with himself.

He looks like he can dance, I thought while trying not to check him out too overtly. The way he moved was hypnotizing, and the twilight only accentuated his dark features.

"This is *almost* like a nightclub," he said.

"This is nothing like a nightclub. For one thing, the music is totally different."

He pointed a finger at me. "Exactly. Club music sucks. This makes it feel like we're *actually* in Rome. Which, in case you didn't notice, we are." He swept his wine glass across the plaza and city while dancing on his balcony.

I smiled as I watched him. He looked remarkably dashing in plain jeans and a T-shirt, dancing with his arm around an imaginary woman. The smell of Rome was in the air, the view of the city was stunning, and the music was setting the mood. I suddenly wished I was on his balcony, filling the empty space in front of him, his hand on the small of my back as he guided me in a circle.

"I wish we could dance," I said wistfully.

"Why can't we?"

"We're supposed to stay six feet apart," I said. "Just in case."

"Do you ever break the rules?"

"Almost never."

Donovan closed his eyes while dancing with his imaginary woman. "You're not living up to your nickname, Feisty. Sometimes breaking the rules is fun."

I watched him longingly, wanting nothing more than to throw caution to the wind, go over to his balcony, and dance with him. I wanted to do something *fun*, something more than just share wine together. If Donovan pushed the issue, I knew I would give in. Part of me wanted to.

Instead, Donovan stopped dancing and leaned on the railing again. He swirled the wine around in his glass and then knocked his head back to gulp it down.

"What's for dessert?" I asked hopefully.

He grimaced. "There's no more chocolate in the vending machine. I think there are a couple of bags of cookies, but I can't do much with that."

I snorted derisively. "You went to cooking school and didn't learn how to bake delicious treats for your neighbor?"

He spread his hands apologetically. "I don't have an oven in the room. Just a single stove top."

"Darn."

I reached for the bottle of wine to refill my glass, but it was empty. I put it back down and looked at Donovan. This was one of those crossroads where a night could go one way, or it could go another. We could open another bottle of wine and hang out more, and see where the night took us. Or we could end things here.

I waited too long, because Donovan glanced at the empty bottle and said, "I'm going to tidy up the kitchen. I only have one pot and one pan, so I have to keep them clean."

I smiled sadly. "I'd offer to do the dishes, but... You know. Six feet."

"A likely excuse." He opened his balcony door. "You going to stay out here a bit longer?"

"Yes!" I said hopefully. Was he going to stay after all? "I am. Why do you ask?"

He gestured at the table. "I'll leave the music on for you. Thanks for the wine. How about a third date tomorrow night? Unless you have other plans..."

"I'll check my calendar," I said, "but I think I can squeeze you in."

He started to go into the room.

"Donovan?" I asked.

He stopped. "Yeah?"

"I'm sorry I yelled at you in the lobby."

Thick black hair swayed as he shook his head. "Don't be. I'm glad you did."

The door closed behind him, and then I was alone.

10

Molly

The Day My Heart Did A Backflip

I couldn't get Donovan out of my head the next day. I felt like a girl who had made a new best friend on the first day of school, and couldn't wait to see them at Recess so we could play together.

I told myself it was purely platonic. Donovan was good company. He was the *only* company I had in the deserted hotel, as a matter of fact. I would have been excited to hang out with him even if he was a balding, middle-aged guy with crooked teeth.

But he doesn't look like that, I thought. *He looks like he was carved out of marble.*

Our care packages came around lunchtime, which gave me an excuse to text Donovan.

Molly: I'm eating the worst bologna sandwich I've ever had. Your pasta is so much better. When it's not dropped off the balcony, I mean.

Donovan: It's good even when it's dropped, Feisty.

Those cats in the plaza gobbled it up!

Donovan: What are you up to on Day Six of the lockdown?

Molly: Watching Seinfeld on the hotel channel. It's actually funnier in Italian. I'm having a blast.

Molly: Okay, that was a lie. I'm bored out of my mind.

Molly: There's not a lot to do around here.

Donovan: Ain't that the truth?

I turned down the TV volume and strained my ears. I couldn't hear him next door. In fact, I hadn't heard him in awhile.

Molly: What are you doing right now?

Donovan: I took a taxi out to the countryside. I'm at my third vineyard of the day. They're letting me do that thing where you smash the grapes with your bare feet.

Donovan: You know, typical pandemic-safe activities.

Molly: Oh God, don't tease me like that. I WISH I were at a vineyard right now.

Molly: What are you really doing?

Donovan: Snooping around the hotel pool. Someone left a pair of goggles in the locker room. I'm going to go for a swim.

Molly: There was a sign on the pool door. It's

supposed to be closed.

Molly: You wouldn't DARE ignore a closed sign, would you?

Donovan: What can I say? I like to live dangerously.

Donovan: Breaking the rules makes it more fun.

Donovan: Feel free to join me. It's better than sitting in the room, right?

I thought about the invitation while watching Seinfeld. It was a good excuse to leave the room, and I *did* want to see him again. The only problem was I didn't pack a swimsuit.

When the episode ended, I turned off the TV and took the elevator downstairs. The lobby was still completely empty, another harsh reminder that we were alone in the big hotel. Everything was silent except for a soft splashing sound coming from the pool.

I walked through the doors into the pool room. Donovan was swimming freestyle in one of the lanes, splashing with every stroke. He reached the end of the pool, did a flip-turn under the water, and began swimming back in the other direction.

His muscular body glided through the water smoothly. He made it look effortless. I watched him from the alcove by the door as he swam three laps, then four, never looking in my direction.

Finally he stopped at the end. After pausing to catch his breath, he planted his hands on the edge and climbed out of the pool. I ducked back out of sight, suddenly embarrassed that I had been watching him for so long. He rounded the corner of the pool and walked away from me.

I should have gone back up to my room, but temptation got the better of me. I peeked my head around the corner again.

Oh my God.

He was wearing boxer-briefs instead of a swimsuit, and they clung wetly to his body like a second skin. I was mesmerized by his ass as he walked down the length of the pool. Rivulets of water ran down the nooks and crannies of his muscles, making his entire body glisten.

He looks like a freaking cologne model. I half expected him to suddenly stop, face the camera, and say the name of a cologne in a sexy voice. *Pandemic, by Armani.*

Donovan reached the end of the pool and climbed the ladder up to the diving board. I watched him from my hidden alcove as he stopped at the top. Rolling his arms in their sockets, he took a deep breath, then strode out onto the diving board. He bounced on the end and launched into the air. Like a professional diver, he tucked his legs into his body, spinning in a full backflip, then extended his arms and legs until he was straight as a pencil. As he sliced into the deep end of the pool, a small splash fountained up from the languid water.

I was grinning from ear to ear as he returned to the surface. This time he swam over to the pool ladder that faced my direction. He grabbed the rails and pulled himself out of the water.

He stopped and cocked his head. "Molly?"

Shit, shit, shit.

Embarrassed that I'd been caught, I quickly exited through the doors.

By the time I got back to my room, I had a text waiting for me.

Donovan: Caught you watching me again. If I didn't know any better, I'd say you were stalking me.

Molly: I don't know what you're talking about

Donovan: You know you could have joined me, instead of watching from afar like a creeper.

Molly: The pool was closed. There was a sign on the

door, remember?

Donovan: You still walked through them.

Donovan: Since you already broke the rules, you might as well have come all the way into the pool.

Molly: What's for dinner tonight?

Donovan: Dinner?

Donovan: I'm not making dinner

Donovan: I'm planning on drinking wine and passing out

Molly: That's not very healthy!

Donovan: Wine comes from grapes. Grapes are fruit. Fruit is good for you.

Donovan: Trust me, I'm a chef.

Molly: Can't argue with that logic. Count me in for a liquid-fruit dinner. Same time and place as last night?

Donovan: It'll be our third date

Donovan: Things are getting serious.

Unfortunately, a storm rolled over Rome that afternoon. Lightning flashed across the cloud-filled sky and thunder echoed through the plaza, shaking the windows. There was no way we could eat on the balcony tonight.

Donovan knocked on the divider at six. A plate of food was waiting for me inside the partition. I swapped it for a bottle of wine and knocked, but this time I left my door open.

When Donovan opened his door, he blinked in surprise to see me sitting on the bed. A roguish smile filled his handsome face.

"Guess our date's canceled, huh?" he said.

"Looks like it. Rain check?"

He picked up the bottle of wine and held it in both hands, examining it, and I imagined his hands on *me* instead, cupping, squeezing, and holding me like he needed me as much as he needed the wine. His eyes raked over me for a moment, taking in the dress, my hair and makeup. Tonight there was a spark of something in his gaze when it lingered on the curves of my body. Like he didn't want the rain to ruin our date.

Invite yourself in, I pleaded with my eyes. *Ignore my rules and come sit down. Keep me company and make me laugh so I don't have to drink alone.*

But Donovan said, "Rain check, Feisty. Thanks for the booze."

He hesitated a moment longer, as if waiting to see if I would invite him in, then he closed the door.

I fell back on the bed and groaned.

I definitely have a crush on my neighbor.

11

Donovan

The Day She One-Upped Me

I have a fucking crush on my neighbor, I realized as I stared at Molly through the room divider.

She looked as pretty as a peach, sitting there on the edge of her bed with a glass of wine in her hand, one leg crossed over the other and staring at me expectantly. If it were any other time, in any other place, I would've sworn she wanted me to join her. She was giving me the *fuck-me eyes* to end all *fuck-me eyes,* like she wanted to forget our dinner and skip straight to a sweaty, naked dessert. To lose ourselves in the mindless drive of our bodies until neither of us could breathe.

And the way she smiled at me? My cock was *screaming* at me to cross the space between us and take her.

But even though I ached to give her everything I had and leave nothing on the table, I knew it wasn't what she wanted. She was the kind of girl who moved slowly. We barely knew each other. Even if this were a *real* third date, sex wouldn't be on the table.

Which is a shame, Feisty, because the things I would do to you...

I shook it off and thanked her for the booze before I could do something I regretted.

She ran through my dreams that night, all puckered lips and soft whispers, and lusty, leering smiles.

I woke up as hard as a rock. I closed my eyes and she reappeared in my mind, sitting on the edge of the bed with her legs uncrossed, open *just enough* to give me a peek at the panties underneath her dress. I stretched on the bed, pushing the comforter off my chest and letting my hand drift down to my cock, squeezing myself the way I imagined *her* squeezing me with those long, pink-tipped fingers. I stroked myself lazily while thinking about what I wanted to do with her. What I wanted to do *to* her. Within moments the spark of lust inside me was a wildfire burning out of control, and my hand moved furiously as I pictured her perfect tits pushed together in her dress, begging to feel the caress of my tongue, and I thrust into my palm until my dick throbbed and I exhaled Molly's name to the ceiling.

My hand and stomach were a hot, dripping mess as I lay in bed, panting.

Yeah, I thought, *I definitely have a crush on my fucking neighbor.*

Even after that, Molly was stuck inside my head like a bad idea. To try to get her out, I went to the gym in the morning rather than the afternoon. Jogging was like meditation to me. It helped me turn off my brain and focus on a simple, physical act. Putting one foot in front of the other, over and over, until I was sweaty and exhausted.

But soon after I started, I saw Molly in the mirror. She had her earbuds in and was walking down the hall in front of the gym windows. A few minutes later she walked by again. She must have been doing laps around the floor, like the other day. And she was conspicuously *not* looking in my direction.

My phone lit up on the treadmill holder.

Molly: Before you ask, I'm NOT stalking you. I

came out for my walk at this time because you normally exercise in the afternoon.

I slowed the speed enough that I could respond.

Donovan: You know my workout schedule? You sound like a stalker to me.

Molly: [eye-rolling emoji]

Donovan: Admit it. You like looking at me.

Molly: Not even a little bit.

Donovan: Prove it. Go walk on another floor. Unless you can't keep your eyes off me.

Molly: I'm not changing my routine because of you!

Molly: You're probably the one who wants to ogle ME.

Donovan: I was here first.

Molly: I can ignore you. I doubt you can do the same

Donovan: Trust me, Feisty. I've got the willpower of a saint

The next time Molly walked by the gym, she paused in front of the window. She turned toward me and pulled her arms behind her back like she was stretching, but the effect pushed her tits up like they were going to pour out of her tank top.

I'll admit: I couldn't look away. And when she was done she gave me a smug little nod before continuing her walk.

Two can play at this game, I thought with a smirk.

When she was gone from view, I paused the treadmill and went to the window. I waited until she walked by again, then slowly peeled my shirt over my head. I wasn't as ripped as some of the guys at the gym back home, but I stayed in shape and knew I looked good. I flexed my arms and chest muscles as I removed my shirt, giving her the full show.

She glanced at me and rolled her eyes. But she blushed, too.

I returned to the treadmill, content that I had one-upped her.

Boy was I wrong.

The next time she walked by the windows, I gawked at the sight. Her shirt was gone and she was only wearing a bra, which showed a *lot* of skin. Her full breasts gently bounced up and down as she walked by. I may have been imagining it, but it looked like there was a small smile on her face.

Touché, I thought as she disappeared around the next wall.

I couldn't help but watch her when she walked by again. My eyes followed her in the mirror, drinking in the sight of her fair, exposed skin. She looked soft and smooth, and I began fantasizing about what it would feel like to hold her in my arms without any clothing between us. To get a handful of her curves, cupping her breasts and lowering my mouth to her nipple so I could give her a playful lick...

"Focus, man," I said to myself after she was gone. "You're supposed to be taunting *her*, not the other way around."

I increased the speed on the treadmill and ran faster.

The next time she passed, she had gone a step further. Her jeans were gone, and a perfect pair of cotton white panties clung to her hips. This time she walked *extra* slow to make sure I got an eyeful. She even leered at me through the window.

I tried to stare straight ahead at the mirror, but there was no way I could ignore the way she looked. She was gorgeous fully-dressed, but half-naked?

This girl is a bombshell.

I was half-hard in my jogging shorts, which made for an awkward running motion. The clock on the treadmill said I had ten minutes left. I didn't want to cut my workout short.

Stick it out, I thought. *Get an eyeful the next time she walks by, then ignore her.*

The *whir* of the treadmill changed in pitch as I increased the speed again.

I waited for Molly to reappear, and then I waited some more. My feet pounded on the treadmill with every stride. Had she gone back to her room? Not seeing her again suddenly felt more torturous than having her strut her stuff.

Finally she appeared. She walked like a runway model milking her time for all it was worth, strutting down the hallway. I didn't try to hide the way I watched her in the mirror this time. I grinned widely at her.

You want to distract me? The joke's on you. I don't mind a bit.

Molly's smile disappeared as she realized I wasn't fighting it. An annoyed look flashed across her dark eyes, and then was replaced with something like inspiration. She looked like she had a really good idea.

She suddenly stopped and held out her phone. She let go of it, dropping it on the floor. She covered her mouth with her hand, like a mime acting out a scene.

Then she turned around and bent over to pick up the phone.

Ah, fuck.

My eyes locked onto her ass automatically. The white cotton panties were molded to her skin in a way that left nothing to the imagination. Her ass was perfectly heart-shaped, tapering up to a narrow waist that I desperately wanted to wrap my hands around. Flashes of what I wanted to do ran through my head. Bending her over just like that, pulling the panties down slowly. Burying my face in her pussy from behind. Sliding my tongue as deep as I could to taste every delicious inch of her.

I was so distracted that my foot landed on the edge of the treadmill, the part that wasn't moving. I stumbled forward and tried to regain my stride, but my other foot was off-balance now. I started to fall, flailing around with my hands, finally grabbing onto the treadmill rails before I face-planted on the ground.

I regained my composure in time to see Molly stand back up, holding her cell phone and laughing. She tossed her hair and strutted away with a victorious smile on her face.

I'm going to get you, Feisty, I thought while resuming my workout. *Just you wait.*

12

Molly

The Day Shit Hit The Fan

With nothing else going on in my life, one-upping Donovan felt like winning the Super Bowl. I giggled as I finished my lap around the hotel, then went back to my room and sent him a few taunting texts.

Molly: So that's what having the willpower of a saint looks like?

Molly: Don't worry. Next time I'll walk around the fourth floor.

Molly: For your safety.

Donovan: Yeah, yeah. You win this round, Feisty.

I pumped my fist at his admission of defeat. His text also held an unwritten promise: he was going to win the *next* round. I couldn't wait to see what that was.

I heard Donovan return from the gym five minutes later. Then came the soft hum of the water being run in his bathroom. He was taking a shower.

A naughty thought came to me, the kind of thought that I never would have considered before meeting Donovan: *I wonder if he's jacking off in the shower while thinking of me.* Guys did that, right? I was normally too shy to flaunt my sexuality, but I knew I had a great ass.

Maybe I should ask him. I immediately shook my head. That was way too forward for me. Heck, doing what I had just done—stripping off my clothes and walking around in my underwear—was far more scandalous than I normally acted. The old Molly never would have done that, and if she *had*, she would have been mortified by it.

Being here in this empty hotel was bringing out another side of me.

But I knew it wasn't the setting. It was Donovan's friendly, flirty attitude that was pulling me out of my shell. I wanted him to look at me the way he had in the gym mirror, eyes wide and thirsty, drinking me in like I was the Gatorade he needed after a run.

It was a good way to pass the time, too. Flirting with him was much more fun than being alone.

I was watching TV when suddenly there came a knock on my door. Not the divider between our rooms. The *front* door.

I slowly walked to the door and gazed through the peep-hole. Donovan's gorgeous frame was distorted in the fish-eye lens.

"What are you doing?" I asked.

"I want to ask you something."

"Why do I have the feeling you're going to go all Hannibal Lecter on me?"

He laughed. "I promise it's nothing that graphic. Come on, open up."

I hesitated. This felt like it was part of his plan to get even with me, whatever that may be. Coming to the front door instead of the divider...

But deep down, I wanted to know what he was going to do, so I unlocked the door and opened it.

"Was that so hard?" He pointed over his shoulder with his thumb. "Come watch TV with me downstairs."

TV? That's all you want to do?

"I'm watching TV right now," I replied.

"I'm sick of my room," he insisted. "I know you feel the same way, especially since it's been raining outside. We have this whole big hotel to ourselves, so I figure we should take advantage of it."

I glanced back into my room. "I don't know. Italian George was just making fun of the way Italian Elaine dances..."

"We can watch Seinfeld on the TV in the lobby. It'll be our socially-distanced third date. The lobby creeps me out when I'm the only person down there."

In a taunting baby voice I said, "Well, I wouldn't want you to be *scared* in the lobby all by your lonesome..."

I put some shoes on and followed him into the hall. Now that we were in the same space, without a balcony or door dividing us, I was struck by just how *strong* he appeared. He was broad-shouldered and walked with the easy gait of an athlete. He certainly didn't look like a mere line cook.

And as I followed behind him, I caught a whiff of his scent. It was cologne, or after-shave, or a really nice deodorant. Whatever it was, it lit a fire in my chest and made me want to walk closer to him and breathe deeper.

To be safe, I took the elevator and Donovan took the stairs down to the lobby. We walked over to the sitting area across from the concierge desk, which had an array of couches and chairs around a flat-screen TV. I took an armchair and Donovan spread out on the couch a respectable distance away, stretching his legs out and putting his arms behind his head.

"You're right," he said after a few minutes. "It *is* funnier in Italian. The guy voicing Kramer is nailing it."

I grinned over at him. "Wait until you see Newman."

We laughed and relaxed together while watching TV. Despite the flirting and sexual tension of the past few days, I felt totally comfortable in his presence. Neither of us needed to talk. We were happy just watching TV together in silence.

It helped that he didn't mention the lobby incident.

After three episodes, Donovan got up from the couch and stretched. "Hungry? I could go for a snack."

"Sure. What are you making me?" I shot back at him.

"You have two choices. Whatever's in vending machine number one, or whatever's in vending machine number two."

"Hmm, those both sound tasty," I said. "You wouldn't happen to have any oranges in your room, would you?"

He blinked. "Oranges? Afraid not."

I sighed wistfully. "I would kill for an orange right now. I normally eat an orange with lunch every day, and I've got a bad craving. Um, I don't know what I want. Surprise me?"

While he was gone I checked my phone. I had several news alerts. I scrolled through Twitter and gasped at what I saw.

"Shortbread, or lemon?" Donovan said when he returned, holding out two bags. All of his muscles stood out in wonderful contrast beneath his polo, but I was too stunned to eye-hump his sexy body.

"There's news. From America."

He lowered the cookies. "What happened?"

"California just shut everything down," I said, holding up my phone. "Oregon and Washington are going to follow suit tomorrow."

Donovan whistled. "The whole west coast?"

He lowered himself onto his couch and pulled out his phone. For the next few minutes we ate cookies and scrolled through the news, sharing with each other everything that we saw.

Sports leagues were suspending all games.

Restaurants and retail stores were closing.

Panicked Americans were rushing to the grocery store to stock up on supplies. It was still the afternoon back home, but people were already complaining about empty shelves.

"Toilet paper?" I said out loud. "Apparently everyone's buying up all the TP?"

"That's how you know shit *really* hit the fan," Donovan said.

I rolled my eyes, which made him grin harder at his joke.

We started doing research on ways to get home. With different countries around the world implementing varying levels of travel restrictions, the U.S. Government had created an online form for all Americans overseas who needed to return home. Donovan and I each filled out the form. We were then told that we were on a standby list, and would be contacted when travel arrangements could be made.

"Estimated wait time: between ten and thirty days?" I gasped when I read further down the page.

"They have no idea," Donovan said. "They're just guessing because everything is crazy right now. It could be next week for all we know."

"Guess we won't be going home soon after all," I said.

Donovan sighed and kicked his feet up on the couch. "Look on the bright side. If we have to be stuck somewhere, the view is much better here."

I glanced out the lobby window. The rain had faded enough that I could see across the plaza again. "Rome is definitely more beautiful than Indiana."

He gave me a sly grin. "Wasn't talking about the city."

I smiled in spite of myself. "Is that what you do on a third date? Flatter girls with compliments?"

"Normally, by the third date we're *well* past compliments." His grin deepened, and he looked at his watch. "Speaking of which, want to go upstairs?"

"I thought you were sick of being up there," I said.

"I am, but there's something I want to do." He slid his feet off the couch and fixed me with his stormy gaze. "Something I've been doing by myself, but is a *lot* more fun with two people. And it's messy. At least, it's messy when you do it right. What do you say?"

I waited for the punchline. Donovan kept staring at me with his sexy poker face. Letting the invitation linger in the air like expensive cologne.

Is he really being so forward? Is he bluntly inviting me upstairs for sex? Last night he had wanted to cross the divider into my room, I was certain. And our flirting had escalated quite a bit when he was in the gym. Was he finally saying *fuck it* and shooting his shot?

For a few heartbeats I let myself imagine it. Donovan pushing me down onto the bed with a hungry, desperate look in his eyes. Tearing off my clothes like they offended him. Nuzzling and licking and *filling* me with everything he had...

"Sure," I found myself saying in a voice that was hardly more than a whisper. "Show me what you have in mind."

He smiled like it was exactly what he wanted to hear.

13

Molly

The Day We Got Dirty

"This wasn't the kind of messy I expected."

I was standing in front of the divider between our rooms, which was open. I had dragged my desk over, cleaned it thoroughly with soap, and then when it was dry I sprinkled flour across the surface. Donovan was directly in front of me in his kitchen, punching a big roll of dough and sending bits of flour in all directions.

"I promise it will leave you satisfied," he said over his shoulder in a sexy voice. "What's more satisfying than being *filled* with thick, salty pasta?"

I laughed and said, "You're not wrong."

Together, on either side of the dividing doorway, we made pasta together. Donovan had a technique where he cracked an egg open on the counter, then spun it around the flour until it slowly began coalescing into dough. Every so often he splashed a little water or oil on the counter too. When he was done, he tossed the dough to my side of the room, where I continued kneading it with my fingers and rolling it smooth.

"Punch it," he instructed.

"I'm not a violent person."

"Trust me, the dough is asking for it. Go on. Make a fist and *pound it* like you're on a real third date." He said it with a wink.

I bent my head to the dough so he couldn't see my cheeks redden. I rolled the dough into a ball, then sank my fist into it with a satisfying *smack*.

"Atta girl," he said in a husky voice.

"Stop making it sound so dirty!" I laughed while using the dough as a punching bag. "This *is* fun. Forget dinner. I want to do this all night."

"Easy there, Rocky," he said. "I think you finished it off. Give it here."

I tossed it through the doorway, and Donovan caught it like a football receiver. He fed the dough into a pasta strainer, which spit out flat fettuccine noodles onto the kitchen counter. I made *ooh* and *ahh* noises while watching. When all the dough was converted into noodles, he dumped them into a pot of boiling water. Then he began heating the sauce in a pan.

Even if it wasn't the kind of dirty that I expected, it was still a lot of fun. Helping make the dinners I was eating made me feel slightly more useful, too.

"You said you own a shop? In Indiana?" Donovan asked.

"Yeah," I said while cleaning the flour off my desk. "A clothing store."

"What's it called? *Feisty Fabrics?*"

I laughed and said, "*Nellie's Boutique.*"

"Who's Nellie?"

"My mom. She was the one that opened the store."

He nodded along while stirring the pasta with a wooden spoon. "And you help her run it?"

How much should I tell him?

81

"I pretty much run it all by myself," I said carefully. "Along with the manager I hired, Andrea."

"Did your mom retire or something?"

I hesitated. Opening up wasn't easy for me, even in the best of circumstances. My every instinct was to brush off the question and change the subject.

But I felt like I could trust Donovan. I *wanted* to open up to him.

"My mom... died last year. She and my dad both."

He stopped stirring the pasta and turned to face me. Alarm and concern were painted on his face. "What happened?"

"There was a big ice storm last October," I explained numbly. Like I was talking about something mundane, like the thickness of the pasta dough. "Roads were slicker than a hockey rink. Traffic on the interstate came to a stand-still, but a semi-truck didn't realize it until too late. My parents were in the car in front of him, and..." I paused as my throat tightened. "They never saw it coming."

"Oh, Molly," he breathed. "I'm so sorry."

"That's the reason for this trip," I said. "My girlfriends wanted to take me away for a week. Help me forget everything. The funny thing about it all? The pandemic *has* helped take my mind off of it. It's the first thing that has distracted me since they died. How's that for irony?"

And you, I thought to myself. *You've helped distract me, Donovan.*

He gazed at me like he wanted to do something. I'd seen that look a hundred times, whenever I told someone about my parents' accident. Sadness and pity and regret all mixed together in his storm-cloud eyes. It reflected back onto me and made *me* want to cry all over again.

Then he walked to the divider, reached across my makeshift pasta desk, and pulled me into a hug.

It was the first time we had made any sort of contact. It was the kind of hug given with his entire body, like he wished he could hug my soul, too. After the shock of touching another person wore off, I relaxed and savored the way he felt. Chiseled arms and a hard, wide chest. Flour-coated fingers laced into my hair, holding my head against his shoulder.

It was the kind of hug that made a little piece of my soul untwist. Like a knot was being removed.

Finally he pulled away. He cleared his throat and said, "I know we've been trying to keep our distance because of the distancing rules, but I just thought... You needed that. I won't do it again if you don't want. I'm sorry about your parents."

"I don't want sympathy," I said. "I just wanted to tell you. So you know."

He gave me a sad smile. "I'm glad you did, Molly."

Donovan strained the pasta and added it to the sauce. We carried our bowls out to our respective balconies to eat while watching the sunset. Neither of us talked for awhile—we just savored the comfort of each other's presence. It felt the way it had when we watched TV together in the lobby, but on an entirely different level. More intimate, somehow, even though we were just making dinner.

"This is the best pasta I've ever made," I said.

One of his dark eyebrows rose. "The best pasta *you've* ever made?"

"Yes, I'm taking full credit for it."

"It would be better if I could make the sauce from scratch," he muttered while stirring his food. "I hate using pre-made sauce in a jar. If I could get fresh ingredients..."

"I think it's fantastic! The fresh pasta makes a *huge* difference, regardless of the sauce," I said. "When you get back, you'll get a job wherever you apply."

"I don't know..."

"Just make them this and they'll hire you on the spot," I insisted. "I'm certain of it."

He smiled to himself while eating. If I didn't know any better, my flippant compliment meant a lot to him.

"Want to go out?" Donovan asked as we finished up.

"Go out where? The front door is locked."

He swept his hand at the hotel behind us. "We've got the entire Residencia Al Gladiatore at our disposal! Let's get into some trouble. But I'll warn you now: we might have to ignore a *closed* sign. If you can handle that."

"You know what? I think I'm in the mood to live dangerously. What did you have in mind?"

14

Molly

The Day I Broke The Rules

We went down to the lounge on the second floor. It extended away from the main building, which allowed it to have a vaulted ceiling with glass that showed the night sky high above. It was decorated like a cigar room from the nineteenth century, with dark wood and earthen tones. There were two pool tables, some leather couches and chairs, and a projector aimed at one wall.

"They host movie nights in here when things are normal," Donovan explained. "I didn't go to any of them, but the concierge told me about it. Drinks are free."

I went to the bar and gently pulled on the glass. "They're not free now. The bar is locked."

Donovan came over to check them. He pointed. "Damn. It looks like the pool cues and balls are locked away, too. I don't think I'm desperate enough to break the glass."

"Maybe when we run out of wine," I said.

It felt like the wind had been taken out of our sails. We stood around, not sure what else to do.

"Seinfeld in the lobby?" Donovan suggested.

I frowned while thinking about our options. "Do you know how the supply delivery guy gets in every day?"

"What do you mean?" he asked.

"The front door is locked," I said, thinking out loud. "He must have a key. Maybe he has a key that can unlock this, too." I tapped the bar cabinet. "We can ask him tomorrow."

Donovan's eyes brightened. "I have a better idea."

We descended another floor to the lobby. Donovan led me behind the concierge desk, where he began opening drawers at random.

"There *has* to be a spare key around here," he said. "The concierge and everyone else left in a hurry. I bet if we search hard enough..."

The concierge desk didn't turn up anything, so we went into the back office. There was a desk with an array of computer monitors showing security camera feeds from around the hotel: outside the front door, by the loading dock, the lounge, the lobby, and the pool room. Donovan went under the desk, and seconds later the monitors all turned off. He crawled back out and held up an unplugged power cord.

"Don't need anyone recording all the rules we're breaking," he said with a smile. "I'd hate for you to get in trouble for ignoring a sign."

The other desks in the office were used by administrators, and were covered with paperwork. One had a lunch bag open with the contents spread out on the desk. A half-empty can of Coke was next to it.

"Everyone left in a hurry," I said. "Probably rushing home when the lockdown was first announced."

Donovan opened a drawer and made a victorious sound. "Found them!" He held up a big ring of keys.

"There must be thirty keys on there," I said.

"Which means one of them has to work. Come on."

We rushed back upstairs like kids who had solved a puzzle. Donovan opened the key ring and dumped out half the keys on the bar top so we could try them simultaneously. One by one we jammed keys into the lock and jiggled them.

"Bingo!" I said when my sixth key opened the liquor cabinet. "And God said, *let there be booze!*"

Donovan quickly put his hand on the cabinet to keep it closed. "Hold on a second, Feisty. As soon as we open this cabinet, there's no going back. You're living a life of crime from that moment on. Are you sure you want to take that step?"

I nodded solemnly. "I'm ready. Even if it means I have to get a gang tattoo on my ass."

Donovan laughed, then took the key from me and opened two more cabinets. "Take the pool balls and rack a game. I'll make us a couple of drinks."

"How do you know what I like?" I pointed out.

"I don't." He pulled down a bottle of Campari. "But we're in Rome, so I'm making you a Negroni."

I carried the pool balls to the table. "I thought you were a line cook, not a bartender."

"I can do both," he said, "but I've only ever been paid for one."

I had the balls racked and ready by the time he brought me an amber-colored drink in a highball glass. It tasted like dark licorice and fruit, with a bitter aftertaste.

"It's better with an orange garnish," Donovan said while grabbing a pool cue. "But alas, no oranges."

"I like it!" I took a deeper sip. "I'm not very good at pool, by the way."

Donovan placed the white cue ball at the end of the table and stretched out the cue. "That's okay. I'm not very—"

He jabbed the stick forward, but it only glanced off his target. The cue ball rolled off at a diagonal angle, bounced off the railing, and then hit the rack of colored balls weakly. They drifted apart a few inches, but remained clustered down at the other end of the table.

I raised my glass and said, "You may not be a good pool player, but you make a good drink."

"Apparently." He looked at the tip of his cue stick and frowned.

I eyed the table. I didn't have any good options thanks to his bad break. I lowered my pool stick to the table, gripping the front of it while using my other hand to push it forward. The stick hit the cue ball flush, but it wasn't very hard, and my aim was so poor that I didn't even hit the ball I was aiming at.

"You may not be a good pool player," Donovan teased, "but you... Huh. What *are* you good at, Feisty?"

"Oh, I'm good at plenty of things."

"I bet you are," he said while chalking his cue.

We played pool while flirting and teasing each other. I smiled at Donovan while watching him bend over the table to line up a shot. It felt like a weight had been lifted from my shoulders now that I had told him about my parents. It wasn't that I was trying to hide it from him. It's just that people always reacted so *awkwardly* when they found out. They looked at me with pity, like I was a poor orphan girl who was suddenly all alone.

But Donovan had reacted perfectly. He hugged me, told me he was sorry, and then helped take my mind off things with food and drinks and pool. He didn't treat me differently now that he knew.

That meant more to me than all the pasta he'd been sharing. It made me feel like things were *normal.*

"You're holding the pool cue wrong," he said casually. "Want me to show you how it's done?"

I leaned on my cue and said, "Not sure I want to take pointers from the guy who couldn't make a solid break."

"I'm rusty, but I know how to play." He held his cue stick out and motioned. "Curl your index finger over the tip. You've been gripping it like you're giving it a hand-job."

The strong liquor was going to my head, which made the sexual metaphor sound *extra* dirty. Especially the way he said it while motioning on the stick and narrowing his eyes suggestively. I tried to think of a good retort, something funny *and* dirty, but nothing came to mind.

"Like this?" I followed his suggestion with just one finger.

"Almost. You still need to use the other fingers to stabilize it. Here."

Donovan rested his stick against the wall and came up behind me. He wrapped his arms around me, pressing his strong body against mine and surrounding me with his warmth.

"Bring your other fingers up." His breath was hot on my neck and unleashed a flurry of butterflies in my stomach. Aside from our hug, this was the closest we had been together.

"Like this?" I asked.

"Exactly," he whispered. "Just like that. You're a natural."

Is this his way of getting even with me? I wondered. If so, it was working. The entire world had narrowed to Donovan's ridiculously-hot body, a body which was currently pressed against mine like a sexy shadow.

The front of his jeans brushed against my ass. He pulled away slightly, but I could still feel his body heat just out of reach. The liquor in the Negroni was strong, and it made me want to have some fun. The kind of fun I was normally too chicken to try.

What are you good at, Feisty? he had asked.

I wanted to show him.

His hands were still on the pool cue to show me what to do. I

89

bent over the table and stuck my ass back until it pressed against his crotch. If this were a poker game, then I had just called his bet *and* raised him.

"How's this?" I asked softly.

"That's good," he rumbled. "Really good."

Something *twitched* against me. Something warm and hard and rapidly growing. Feeling bold, I pushed my ass harder against him until there was no denying it.

"Now what?" I asked.

He let out a strained sigh. "Pull the cue back smoothly. See how it feels in your fingers this way?"

"It feels good," I breathed.

"Whenever you're ready," he said in a tight voice. "Give it a shot."

I gave the cue a few slow, steady strokes. Like I was holding *him* in my fingers instead of the polished wood of the cue. The fabric of my dress was so thin I could feel his cock pressed firmly between my cheeks, grinding against me slowly. I got the sense he was holding himself back. Like he was on the edge of throwing aside all pretext and pulling my dress over my ass, ripping my panties aside, and burying himself into me from behind.

I want him to do it, I realized. *If he made his move now I would surrender and never look back.*

I pushed my ass into him a little more, then swung the pool stick. It hit the cue ball firmly, shooting it across the table at the seven ball, my target. The ball rolled toward the corner pocket, bounced against both rims, and then rolled away.

"*So close,*" Donovan sighed in my ear. Then he pulled away from me. "But your form was good."

He retrieved his stick and rounded the table to set up his next shot. There was a noticeable bulge in his jeans which pulled my eyes like a magnet.

Okay, maybe he does have the willpower of a saint, I thought as we continued playing.

Donovan was rusty, and missed more shots than he made, but that was still good enough to beat me. He racked the balls and we played another game, but there wasn't any more sexy grinding or thinly-veiled pool euphemisms. The moment we had shared was gone.

When we went to make two more drinks, he eyed the key ring for a long time. "What's up?" I asked.

"I just realized something," he said slowly. "You know what else these probably unlock?"

"What?"

"The front door."

15

Donovan

The Day I Went Outside

"Are you sure you feel comfortable doing this?" Molly asked me the next morning while we rode the elevator down. Neither of us acknowledged the fact that we were sharing the cramped space. I felt safe around her, and she felt safe around me.

"We're running low on food," I told her. "I didn't expect to be sharing it with my hotel neighbor."

She gave me a playful little glare.

"I didn't say you weren't worth it," I clarified. "But unless you want to eat plain pasta noodles, I need to get supplies."

"I don't like the idea of you risking yourself out there."

The elevator opened on the first floor and we walked across the lobby. "I'll be okay. I've got my mask, and a pair of sunglasses to cover my eyes." I put them both on and turned to her. "How do I look?"

"Like the Unabomber, but sexier," she said.

"Sexy Unabomber. Now there's a Halloween costume I've never seen before."

I went into the office behind the concierge desk. There was a panel on the wall for the exterior alarm. The light indicated that it was currently armed. I found the right key on the key ring to open the panel, then pressed the button marked "DISABILITATO." The light winked out.

"Any last minute requests?" I asked.

"Oranges!" she said. "I've been craving orange slices like you wouldn't believe. If it's not too much trouble, I mean. Don't go out of your way just for me."

"I'll see what I can do. Wish me luck." I unlocked the front door.

"Good luck. Watch out for zombies."

I chuckled, but said, "Not sure how I feel about dark humor right now."

"If I didn't laugh about it, I'd probably be crying!" she said cheerfully. Then her tone softened and she said, "Be safe. Seriously. Text me if anything happens."

I was touched by her concern as I walked out of the hotel. But the feeling quickly dimmed as the reality of the situation sank in. I hadn't left the hotel since I got supplies at the beginning of the lockdown, a week ago. Things still felt normal back then, with people crowded in the plaza and the sound of markets and tourists and street performers. Now everything was deserted and silent.

And experiencing the silence down in the plaza itself was a *lot* different than experiencing it from my hotel balcony. It was like the difference between watching a shark at the aquarium and being in the fucking *tank*.

I turned back to look at the hotel. Molly was watching me from the front door, and she gave a little wave.

It really did feel like I was walking around in a post-apocalyptic movie. Humanity had been wiped out and I was the only person left. It was unsettling. Like swimming too far from the shore and suddenly realizing that there was only empty ocean in all directions.

93

"Relax, Donovan," I said out loud. "Everything's fine. Just a quick trip to the market."

The market I had used the other day, a quarter mile from the hotel, was closed. The city had sent out a map with the locations of open grocery stores which people were allowed to visit in a four-hour window. Unfortunately, that store was over two miles away.

Three kilometers, I corrected in my head. *When in Rome...*

The farther I got from the tourist center of Rome, the more signs of life I saw. I passed an apartment building with balconies that were full of life: plants, laundry, even an old woman smoking her morning cigarette. Her eyes followed me down the street.

At the next intersection I saw a police officer. "Dove stai andando?" he asked me.

It was one of the few phrases I had learned in my week of cooking school. "Cibo," I replied back. "Il mercato."

Food. The market.

The officer pointed up the street and waved me on.

The walk was long, but I didn't mind. It actually felt nice to get outside. *Actually* outside, not just sitting on the balcony. It felt good to stretch my legs beyond just running on the treadmill, too. Back home, I had to walk three miles to get to the diner where I worked. I liked to walk.

Soon I came across two other masked pedestrians walking in the same direction. I slowed my pace so that I wouldn't catch up to them. Then another person fell in behind me from a side street. They kept their distance, but I couldn't help but wonder if any of them were infected. Was I breathing the same air as the people in front of me? I pictured them exhaling, breath droplets hanging in the air like smoke, waiting for me to walk through. Realizing that I was holding my breath, I tried to make myself relax. It didn't work.

As I drew closer to the market, the street grew more crowded. Somehow the crowd made things feel normal again, and also eerily different. Nobody talked—we all walked along, silent except for our footsteps, like mice who were too afraid to make any noise.

The grocery store was called *DESPAR*, which looked unnervingly like the English word *despair*. There was a line of people waiting to get inside, with police officers patrolling the area to make sure everyone stayed two meters apart. Their presence was surprisingly calming for my nerves. After being isolated in the hotel, it was good to see that there were people in charge. Lines were a byproduct of civilization. The world might feel like it was ending, but at least it was an *orderly* apocalypse.

The line moved slowly. I pulled out my phone to kill time.

Donovan: I'm here. There's a long line, so I probably won't be back for another hour.

Donovan: Don't throw any parties while I'm gone.

Molly: Too late. I'm inviting all my friends over and we're drinking ALL the liquor in the lounge.

Donovan: If there's no booze when I get back, I'm making you eat vending machine chips for the rest of the week.

Molly: That's not nice!

Donovan: Neither is drinking all the alcohol!

Molly: Fine. I promise not to drink all the booze.

Molly: Are you doing okay?

Donovan: I think so. It's kind of surreal out here.

Molly: I bet. Be safe.

Molly: I'm thinking of you.

I'm thinking of you. My eyes scanned over the last text again and again. It was such a simple, straightforward statement of care and concern.

But it made me grin like an idiot while standing in line.

While I waited in line, I replayed the events from last night in my head. I thought I was so smooth, showing her how to use a pool cue as an excuse to get close to her. Oldest trick in the book, right? But rather than turn her into the awkward, nervous woman I expected, she leaned into it by leaning into *me*. Pushing that sweet ass against my crotch until my dick was wedged between her plump cheeks. Her dress was thin, so I felt *everything*. And I knew she felt everything from me.

Even now, a day later, my cock twitched just thinking about it. I had to quickly think about something else to keep from getting hard there in the line outside the store.

But one thing was certain: I needed to think of a way to get even.

When it was my turn to go inside, a grocery store employee used a laser thermometer to check my forehead temperature. I must have been fine because he waved me inside. Another employee wiped down a basket with a disinfectant cloth and handed it to me.

The thing about European grocery stores was that they were small. Back in America, our stores had wide aisles that could fit two or three carts across. That wasn't the case in Rome. The aisles in *DESPAR* were so narrow that a single shopping cart blocked the path, and there weren't big open walkways at the end of each aisle.

This may have been annoying in normal times, but it was debilitating during a pandemic. It was a challenge to stay two meters from everyone as I darted through the store, grabbing supplies. It was like a game of tag, except everyone was "it" and nobody wanted to win.

Even when I managed to navigate through the store like an art thief dodging lasers, I couldn't get everything I needed. Many of the shelves were empty, especially in the dry goods section. The pasta aisle was totally wiped out. A single box was open on the floor, dry macaroni scattered in all directions like a crime scene.

My grocery list quickly became unrealistic, so I changed my game plan. I grabbed whatever food I knew I could use to make a meal. Canned tuna. Two packs of ground beef, and one of ground sausage. A head of broccoli that had seen better days. I was in emergency mode now. We had to eat to survive, not just for pleasure.

The store was out of oranges, so I grabbed a bag of apples instead. I knew it would be heavy to carry back to the hotel, but if it put a smile on Molly's face? It would be worth it.

The check-out line was extra unnerving. The cashier had to pick up every single item, scan them, and then place them in a bag. I wondered how many other objects she had touched today, objects that had been touched by *other* people. She rubbed some hand sanitizer between her palms when she was done ringing me up, but I couldn't shake the feeling that I was carrying a bag full of tainted items.

The fresh air outside felt good on my skin. Little was known about the virus so far, but that was something everyone agreed on: outdoors was safer than indoors. I breathed a sigh of relief through my mask as I made the long walk back to the hotel.

When I walked through the front door, I was greeted by a surprising sight. A figure stood next to the concierge desk, decked from head to toe in a yellow hazmat suit. The face was hidden behind a plastic window in the suit. In front of the suited person was one of the coffee tables from the lobby, and a bucket of water.

"I found this in the janitor's closet!" Molly said from inside the suit. "Does it make my ass look big?"

She turned around and shook her butt, which just a shapeless plastic bump.

I laughed. "You've never been sexier."

"Ha ha, very funny," her muffled voice said through the suit.

"You've actually stumbled upon my kink," I teased. "Dressing up like astronauts is the only way I can get hard."

She giggled inside the suit. "I know *that's* not true. Shut up and start unloading the bags. I have a process for cleaning everything on this coffee table."

So she's acknowledging what happened last night, I thought.

Molly had me place each grocery item on the table one at a time. She then sprayed it down with a can of disinfectant spray, then used a big pair of tongs to dip the object into the bucket of water. Then she placed the clean object to the side where it could dry.

"No oranges," I told her when we got to the bag. "But I got apples instead."

"I like apples too," she said, but I could tell she was a little disappointed.

It took ten minutes to individually clean every grocery item. "Okay, your turn," she said, when the last one was done.

"You're not spraying me with that," I said.

She laughed and said, "No, we're getting you clean another way. Come on!"

I followed her suited shape down the hall to the pool. The hot tub was bubbling gently. Next to it was a towel.

"*You* walked into the pool room?" I asked. "Woah now. You're breaking the rules, Feisty."

She stuck her tongue out at me. "The *closed* sign fell off the door, so technically I'm not breaking any rules by being inside."

"So you're excusing your criminal behavior based on a technicality. I see how it is."

"Get in," she insisted. "Scrub yourself clean!"

I smirked at her. "You just want to see me naked, don't you?"

"I already saw you in your underwear when you were swimming laps," she said curtly. "This is just like that."

"You mean when you were so embarrassed that you ran out of the pool room?" I asked.

98

"It's different now," she said. "I've gotten to know you better. Strip down to your underwear."

Molly turned away from me slightly to give me a little bit of privacy, but I could tell she was looking at me out of the corner of her eye. *You just gave me a way to get even,* I thought while removing my shirt, then my shoes. I scrambled out of my jeans until I was only wearing my boxer-briefs.

"Good," she said, like a nurse giving instructions to a patient. "Now jump in the hot tub and—"

She cut off as I bent down and yanked my underwear off. I stepped out of it and tossed it aside with my toe, then struck a pose with my hands on my hips. I didn't need to flex much, but I sucked in my gut to make sure my abs really *popped.*

My move had the desired result. Molly gawked at me. She was unable to look away. Her eyes were wide behind her plastic suit as she took in my nude body, eyes moving down my chest, then my abs, then pausing extra long at my groin.

"If we're going to be safe," I said, "we might as well be *totally* safe. Right?"

Her eyes shot back up to my face like they were pulled by magnets. "Right. Good idea." Even with the plastic suit on I could see that her cheeks were as red as a Miami sunburn.

I paused for three long heartbeats. Only then did I turn toward the hot tub and slowly step inside. I took my sweet time so she could get a long look at my ass before I finally dipped all the way beneath the surface. The water was scalding, right on the edge of *too* hot, but after a few seconds my skin adjusted.

Only then did Molly unzip her hazmat suit and climb out of it. She was wearing normal clothes underneath. She sat on the edge of the hot tub, rolled up her jeans, and dipped her feet inside. Then she handed me a bottle of body wash.

"Scrub everything," she said.

"I know how to clean myself," I pointed out.

"Just making sure you do it right. If you get sick, then I'll probably get sick too."

"Good point," I said casually. "I'd hate to give you an excuse to not grind your ass up against me."

She cleared her throat. "I was talking about the food. If you get sick, I can't keep mooching dinners off you."

"Food, right," I said with a smirk.

When my body was pink, I climbed out and toweled off. This time Molly had enough willpower to totally face the other direction until I had wrapped the towel around my midsection. She picked up my old clothes with a big pair of tongs.

"I'll take these to the laundry room and wash them."

Where'd you get those tongs?" I asked. "The same place you got the funky hazmat suit?"

Molly's eyes brightened. "Oh, yeah! I forgot to tell you. I have a surprise."

"I like surprises."

She picked up the ring of keys and gave them a jingle. "There's another place these keys open. And it's going to make you the happiest man in Rome."

16

Molly

The Day With Pie

"The kitchen!" Donovan shouted. "We can get into the kitchen!"

After putting on fresh clothes, Donovan ran inside the unlocked kitchen like a kid on Christmas morning. He gazed in all directions, running his fingers along the stainless steel counters and appliances.

"They have a twenty-range industrial stove. And a flat-top for burgers and other grilled items. That's what I used at the diner. Oh! A deep fryer!"

"I realized the keys unlock the kitchen when you were already at the store," I told him. "I'm sorry you made the trip for nothing."

"Why did I make the trip for nothing?" he asked, confused.

I opened the door to the giant industrial fridge. "This is why."

His eyes widened as he stared inside. The fridge was full of food: eggs, chicken, beef, pork, fish, milk. All the supplies needed to run the hotel restaurant during a normal week.

"There's a lot more in the pantry," I said. "Like, a *lot* more. I think they bake their own bread."

"Ovens!" Donovan suddenly exclaimed. He ran across the kitchen, where an industrial-sized oven covered the entire wall. "This is the big kind used by bakeries."

"Does this mean you'll be making me cookies?"

He gave me a perfectly-sweet smile. "Feisty, I'll bake you whatever you want."

It was cute how *giddy* he was while examining the kitchen. He told me it was so much nicer than the diner he cooked at, which was basically just a single flat-top with a grease trap.

"I could cook for the entire hotel in a kitchen like this," he said.

"That's good, because right now the entire hotel is *me*. What's for lunch, Chef Russo?"

He grinned harder than I had ever seen him smile. "First we need to know what we have, and how long it's been here."

We spent the afternoon taking inventory of all the food. I called out the item and the expiration date, which Donovan then wrote down in a notebook. The expiration date was important because it gave us an idea of what food we should cook first, and which we could save for later. Since we didn't know how long we would be stuck here, we needed to plan.

"First the pool, then the kitchen?" Donovan said while we worked. "I'm impressed. You're breaking all sorts of rules."

"Nothing says we're not allowed in the kitchen," I argued carefully. "We used a key to unlock the door, but it doesn't say *employees only*. No rules have been broken."

He ran a hand through his dark hair. "I don't buy it. You've *clearly* turned to a life of crime. Next thing I know you'll be sneaking into my room to cuddle."

"That would *definitely* be breaking a rule. The concierge said not to allow anyone into our rooms. For our own safety."

"Oh, well if the concierge said so..." Donovan chuckled. "So if I hear you choking on a pasta shell in your room, you wouldn't want me to rush over and save you?"

"Hmm." I made a show of stroking my chin and considering it. "*Maybe* it would be okay then. But only if it's a life and death situation."

Once the fridge was inventoried, we went into the pantry and started counting the dry items. "Five sacks of black beans," I called out.

Donovan was sitting on a crate full of olives. "How big are the bags?"

"Five pounds. No, five *kilograms*," I said. "So, twenty-five kilos of black beans."

"Got it." He made a note on his sheet.

"This reminds me of taking inventory at the boutique," I said while moving the beans out of the way. "Mom always recruited me to help her. I *hated* it at the time. It was boring, and I just wanted to go outside and play. But she made me do it at the end of every month. It's kind of funny, thinking about it now."

He looked up from his notebook. "Funny how?"

"Doing inventory was my least favorite thing in the world, at the time," I explained. "But now? I would give anything to do inventory with her one last time."

"I can't imagine losing my parents." He lowered his notebook. "Did your mom have any special recipes?"

"Special?" I asked.

"Something she would make on special occasions. A type of cake, or homemade brownies. Something that reminds you of her. I could make it for you."

He smiled hopefully. He was so eager to do something sweet for me, and the gesture made my throat tighten.

"Mom wasn't much of a baker," I said. "She bought those pre-

103

made rolls of cookie dough and made cookies that way. That's about it."

"Ah, okay." He looked disappointed for a moment, then suddenly jumped to his feet. "If you don't have a family recipe, then I'll share one of mine. It's a special pie recipe that's been in my family for generations. Russo Pie. It's deceptively simple."

"What about inventory?" I said. "We still have most of the pantry left."

"The dry goods can wait until later," he insisted. "Come on."

He led me back into the main kitchen and started throwing open cabinets to search for mixing bowls and measuring cups. Donovan gave me instructions on how to make the filling: beaten eggs, melted butter, flour, sugar, and chocolate chips. While I mixed all of that together in the bowl, Donovan rolled out the pie crust.

"Pour it in," he instructed, standing behind me with a gentle hand on my back. "Spread it around so that it fills the crust evenly. Good. See the batter at the bottom? Make sure you scoop that out too."

It was similar to our pool game when he stood behind me and showed me what to do: his voice was a soft rumble in my ear, and his breath tickled the back of my neck and stirred my hair. But it wasn't purely sexual. It felt more intimate than just grinding our private parts together.

Donovan's hand lingered on my shoulder, then he opened the oven and gestured. I picked up the pie and slid it inside. He closed the door and wiped his hands together.

"In thirty minutes we'll have a delicious Russo Pie."

"That's it?" I asked.

"That's it. I told you it was deceptively simple. The homemade crust is the hardest part."

"There were pre-made crusts in the fridge," I said.

Donovan's face twisted in disgust. "I'm going to pretend that was a joke."

We finished the rest of our inventory while the pie baked. There were a *lot* of dry goods in the pantry. Especially basics like flour, sugar, and boxes of dry pasta. We could live here at the hotel for months if we had to. And as long as I was with Donovan, that didn't seem like such a bad prospect.

A sweet and chocolaty smell filled the kitchen when Donovan pulled out the pie. The crust was golden brown, and my mouth watered at the sight of it.

"It needs to cool," Donovan said. "But it will be ready by the time dinner is done."

Out of all the food items in the fridge, the ground beef and cream had the most recent expiration dates, so Donovan made spaghetti bolognese for dinner. Even though we had boxes upon boxes of dry pasta in the pantry he insisted on making the pasta from scratch.

"Can you watch the garlic bread for me?" he asked when everything was almost ready. "I'll be right back."

I watched the bread through the oven door, pulling it out when it was toasted to a perfect golden brown. Donovan returned moments later with two plates.

"Perfect timing," he said while spooning bolognese onto each plate.

"Want to eat this in the lobby?" I asked. "We can watch Italian Seinfeld."

"I have something else planned." He carried both plates out of the kitchen.

I followed behind him, wondering what he meant.

The restaurant was dark, as it had been all week. All the chairs were still stacked on their tables except for one table where they had been pulled down. A cluster of candles were glowing softly in the middle of the table, casting flickering shadows across the room. A bottle of wine and two glasses waited.

Donovan placed both plates on the table and then held a chair for me.

"Donovan," I said while sitting down. "This is wonderful."

He pushed my chair in and sat across the table. "I wanted a special night with you," he said. "To take your mind off things. The way this trip *should* have gone."

I didn't know what to say. I reached across the table and squeezed his hand.

He popped the cork on the wine and began filling my glass. "This isn't from your room. This is a *nice* bottle. From the dusty section of the wine closet."

"You don't think we'll get in trouble for opening it?" I asked.

"Who's to say we opened it?" he replied with a sly grin. "The security cameras are all off."

"It was probably the daily delivery guy," I agreed. "He's been known to steal wine, after all."

We laughed together and enjoyed our candlelight dinner. The bolognese was tangy, and creamy, and absolutely delicious. And the garlic bread was crispy on the outside and soft on the inside.

Donovan served Russo Pie for dessert. I made a soft moan when I tasted the first bite.

He nodded smugly. "What did I tell you?"

"It's all gooey on the inside!" I said as I took another bite.

"That's why it's been a family recipe for generations," he said. "It's easy *and* delicious."

My plate was empty less than a minute later. I looked at it sadly.

"Want seconds?" he asked.

I glanced up at him. "You won't judge me?"

"You're on vacation, Feisty," he said while taking my plate. "You can do whatever the hell you want."

I grinned and admired his sexy shape as he went back into the kitchen to get me another slice.

17

Molly

The Day We Danced

We drank expensive wine and talked about everything—home, work, other countries we wanted to visit—until the candles burned low. When Donovan went to refill his glass, the bottle was empty.

"How about I grab another bottle from the wine closet and we drink it on our balconies?" I asked. "The rain has finally stopped, and we haven't had balcony wine in days."

He chewed the inside of his lip, then smiled sadly. "I should probably clean the kitchen and put the food away."

"I can help!" I said. "It's the least I can do."

But he waved his hand. "I don't mind. Besides, I want to tinker with some of the kitchen gadgets. I've never had access to a *real* kitchen before. I feel like a kid in a toy store, and I don't know what to play with first."

"Fine," I teased. "Play with your *toys*. Thank you for a wonderful evening."

We smiled at each other, and I was struck by just how much I wanted to kiss him. Donovan wasn't a stranger anymore. We'd been stuck together for over a week, and had been on the equivalent of five or six dates. I didn't have any excuses anymore.

Not to mention he *radiated* sex appeal. As we stood on either side of the table, the sexual tension between us was the strongest it had ever been. Even more than when we played pool last night. That felt like playful teasing, but this? This had been a *real* date, with cooking and wine and candles.

Kiss him, I told myself. *Go around the table and push your lips against his and make him respond.*

Before I could work up the courage to do just that, Donovan grabbed our two dessert plates and carried them into the kitchen.

I snatched a bottle of red wine from the kitchen closet and carried it upstairs to my balcony. The sky was perfectly clear and the stars were shining above the city, despite the light pollution. A cool breeze blew across the balcony, stirring my shirt.

I thought about my date with Donovan. Something had changed between us, for the better. His playful flirting had been replaced with genuine interest.

It's probably the kitchen, I thought while sipping my wine. *Now that he can cook real food, he's happier than I've ever seen him.*

As I thought about him, my mind drifted to the hot tub this morning. The way he fearlessly removed his boxer-briefs and stood in front of me like it was totally normal to be naked. I had *never* been that comfortable in my nudity, even with my serious boyfriends. Letting Donovan see me in my bra and panties, and bending over in front of the gym window, was a huge step for me. Yet he one-upped me by the hot tub with ease.

Confidence probably came easy when you looked like *that.* Because everything I saw while he wore his birthday suit made me tingle with unrestrained arousal. Bulging arms, broad chest, abs like buttery dinner rolls leading down to a penis that looked smooth and long, even when he wasn't hard...

Suddenly the door to the neighboring balcony opened and

Donovan walked out. "I changed my mind. The kitchen can wait."

I couldn't stop a smile from filling my face. "I'm so glad! I mean, because I didn't want to drink alone. This is an expensive bottle of wine, and I don't think I can finish it by myself."

He leaned his wine glass across the railing toward me and flashed his most charming smile yet. "Happy to help with that."

His portable speaker chimed to life and began playing classical Italian music. We stood on our balconies and gazed out at the city. Some cats wandered across the plaza and *meowed* beneath our balcony. Wondering if we were going to accidentally drop more food.

"I wish I was dancing right now," I said out loud.

"Yeah?"

"It's the only physical exercise that I actually like. I hate running, and I can tolerate walking but I don't enjoy it. But dancing? It always takes my mind off things. It gives me a *release* that I can't really explain."

He nodded along. "I get it. That's how I feel after working out."

"We had four different clubs we wanted to visit while we were here. I know I sound like a broken record but..." I sighed. "This was supposed to be the day I flew home. The end of my trip. I thought I would return to Indiana with a new perspective on life, refreshed and rejuvenated. But I feel the same as I did a week ago. I know I should be happy that I'm healthy and safe, but..."

"It's okay to be disappointed," Donovan said. "Yeah, shit is crazy right now. But you're still allowed to be sad over the trip that didn't happen."

"You don't think I'm whining too much?"

He gestured with his wine glass. "All things considered? I think you're whining the perfect amount. It would be weird *not* to complain about the circumstances."

"I haven't heard you complain much," I said.

110

"I don't have much to complain about," he replied while leaning on the railing. "I've got a four-star kitchen and months of food supplies at my disposal. Instead of being stuck in this hotel alone, or with a bunch of assholes, I'm neighbors with a pretty cool girl from Indiana. And she's gone seven days without yelling at me, which is nice."

I chuckled and said, "Surely you have something to complain about."

"Right now? My only complaint is that I'm not dancing with you."

Before I could respond, Donovan gulped down the rest of his wine and put down his glass. He walked to the edge of the balcony and threw a leg over the railing.

"What are you doing!"

He climbed over the railing until both feet were on the other side, totally open to the ground three stories below. He jumped across to my balcony, clutching the railing with both hands and making the whole structure shake. Then he climbed over until he was standing in front of me.

"I really want to dance with you," he said. "We've been around each other a lot lately. Hell, I even hugged you yesterday. I think this is safe."

My stomach was a roller coaster of twists and turns. "Okay. If you think so."

"Besides," he said, "you said I'm not allowed in your room. But the balcony is *outside*. No rules are being broken."

The upbeat music ended and a slower song began, one with violins and soft reedy sounds. Donovan put his hands on my hips, fingers sliding against the waistline of my jeans. Respectful, but on the edge of doing *more*. After a moment I wrapped my arms around him too.

I knew what Donovan's body looked like. I'd seen him shirtless plenty of times by now, and he'd stripped totally nude this morning. I felt his body against mine when we hugged yesterday. But this was totally different. Donovan *held* me against him with strong hands, assertive and commanding, pulling my breasts against his mile-wide chest. Wonderful smells surrounded me—that spicy cologne or aftershave he wore, warm baked bread from the kitchen, and underneath it all, his musky, masculine scent.

He feels better than I ever could have imagined.

My heart raced as Donovan began guiding me back and forth in a slow dance. We didn't have much room in the small balcony space, but we didn't need it for our gentle sways. This wasn't the kind of dancing I meant when I talked about feeling release, but it suited my mood after our candlelight dinner date. And it meant I got to rest against his boulder-hard body.

"You could have walked over through the door separating our rooms," I said softly.

"Hopping the balcony was more dramatic," he said. "Plus, this way I'm not breaking your rule about going in each other's room. Right?"

"Getting off on a technicality. I like the ingenuity."

"I can be creative when I need to be." He sighed. "I'm sorry your trip turned into a disaster, Feisty. Hopefully this is almost as good as going to the club with your friends and grinding with random Italian dudes."

It's better, I thought while we danced.

His hands moved down a little, until they were dangerously close to the top of my ass. I responded by holding onto him tighter. After a week of little-to-no physical contact, it felt so *good* to hold onto something steady. Like as long as I was in his arms everything would be okay.

His hands were warm, and his smile was bright, and I surrendered to the gentle, swaying motions. I leaned into his warm body and rested my head against his shoulder. I wanted to cling to him all night long and never let go.

"I'm glad you changed your mind," I whispered.

One of his hands caressed up my back and laced into my hair, fingertips gently massaging the scalp. "Playing with you is more fun than playing with the kitchen toys."

"Are you sure?" I asked his shoulder. "I'm not sure I can compete with the big baking oven thing."

His warm breath stirred my hair. "Good point. You don't have as many dials and knobs. In fact, I can only think of two, *maybe* three parts of your body I can twist..."

I giggled and playfully slapped at his arm. It was like hitting a brick wall of muscle.

"Hey, Feisty?"

"Yes?"

"I do have a confession to make."

He cupped my chin and tilted my head up so that I was facing him. His grey eyes reflected the moonlight, and the edge of his lip twitched in a smirk. I held my breath and waited to hear what he had to confess.

"I didn't come over here just to dance."

18

Donovan

The Day We Fooled Around

Being this forward was a huge risk. I barely knew this girl. The suggestion might offend Molly, or push her beyond her comfort level.

But I didn't care. It felt like the world was ending around us. And if that were the case, then I wanted to shoot my shot, consequences be damned.

Because at that moment: I wanted Molly badly.

And I was pretty sure she wanted me too.

I hadn't been able to keep my eyes off her since our dinner date began. She was *so damn stunning*. A tight little package in her jeans and close-fitting blouse. She was cute and funny and smiling like the world *wasn't* going to shit around us. Even if the hotel was full of people and things were normal, she would have stuck out to me in the crowd. I would have done everything in my power to win her over.

Her eyes were dark, wide orbs as she looked up at me. Waiting.

I gently spun her around so that she was facing the view of the city, then danced with her from behind. I lowered my lips to her neck but didn't kiss her—I stopped just short, where she could feel my breath and sense me so close to her skin. She cocked her neck to the side, practically *begging* me to kiss her skin, but I held back.

Instead, I snaked a hand over her hip and held her against me. I wrapped my other arm over her chest, my bicep and forearm pressed against her plump breasts. Holding her like she *belonged* to me, the way I'd been dreaming of holding her for the last week.

Her body melted into my arms, all the tension evaporating as she relaxed. Her hips inched backward until her ass was brushing against the front of my pants with every movement, soft caresses against my cock. We rocked back and forth along with the music coming from the speaker on my balcony. Swaying like we were the only two people in Rome. Like the city was *ours*.

I explored the outline of her body with my fingers. The curves beneath the jeans, the bump of her panties along her hip. The plumpness of her ass, even just the edge of it on my fingertips. Everywhere I touched she responded eagerly, relaxing and sighing, while clinging to me.

I slid my hand up along her neck and into her silky hair. The brass instruments in the music rose dramatically before falling back down.

Our bodies were pressed tightly together, now. It took all my willpower not to drag her into the bedroom and *really* show her what I wanted.

Not yet, I thought. *No matter how much I want her, she needs to be eased into it.*

I let my hand explore the top of her thigh. I could feel the warmth of her skin through the denim. But I wasn't interested only in what was on the outside.

I reached across her hip, sliding my fingers into the front of her jeans. The bare skin of her navel was soft and smooth, and she responded by trembling in my arms. My fingers pushed deeper and she widened her stance a few inches. It was a subtle movement, but it made my cock *pulse* against her ass. It was the green light I had been waiting

115

for.

Better give her what she wants.

I flicked open the button on her jeans and dove into the waistband of her panties, down into the soft warmth of her pussy. She was already soaked for me as I held her in my arms and began rubbing her slit. She trembled and let out a soft moan, leaning her head back against my shoulder while I got acquainted with what my fingers found.

"What if someone can see us..." she breathed.

"Nobody can see us," I whispered, lips only an inch from her ear. "The city is ours tonight. There's only me, and only you."

She surrendered as I slid my fingers up and down her wet heat— the only sounds that came from her were soft moans, noises that disappeared into the descending Roman night. I used my free arm to squeeze her, holding her against me while I fondled her. I slid my fingertips up and around her clit, giving it some caressing attention before returning to her soft lushness.

Molly tilted her head back and moaned louder, and I finally took the opportunity to kiss her neck. I started beneath her ear and kissed a trail down to her collarbone. She clung to me, pushing her hips into my massaging fingers while I rubbed and kissed her.

I savored the feeling of her body in my arms, soft and warm and inviting. She felt better than I ever could have imagined.

Molly drew rapid breaths and pushed her hips into my working fingers, begging me for more. My cock was screaming at me to rip her clothes off, to bend her over the balcony and *take her* while her hands gripped the railing so tightly the paint came off.

I pried my lips away from her neck and she twisted to gaze up at me. Her dark eyes were round and full of desire, and also something close to surprise. Her chest swelled and her cleavage heaved against my possessive arm.

She began moaning and then her hand was reaching behind

her, scrambling and clutching at my pants, grasping for my cock. When she found it she wrapped her fingers around my shaft, squeezing me through the fabric of my jeans, but I was totally focused on my job. Right now this was about *her,* and I wouldn't let myself get derailed. I wanted to make Molly squirm.

After all, you never got a second chance to make a first impression.

She didn't just squirm—she screwed her whole body into my hand, whimpering adorably as her breath came in ragged little gasps. I squeezed her tighter against my body and rubbed a fire into the nub of her clit with my palm. She arched her back and twisted her plump lips toward me, demanding to be kissed as I steered her toward the oblivion of ecstasy, and then she started gasping. She bit down on the collar of my T-shirt, teeth raking against my neck through the fabric, and then she let out a cry of ecstasy so intense it sounded like she was in pain.

"Oh God! Oh my God!" she cried, eyes wide and full of bliss. Her prayers turned into a wordless wail of pleasure, a siren that began deep in her lungs before shuddering out through her throat. I held her like my most prized possession while she shivered and trembled underneath my touch, until finally she became still.

She exhaled like she had been holding her breath, then rested her head back against my chest. I slid my fingers out of her panties and held her against me while she panted.

"I can't believe..." She blinked in horror. "The whole city must have heard that!"

"Just the cats, Feisty," I said.

Molly sighed while still clinging to me. Her hands ran over my arms like she was trying to remember where she was, snapping herself out of an erotic daze.

"Is *that* the kind of release you get from dancing?" I rumbled into her ear.

She shook with silent laughter as I held her in my arms.

19

Molly

The Day He Left Me Standing There

Did that really just happen?

I came down from my high and melted into his arms. Now *that* was the Donovan Russo I had been waiting to meet. The man who took control and made me squirm and gasp and scream on the freaking hotel balcony.

But I knew we were just getting started.

I twisted in Donovan's possessive grasp, and he eased up on his grip so I could turn around and face him.

"Now what?" I asked.

Donovan grinned down at me. There was a mischievous look in his storm-grey eyes, like he was thinking of all the things he was about to do to me. I tingled with anticipation and his smile deepened.

He brushed a strand of hair away from my face and said, "Thanks for the dance." He kissed me on the forehead, then let go of me.

I watched in disbelief as he stepped over the railing, hopped the gap, and then climbed over to his balcony. He picked up his portable speaker and turned it off.

"Where are you..."

"See you in the morning. Breakfast is on me." He winked before disappearing into his hotel room.

I stood there, dumbfounded, for a long time.

I thought about it while laying in bed, trying to fall asleep. I don't know what had come over me. I had *never* come that quickly before, not even on the rare occasion when I touched myself. Maybe it was the isolation and the loneliness, or maybe the thrill of being with someone who I only just met last week. I was more sensitive than normal, and his touch was intense in new and exciting ways.

Emotionally, Donovan was replacing everything I had hoped to experience on this trip. He was a sexy, muscular placeholder for tours and wine-tastings and fun with my friends.

Whatever the reason, being in a gorgeous man's arms on a balcony overlooking the city, dancing while romantic music played, letting him caress me in all the right ways with his long, warm fingers until I arched my back and cried out...

But as good as it was, I couldn't stop thinking about the way it ended. What kind of guy fingered a girl and then just *left?* I thought I had given him all the right signals that I was ready to do more. I had intended to push him into my room and climb all over him like he was a big, sexy jungle gym.

And it's not like he wasn't interested. He was hard as a rock when I rubbed him through his pants, even more than when we had grinded together playing pool.

So what was the problem?

When I woke up the next morning, our balcony dancing felt like a dream. I had a text waiting on my phone.

Donovan: Breakfast is served in the restaurant

119

whenever you wake up.

I showered, fixed my hair, and then went downstairs in a daze. Donovan was in the kitchen, hunched over the flat top while flipping pancakes.

"Was wondering when you'd wake up," he said over his shoulder. He was wearing a Residencia Al Gladiatore apron. "It's almost lunchtime. You must have been sleeping *very* well."

I cleared my throat and replied, "Breakfast isn't over, is it?"

"Normally we stop serving it at eleven," he said. "But here at the Residencia Al Gladiatore Hotel, we want to give our guests the perfect Roman experience. I'll make an exception for you. Pick a dish and tell me what you want."

He was pointing at a prep table where there were eight plates of food. There was a plate with an omelet, a plate with a poached egg on toast, waffles and pancakes and bacon and every other breakfast combination imaginable.

"You made all this for me?"

"I just wanted to take the flat top grill for a spin. For practice. I made those hours ago, so they're cold. But tell me what you want and I'll make it again."

I wanted to walk up and hug him from behind. To kiss him, *really* kiss him this time, and tell him I had fun last night. But he looked busy as he moved from the grill to the prep station and back to the grill, cooking up a storm in his kitchen.

"Pancakes sound lovely."

"Coming right up! I'll bring them to you."

I waited in the restaurant while checking emails on my phone. Donovan brought a big stack of pancakes shortly thereafter, with a glass jar full of warm maple syrup and a tin of soft butter.

"Aren't you going to eat with me?" I asked.

120

He waved his spatula like a music conductor. "I already ate. And I'm going to try a new recipe with the pork cutlets in the fridge. I'm going to have a *lot* of fun in this kitchen."

You could be having a lot of fun with me instead.

I let him return to the kitchen while I ate breakfast. The pancakes were soft and fluffy and perfect. When I was done, I carried my dishes into the kitchen and eyed Donovan. He was watching a YouTube video about pork cutlets while wielding a butcher's knife, so I decided to leave him alone and returned to my room.

He didn't leave the kitchen all afternoon. I went down to check on him around six. The kitchen smelled like delicious roasted meat, and Donovan was rushing from one station to another.

"What's for dinner, chef?" I asked.

He grinned when he saw me. "I was just about to text you. Tonight's menu is roasted pork loin in an apple-vinegar glaze, with steamed vegetables. Where do you want to eat?"

The memory of last night was still fresh in my mind so I said, "How about the balconies again?"

Donovan nodded while tossing a bowl of vegetables with salt and pepper. "This time I'll follow the rules and stay on my balcony."

"Oh?" I said. "Suddenly you care about the rules?"

He flashed a smile and said, "No, but I know how particular *you* are about them, so I'm going to try my best. Dinner will be ready in five minutes, so grab a bottle of wine and I'll meet you up there."

I hoped he was just joking around, because I didn't want him to stay on his balcony. I wanted him to come over to mine so we could continue where we left off last night. I wanted him to drag me into my room, throw me down on the bed, and take my body like it was his to play with.

Mother nature ruined our plans. By the time I returned to my room, clouds had rolled into the sky above the plaza. It wasn't storming yet, but thunder rumbled across the city and promised rain.

So much for another balcony date, I thought gloomily.

20

Molly

The Day I Got Even

There came a knock on the dividing door between our rooms. "Room service."

I opened the door and found Donovan standing there, holding two plates of food. "Probably best to avoid the balcony, right?"

"It looks like it's about to pour," I agreed.

He handed a plate to me and we stood in our respective rooms, at a loss for what to do. Then Donovan sat on the ground in his room, resting his back against the wall next to the door. I could see his legs sticking out, and his arm, but that was about it.

"Wouldn't want to break your rule about going in your room." He jabbed his wine glass into the doorway. "Wine me."

I filled it with red liquid and said, "This bottle was *very* dusty, so I'm assuming it's expensive."

"Grazie," he said in an exaggerated Italian accent. "Expensive wine is my second-favorite kind."

I sat down next to the divider with my back against the wall, just like Donovan was doing on his side. "What's your favorite kind?"

123

"*Free* wine."

I laughed and said, "This is expensive *and* free. So you should really like it."

"A double-whammy."

The pork loin was tender and the apple glaze complimented it perfectly, with a delicious combination of sweet and salty. Every bite tasted like heaven, and I wolfed it down as rain began to patter against the glass windows.

"This wine is definitely better than the stuff we were drinking before," Donovan said from his room.

"That was cheap wine I bought in the duty-free section of the airport. My girlfriends aren't picky, they just like to get drunk. Sara especially. I love her to pieces, but a nice bottle of wine would be wasted on her."

"Sara sounds like a lot of fun. Can I get her number?"

"I'm going to pretend you didn't just say that."

"I bet she's a rule breaker," Donovan said with a laugh. "She'd probably let me into her room."

"That's true, but she's currently five thousand miles away."

He sighed dramatically. "Our love isn't meant to be."

I took a long gulp of wine, hesitated, and then said, "You can eat in my room, if you want."

"Woah, let's not get carried away," he teased. "I know how you are about the rules. I'm staying put."

He's toying with me again, I thought. Just like last night.

The memory reignited my curiosity. I drank the rest of my glass of wine, poured myself a refill, and then dove headfirst into the topic I'd been avoiding all day.

"So, Donovan."

"So, Molly."

"What happened last night?"

I heard him chuckle. "We had a good time. We danced. We kissed. We did other stuff. You don't remember?"

"Of course I remember. What I meant was, what happened *after* that? We were having a lot of fun, and you were doing *very* nice things with your fingers, which made me scream so loudly that I probably woke the Pope. Then you just... left."

"Your screams reminded me of being yelled at in the lobby, actually," he replied. "It was very traumatizing, you know."

I groaned. "Now you've done it. I'm embarrassed all over again and I'm going to hide in my room until the pandemic is over."

"It was fun while it lasted."

We laughed together. It felt good to laugh about it.

"Seriously, though. Why the sudden departure? And don't you dare say it was my rule about the room, because I was giving you *every* signal to come inside."

He was quiet for a few seconds while he ate. I heard silverware scraping against his plate.

"You know what the secret to a good appetizer is?" He finally asked.

"Is this going to be a cooking metaphor?" I asked.

"The secret," he went on as if I hadn't spoken, "is for the appetizer to be good, but don't let it be *too* good. It can't overshadow the main course. You want to leave people hungry for more."

"Yep, a cooking metaphor." I sipped more wine because it helped me talk openly. "I guess I'm just surprised. You were as hard as a rock. Don't guys get, like, blue balls?"

"Just because a guy gets hard," Donovan said, "doesn't mean they have to finish."

"Now I *know* you're lying!"

"It's the truth. At least, it is for me."

I put down my empty plate and turned to face the doorway. He was wearing jeans. I was turned on from thinking about last night, and the urge to charge through the door and climb into his lap was strong. He wouldn't have been able to walk away, then.

But then another idea came to me. An idea that would help me repay what he had done last night.

I reached through the door and around the corner. My fingers found his bicep, hard and warm beneath the soft fabric of his shirt.

Donovan snorted. "Copping a feel through the door? I feel used. Here, at least let me flex for you."

His bicep bulged underneath my fingers. I gave it another squeeze, but that wasn't the part of his body I was looking for. I pressed my cheek against the wall and reached farther until I felt the front of his jeans. I blindly unbuttoned them and pulled down the zipper.

"I've changed my mind," Donovan said slowly. "I don't mind being used."

There's no going back now, I thought.

I bit my lip and reached into his pants, underneath his boxer-briefs. And then I found it. The dick he'd flaunted in front of the hot tub yesterday, which had been pressed against my ass while we played pool and when we danced last night. It was smooth and warm and thick, and within seconds it grew fully hard in my fingers.

I pulled it out of his pants and began caressing his shaft in long, slow strokes.

He let out a long sigh on the other side of the door. "A few days ago you were awkwardly watching me in the pool, too nervous to join me. Now you're doing *this?*"

"The key difference is wine," I breathed. My fingers tightened. "How do you like it?"

"Your pink fingernails are very nice."

"And do you like what those fingers are doing?"

126

"Yeah," he said in a husky voice. "I like it a *lot*."

I can't believe I'm doing this, I thought. *I'm jacking him off through the door.*

I had never been naughty like this before, but the wine was giving me a perfect buzz and there was nothing in the world I wanted more than to please Donovan, to make him feel the way he made *me* feel last night when I cried and gasped in his arms on the balcony.

He groaned deeply as I stroked him faster. I could sense his body reacting to my touch; he pushed his hips up against my fingers, and his back rubbed against our shared wall. Even though I couldn't see him, I pictured what he looked like in that moment. Leaning against the wall, cock sticking out the front of his pants. Closing his eyes, parting his lips, and letting out a long moan. The muscles of his arms flexing in his tight T-shirt as he came closer and closer...

And then I was imagining what we *could* be doing. Instead of stroking him I could be riding him. Lowering myself onto him, allowing his thickness to part my lips. Surrendering to gravity and letting him fill me. Clenching him inside of me while I grabbed a handful of his thick black hair and tilted his head back so I could kiss his neck in that sexy spot right above his Adam's apple.

Soon I was panting as heavily as he was on the other side of the doorway.

"Don't stop," he breathed. He was grinding into my hand now, like he was getting close. His skin was hot underneath my fingers and he was gasping like he'd just swam a mile in the pool. His groaning intensified, filling the air with the sweet sound of his pleasure.

Finally he roared with ecstasy, and his shaft pulsed between my fingers. I felt his come drizzle over my hand, hot and sticky, while he continued moaning and trembling underneath my touch. He clutched my arm while he climaxed, begging me not to let go. As his grunts and gasps dissipated I slowed down, then eventually stopped. I gave his shaft another loving squeeze before pulling my hand back. Ropes of milky white covered my fingers, giving me another tingling sensation of naughtiness.

"You're right," I said. "It's fun to bend the rules a little bit."

Donovan's face appeared in the doorway, more handsome than ever. He flashed me a perfect inviting smile and said, "Come over to my room and we can *break* the rules together."

Oh, it was tempting! I wanted nothing more than to mount him where he sat. To be filled by him rather than simply touching him...

But he had already left me hanging last night, and it was a game that two people could play.

"The secret to a good appetizer," I said sweetly, "is to leave the customer hungry for the main course."

With a big smile on my face, I closed the door and went to wash my hand.

21

Donovan

The Day We Sexted

This girl was *killing* me.

I really thought I had her wrapped around my fingers last night —both literally *and* figuratively. Dancing with her on the balcony, rubbing her wet slit until she was a puddle of moans and gasps in my arms, and then saying goodnight and hopping back over to my balcony.

I expected her to be *begging* me for more tonight. Once the dividing doors between our rooms were open, it was only a matter of time before she caved and crawled over to my side. She was *mine*.

But instead of that, she stayed on her side and reached through...

I wanted to resist. To grab her arm and pull her over so I could show her a *proper* night. But the way her long fingers wrapped around my cock, stroking me while teasing me from the other side with breathless whispers? It left me powerless to do anything but lean back against the wall and close my eyes. Within a minute she had me gasping and coming, spilling my load all over her pretty pink fingernails.

129

And then, just like I had done, she said goodnight and returned to her room.

I was like putty in *her* hands, not the other way around.

Yeah, I know. I deserved it after leaving her hanging on the balcony. Turnabout was fair play, right?

But that didn't stop me from plotting my revenge.

I'll get you back, Molly, I thought as I crawled into bed that night. *Just you wait.*

I woke up the next morning and went down to the kitchen. The leftover smell from last night's meal hung in the air, and I breathed in deeply. I didn't know how long the lockdown would continue, but until it ended, the kitchen felt like mine.

Someday I'll have my own, I thought as I washed my hands.

There were tortillas in the pantry so I scrambled some eggs, chopped some peppers, and made breakfast burritos.

I was halfway done when the phone on the wall rang.

I nearly jumped out of my shoes at the sudden, alarming sound. It was probably best to ignore it. Answering the phone would let the caller know I was using the kitchen. And despite all my teasing about Molly being afraid to break the rules, I did *not* want to get in trouble for being in here.

The phone stopped ringing. I breathed a sigh of relief. But ten seconds later it began ringing again.

Curiosity tingled in my brain, and I carefully reached out to pick up the receiver. "Uh, buongiorno?" I said, butchering the Italian word.

Molly giggled on the other end. *"Excuse me, is this room service?"*

I closed my eyes and laughed with her. "Si, it is indeed! I must inform you that we have a set menu this morning. We are serving breakfast burritos with green peppers and aged cheddar cheese."

"*That sounds perfect. I'll take one of those. Bring it to my room quickly, please. I'm a good tipper.*"

I grinned at her playful, demanding behavior. This girl was fucking *adorable*.

And bringing her food in bed was a good way for me to get even with her.

I carried the burrito upstairs and knocked on the door. "Room service," I said in my best Italian accent, which wasn't very convincing.

A shadow passed in front of the peephole. "Put it on the ground, please. You may leave."

"What about my tip?" I said in a suggestive voice.

"No way," she said. "I'm not opening the door. You might try to pay me back for last night."

"Oh?" I said with mock confusion. "Why would I need to pay you back for last night?"

Silence answered me.

I sighed, then placed the plate on the ground and stepped back.

"I can still see you," she said in a sing-song voice. "You're hiding next to the door. Go down the hall."

I took five more steps backwards. Molly's door opened and fingers with pink nails reached into the hall to take the plate. The door closed quickly like she expected me to try to run up and barge in.

Damnit, I thought as I went back down to the kitchen. I needed another idea.

It came to me a few minutes later when Molly texted me.

Molly: That was delicious. See? I cleaned my plate! Need any help cleaning the kitchen?

There was a photo included. Molly was on her bed with the

131

plate next to her. The photo was taken from her point of view, showing her long legs stretched out. She wasn't wearing any pants, and her pink panties were lined with frilly black lace. In the photo I could barely make out the outline of her pussy lips.

"You don't know what you've just done," I said out loud.

I stripped down to my boxer-briefs. They already fit snugly, but they tightened as I stroked myself until I was hard. Then I positioned my dick so that it ran down one leg, a thick cylinder pushing against the fabric of my underwear.

I stood next to the kitchen prep station and took a photo aiming down. The top half of the photo was the clean countertop, and the bottom half of the photo was my junk.

Donovan: Thanks for the offer, but the kitchen is spotless now.

Molly: Wow. It's not even a little messy. Is it hard keeping it that clean?

Donovan: It's very hard.

Donovan: I'm thinking of going for a swim after this. Want to get wet with me?

Molly: Mmm, that's tempting. But I'm all snuggled in bed right now.

Molly: I kind of want to play with some balls, though.

Molly: Billiards in the lounge this afternoon? Unless you'd rather play with yourself in the kitchen...

Donovan: I do love playing with myself. But I might swing by around four.

Yeah, I was definitely going to get Molly back today. She had no idea what was in store for her.

22

Molly

The Day He Made Me Squirm

I had never sent a sexy text message before. Even though you couldn't see anything in the photo, it felt so *scandalous* to do. Like someone out in cyberspace might intercept it and see my panties.

And Donovan responded exactly as I hoped he would.

I'll be honest: I didn't think the penis was an attractive body part. It was actually kind of ugly. But the photo Donovan sent me, showing the thick ridge of his cock outlined within the grey cotton of his boxer-briefs...

It stirred something inside of me that I didn't know could be stirred.

I was tempted to dial things up a notch right there. To remove my panties, spread my legs a little bit, and take a *real* photo for him. But I chickened out, and instead invited him to play pool.

Donovan joined me in the lounge at four. He looked like he had showered and cleaned himself up—he was wearing a blue button-down over his jeans.

Someone decided to get fancy.

"Ready to play with some balls?" he asked jokingly.

"You look like you're ready to go to a board room meeting."

"I'm running out of shirts. I need to do laundry." He rolled up his sleeves, revealing his tan forearms. "What drink should I make us?"

I went behind the bar and grabbed the two highball glasses I had prepared. "Drinks are on me this time. I'm no bartender, but I can make a Jack and Coke."

His lip twitched in a half-smile. "Jack and Coke is my favorite."

Nailed it, I thought happily as he took a sip.

"This is strong," he said.

"I like it strong."

"No complaints here," he replied. "You break this time. Need a refresher on how to play?"

Need me to grind up against your ass again? was what he meant. I bent over the table and lined up the cue ball. "I think I remember."

I pulled back the stick and hit the cue ball, which slammed into the triangle of balls and spread them around the table.

"Uh oh. You've been practicing," Donovan said while taking a very long pull of his drink.

"I had time to kill while you were playing in your kitchen yesterday." I checked a pocket. "I'm solids. You're stripes."

I examined the table and lined up another shot. My target was right next to the side pocket, so I was able to sink it easily.

"Nice stroke," Donovan said. "Just like last night."

I rounded the table and bent over in front of him. "I'm not sure what you mean."

"The hand-job."

I paused to look back at him. "Hand-job? What hand-job?"

"You have the memory of a goldfish."

135

"You stayed in your room," I said innocently. "With the wall between us, I couldn't see what I was doing. I might have been kneading a roll of pasta dough for all I knew."

Donovan rolled the cue stick in his fingers. "Pasta dough isn't that *hard*."

"You're the chef, not me." I grinned and made my shot, knocking another ball into the corner pocket.

"Uh oh," Donovan said. "Three in a row."

"Getting scared?" I teased.

He flashed a grin. "Not even a little bit."

"In that case, how about we make this interesting?"

"I'm listening," he said in his deep, rumbling voice.

"Whoever loses this game," I said slowly, "has to do *whatever* the other person wants."

He leaned on his pool cue and raised a dark eyebrow. "Anything?"

"Anything," I agreed.

Donovan nodded. "All right. You've got yourself a bet."

I strolled around the table. I was wearing a sun dress today, the one that *really* hugged the curves of my hips and ass, and I made sure to bend over while lining up my shot. I could feel Donovan's eyes on me as I slowly moved the pool cue back and forth, then gently hit the ball. It rolled across the table and hit its target, but the ball didn't drop into the pocket.

"Damn."

Donovan surveyed the table with his steel-grey eyes, then bent over to line up a shot. As a matter of fact, *his* ass looked pretty good in his jeans too. I couldn't help but remember how his body felt on the balcony, holding me against him while his fingers slid inside of me...

Donovan's pool stick flashed, knocking a ball into the corner pocket.

"Nice shot," I said.

He didn't respond to my compliment. His eyes were already scanning the table like a predator, looking for his next victim. He locked onto a ball on my side of the table. As he leaned down and closed one eye to line up his shot, I casually pulled my top down to show a little more cleavage, and then bent forward. My breasts looked amazing from his angle. Surely *that* would distract him.

Donovan leaned low, skillfully maneuvering the pool cue. His muscles tensed and the cue ball flashed across the table, hitting another ball with a loud *CLACK*. The ball bounced off a rail and then hissed into the side pocket.

"Wow," I said with genuine surprise. "That looked much harder than I expected."

He gave me an evil grin as he immediately lined up his next shot.

I watched in horror as Donovan sank another ball, then another, then *another*. Some of them were awfully difficult and required him to bank shots off the rails. But the way he played, he made it look easy.

He sank seven shots in a row, and then all he had left was the eight ball. Donovan hit the cue ball, and before it had even rolled across the table he was walking away to grab his Jack and Coke. He gulped it down as the eight ball gently fell into the side pocket, ending the game.

I gawked at him in disbelief. "You hustled me!"

He grinned. "There was a bar next to the diner where I worked. I always played a couple of games before starting my shift. On good nights I made more money playing pool than I did during my entire cooking shift."

"But the other night when we played..."

"I told you I was rusty. It's not my fault you made a bet before you knew how good I was." He rested his stick against the wall and approached. "Now, as for what I won..."

Part of me had hoped I would lose. I wanted him to *take* what he wanted. No more fooling around or beating around the bush, so to speak. I held my breath as he approached me with hunger in his eyes.

I tilted my head up and puckered my lips, waiting for the kiss I so desperately needed. He had kissed me on the neck the other night, but we still hadn't shared a *real* kiss on the lips. Now, with Donovan gazing down at me mere inches away, filling my nose with his scent, there was nothing in the world I wanted more than for him to crush his lips against mine.

"Kiss me," I breathed.

"Is that what you want?" he rumbled. "To be kissed?"

I bit my lip and nodded. "You won the game. So it's whatever you want."

His hands caressed the sides of my hips, then latched on. "I do want to kiss you."

Before I knew what was happening, he was lifting me into the air. But not into his arms—he was planting my ass on the pool table.

"I do want to kiss you," he repeated, "but I didn't say *where.*"

His fingers slid underneath my dress and danced up my thighs, then pulled my panties off. He lowered his face to my skin and kissed me on the knee, then on the inside of my thigh. The bristles of his beard tickled my skin as he caressed me with his lips, planting a trail of kisses up one leg and then down the other.

Donovan loomed over me for a moment, his steel-grey eyes admiring me. Taking in the view. I bit my lip and tingled with anticipation as his eyes raked over me.

He dove between my legs, burying his face in my sex. I gasped as his tongue slid up my slit, over my clit, then down again slowly. He wrapped his arms around my thighs and held me firmly in place.

"You won the game," I exhaled as he ate me out. "I'm supposed to do whatever *you* want."

He paused to leer up at me. "This *is* what I want. I want to taste every inch of you."

I arched my back on the pool table as he dove back into me. His tongue moved faster, sliding deeper into my pussy this time. His nose pressed firmly against my clit while he buried his tongue deep inside, caressing my inner walls like he was painting every surface. Donovan moaned into me as he did so, a vibrating sound that cranked *everything* up a notch in my body, and I grabbed a handful of his thick hair and held him against me because I never wanted him to stop.

This was what I've been waiting for, I realized as he worshipped me with his tongue. *This is what I've wanted.*

I closed my eyes and surrendered to the feeling.

23

Donovan
The Day I Made Her Squirm

I loved going down on Molly.

The way she felt, her skin soft and supple beneath my grip. The pitiful little gasps she made as I kissed up her thigh, then circled her clit with my tongue. She had the sexiest little patch of hair above her pussy, which I eagerly buried my nose into while jamming my tongue into her pink folds.

And the way she squirmed on the pool table, bucking a little bit like I was giving her everything she wanted?

It was the reaction I'd been dying to see.

I breathed deeply while going down on her, inhaling her womanly scent. Fuck, she smelled amazing. I made my tongue as rigid as possible and then fucked her with it, back and forth with my entire face, brushing against her inner thighs with every motion. Her moans deepened and she grabbed a handful of my hair, pulling me against her and grinding against my face.

This was a totally different Molly. It wasn't the same girl who bashfully watched me swim laps in the pool and then ran away when I caught her. This was the Molly that I knew was hiding just beneath the surface, waiting to come out and play.

I devoured her on the table, worshipping her the way she deserved, until she let out a different kind of moan. She arched her back and clawed at the green felt on the table, and then cried out as loudly as she had done on the balcony two nights before, squeezing my head with her thighs and curling her toes against my arms.

But I never released my grip. I wrapped my lips firmly around her clit, sucking and licking until Molly's voice went ragged and she fell apart in my arms.

Finally she exhaled, and relaxed back onto the table. Her thighs released their vice-like grip on my head and she let out a soft purring sound.

"That's for last night," I whispered into her thigh. I gave it a tender little kiss. "For the hand-job you wanted to pretend didn't happen. Now we're even."

I rose and gave her a wink. My job here was done. Time to leave her wanting more, just like I had planned before the evening started. Just like I had done on the balcony two nights ago.

Molly sat up and snatched a handful of my shirt. "Oh no you don't. I'm not done with you yet." She spread her legs and pulled me in. I could practically *feel* the heat coming off her sex, radiating with need.

I leaned in close like I was going to kiss her. Christ, I wanted to. To feel what those plump lips felt like against mine. To jam my tongue into her mouth the way I had jammed it into her slit. I wanted to make out with her, and take her dress all the way off, and push our boundaries there on the floor of the lounge...

I let my lips linger close to hers. Our breath mingled for a moment—the air smelled like Jack Daniels and possibility. She closed her eyes and in that instant I knew she was mine.

Then I pulled away.

"I need help making dinner," I said. "That's what I want for winning the game."

She was absolutely adorable as she gawked at me. "You're kidding."

"I'm making chicken parm," I said while putting my pool stick away. "It'll go faster with two people. You can be my sous chef. But I *will* make another drink for the road. Want one?"

She made no effort to leave the pool table. "How long are we going to do this?"

"Make dinner?" I said, playing dumb. "As long as we have access to the kitchen. And the liquor cabinet." I hefted the bottle of Jack and made two more drinks.

"Is that how this is going to go?" she asked, eyes narrowing. Her cheeks were still flushed and sweat was beading at her temple. "Pretending like you don't know *exactly* what you're doing?"

I cracked open a bottle of Coke, emptied it into both glasses, and then fixed her with a look. "You mean like thinking you're reaching through the doorway and kneading *pasta dough?*" I didn't wait for a response. "Come on, let's head down to the kitchen. I've worked up an appetite."

"You didn't *eat* enough already?"

"Oh, I did," I said with a grin. "But I can always go for seconds."

Finally she slid off the table and shimmied into her pink panties. I caught a glimpse of her bare ass cheek as she did so, a round globe that made my cock ache for her, but then she lowered her dress and the view was gone.

"I don't want to eat on the balcony tonight," she said.

"You want another candlelight dinner? That can be arranged."

"No," she said while taking her drink from me. "I have something special planned."

142

24

Molly
The Day With The New View

We were in the kitchen making dinner. Donovan was prepping the veggies while I flattened the chicken breasts with a meat mallet.

"That's right," Donovan said lustily while mixing the coating ingredients in a bowl. "Give that meat a *pounding*."

"Oh, *now* you want to be dirty?" I teased. "Not earlier when I was on the pool table, ready to go?"

"Who's being dirty?" he replied in a deep, overly-sexual voice. "I'm giving you instructions on what to do with my *meat*. I like how you're beating it. You're really going to town on it."

I pinched some flour from the bowl and tossed it at his face. His rumbling laughter filled the kitchen.

Days ago, Donovan claimed to have the willpower of a saint. I didn't realize just how true that was until he went down on me in the lounge. Afterwards I was as wet as could be and ready to go. I grabbed his shirt and pulled him toward me. I spread my legs and felt his cock just inches from me. It was impossible to ignore, a thick bulge inside his jeans that was brimming with potential.

I was ready. I *wanted* him. And I knew he wanted me too.

Yet he smiled at me and walked away. Just like on the balcony.

Donovan's comment about appetizers and leaving people wanting more? It wasn't just a stupid metaphor. It was the truth. Because right now, while we were making dinner, my body *ached* for him. I wanted him so badly I could barely stand next to him.

And it infuriated me that his tactic worked.

But I didn't want him to know that. I wanted to play it cool. So I teased him, and laughed, and eye-banged him while we made dinner. He knew his way around the hotel kitchen like he had worked there for years. I enjoyed watching him, too. There was nothing sexier than a man who was totally in his element.

He coated the chicken breasts in an egg bath, then the flour mixture, then grilled them in a pan. When the food was done I grabbed a bottle of wine from the pantry and we carried the plates out of the kitchen and toward the elevator.

"I thought you said we weren't eating on the balcony," he told me.

I pressed the button for the fifth floor. "We're not."

Donovan frowned. "There's nothing up there but hotel rooms. Are we breaking into the penthouse or something?"

"Nope!" I repeated cheerfully.

"Then what are we doing?"

"You'll see!"

We got off on the fifth floor and went into the stairwell. There was a ladder leading up to a hatch in the ceiling, with a sign that said: ROOF ACCESS.

I handed Donovan my plate and climbed the ladder. It took eight guesses before I found the key that unlocked the padlock. I pushed open on the hatch. It was heavy, and the rusty hinges screamed like they hadn't been opened in months. The hatch made a loud

CLANG as it finished opening, revealing the dark sky above.

I climbed through the hatch and then reached down to take each plate, then the bottle of wine. After Donovan followed me up the ladder, he picked up his plate and gazed around.

"Wow," he breathed.

The roof was flat and covered with industrial air conditioners, but there were red brick crenelations around the outer edge. The border was a meter wide, so we could sit on the edge without fear of falling over the side to the plaza below.

"Good call, babe," Donovan said.

"Why thank you, dear," I replied, as if we were two people playing house rather than prisoners in a hotel.

Donovan chewed on his food while gazing around. "We're only thirty feet higher than our balcony, but the view is so much better." He pointed. "That's the dome on Saint Peter's Basilica."

"And we can see a lot more of the Colosseum," I said.

We ate in happy silence for awhile, taking turns drinking straight from the bottle of wine. The wind ruffled Donovan's dark hair, and he squinted out at the city.

"I have a question," he said. "You just inherited your mom's boutique last year, right?"

"Uh huh," I said with my mouth full.

"What did you do before that?"

I paused to swallow the chicken. "It's boring."

"Before I inherited the boutique, I was a logistics analyst for a lumber company."

Donovan blinked. "Okay, I was wrong. That's so boring I don't even know what it means."

I laughed and took a pull from the bottle of wine, savoring the puckering dryness as it ran down my throat. "The company transported lumber around the Midwest. I helped facilitate the transportation on an order-by-order basis. Making sure shipments happened on time, finding ways to improve efficiency by combining certain shipments, moving stock around to our different distribution centers so none ever ran out of a certain type of lumber. That sort of thing."

Donovan tilted his head back, closed his eyes, and started snoring loudly. I tossed a piece of chicken at his face, which bounced off his nose and left a red smear of sauce.

"I told you it's boring," I said with a laugh. "But it was a paycheck. I guess I didn't *hate* it, but I didn't enjoy going into the office every morning. That made it easy to quit my job when my parents died, and then start managing the boutique."

"What did you want to be?" he asked. "Growing up, I mean. Fireman? Astronaut?"

"That's the problem: I never really knew what I wanted to be. I got a degree in business and assumed I would figure out my passion along the way, but it never fell into place."

"What about your siblings?" He paused. "I guess I should first ask: do you *have* any siblings?"

"For someone who came all over my fingers the other night, you don't know much about me."

He gestured with his fork. "Hence the question."

"I'm an only child. No brothers or sisters. I have a boatload of cousins, though."

"I'm an only child too," Donovan said. "Growing up, it sucked."

"How so? I liked being the only one."

"We moved around too much," he explained. "I struggled to make friends because we never stayed in one place. Dad always got a new assignment after a year or two. If I had a brother or sister, then at least I would have had someone to play with. Someone who I was moving *with*, rather than moving away from."

146

I touched his arm. "That's really sad."

He shrugged like it couldn't be helped. "That's why I want kids. Two or three. So they can play with each other, no matter what happens."

I perked up. "You want kids?"

"Someday? Absolutely," he replied. "I want to watch my sons or daughters grow up, take their first steps, learn to talk. I want to teach them how to ride a bike, and how to cook, and help with their math homework even though I suck at math." He looked out at the Colosseum and nodded. "I think I would be a good dad."

"I've always wanted kids too," I said. "Even though I couldn't figure out what I wanted to do for a career, I *always* knew I wanted to be a mom. That's kind of why I broke up with my last boyfriend. He did *not* want kids, not even a little bit."

Donovan shrugged. "All guys say that, but most change. I didn't think I wanted kids until a few years ago, as I got older. Now I'm certain I do."

"He wasn't going to change his mind," I said with a wry shake of my head. "We broke up because he booked a vasectomy appointment."

"Oh, damn."

"Yeah. He had this weird paranoia that all women wanted to trap men by getting pregnant. When I told him he shouldn't make a permanent decision like that while he was young, he flipped out on me. Said that my resistance was proof that he *should* get the vasectomy. I broke up with him when he asked me to drive him to the doctor, hah."

"What a dick."

"And not where it counts," I agreed, putting my hand on Donovan's thigh. The outline of his cock was right on the edge of my fingertip.

"Careful, Feisty," he said. "Don't start something you're not

147

prepared to see through to the end."

"Maybe that's exactly what I want to do," I replied.

"I've got cookies baking in the oven," he pointed out. "I need to take them out in... six minutes. So unless you think we can beat the clock..."

I gave him a coy smile. "What would we do with the other five minutes and forty-nine seconds?"

Donovan grunted. "Ouch. I'll have you know I can last *at least* three minutes."

"You didn't the other night."

He roared with laughter. "You've got me there. But no, we're not having roof sex. That's not how a first time should be."

"How *should* a first time be?" I asked.

"You'll see."

"When?"

"When you're ready," he replied.

I scoffed. "In case you haven't noticed, I've been ready *several* times."

He shook his head while smiling. "Good things come to those who wait. And trust me: it'll be worth the wait."

I rolled my eyes and turned away to admire the view. "I definitely want to come back to Rome."

"You may not be aware," Donovan said slowly, "but you're actually in Rome. Right now. *As we speak.*"

"This feels like it doesn't count. I want to come back when I can actually *see* things. The Colosseum, Vatican City, the Sistine Chapel. And I mean *really* see them, up close. Not from a distance."

Donovan nodded while gazing out at the city. "Yeah. I really wanted to take a tour of the Colosseum."

I sighed and collected our plates. "After we take the cookies out, what do you want to do tonight, darling? Put the kids to bed, then watch a movie in the lounge?"

He was still staring off.

"Donovan?"

"I don't want to stay in tonight," he said. "Let's go out."

25

Donovan

The Day We Explored Rome

I had been having an amazing time with Molly. I couldn't have asked for a better person to be stuck with for the last week and a half. And I wasn't just saying that because of the way she looked in a sun dress, bent over the pool table. We'd been having a *blast* playing house in the hotel.

But tonight, I didn't want to be stuck inside. I wanted to explore Rome with her. I wanted to see the sights, to touch blocks of stone that were older than Christ himself.

And I sure as hell didn't want to wait until a future trip to do it.

"Let's go see the Colosseum," I said.

She looked at me like I had started speaking Russian. "But it's closed."

"So what? I want to see it up close."

"We're under a lockdown," she said, as if it were obvious. "We're only allowed out in the morning, and that's just to get food or medicine."

"Then we'd better not get caught."

"And if someone does catch us?"

I grinned. "What are they going to do? Kick us out of the country? Sounds like a win-win."

She laughed as we climbed down the ladder. "I don't know. I've never broken the law like that before..."

"Here we go with the rules again."

"This is different than stupid hotel rules," she insisted. "This is *serious*. We could get in real trouble if we're caught."

I pressed the elevator button and turned toward her. "Do you trust me?"

She looked up at me and nodded.

"Then I'll make sure everything is okay."

I meant it. I would do whatever it took to protect Molly, while also showing her a good time.

She smiled like she believed it, too. "Okay. I trust you."

We grabbed two of my masks from the room and went down to the kitchen to take the cookies out of the oven. Then I went into the office behind the concierge desk. There was a drawer with a small supply of hotel toiletries. I found a bottle of Italian-brand cough syrup and shoved it in my pocket.

Molly took a big step away from me. "Are you feeling sick? Do you have a cough?"

"I feel fine. Let's go."

I turned off the hotel alarm and then unlocked the front door. Leaving to get groceries felt strange, but that trip was during a designated time when people were allowed to go out to get food. This time it felt like we were crossing an imaginary boundary. Prisoners who were stepping out of their cells.

I closed the door and locked it behind us, and then we hurried across the plaza in the darkness.

"It feels weird being out," Molly whispered behind her mask.

"I know what you mean."

"This is the first time I've left the hotel since the lockdown started," she said.

I held her hand. "Relax. I'm here with you."

Molly clung to my hand as we exited the plaza and walked down a narrow alley. There were small shops and stores on either side, places which should have been bustling at this hour if the plaza were full of tourists, but were dark and deserted now. At the end of the alley we stopped to peek out at the next street. When we were certain the coast was clear we hurried along as quietly as we could.

It only took a few minutes to reach the Colosseum plaza. One minute we were skulking down an alley, and the next minute there was nothing but open ground between us and the ancient Roman structure. A traffic circle wound its way around the Colosseum, but the streets were empty.

Molly's eyes were round and wide in the moonlight. "It's so much bigger than I expected."

"I get that a lot," I whispered.

She gave me a playful shove.

I caught a glimpse of a light on the other side of the structure, so I pulled us back into the dark alley. Moments later a police officer came around the side of the Colosseum. They were masked, and they were staring at a rectangle of light in front of their face. A cell phone.

The officer kept walking along their patrol, and after forty-five seconds they disappeared around the other side of the Colosseum.

"Okay," I said, taking Molly's hand. "Let's go."

"Wait," she hissed. "You want to get *closer?*"

I pulled her into the street and toward the enormous, hulking arena. We were out in the open, totally exposed by the street lamps illuminating everything. If any other police officer stumbled onto the plaza it would be impossible for them to miss us. I tensed as we ran along, waiting to hear a police whistle or siren cut through the night.

But fortune was on our side, and we reached the first barrier of the Colosseum without anyone seeing us. The outer facade loomed above us, three levels of curving arches and a solid top section. From this angle I couldn't see any of the gaps or damaged parts of the structure. It looked totally intact. I could use my imagination and pretend we were actually back in ancient Rome.

"Okay," Molly whispered. "This is impressive. I'm glad we got this close!"

I examined the fencing. It was a temporary barrier ten feet tall, and comprised of interlocking metal sections. I approached the place where two sections connected together.

"What are you doing?" she asked.

"Looking for a way in." I lifted the metal an inch off the ground. There was a hook where the section locked into the other one. If I could raise it high enough...

"We can't go in!" Molly hissed.

"I didn't come halfway around the world just to miss out," I insisted as I raised the barrier. Just a little bit higher...

The hook slipped out of the metal barrier. I pushed it inward, then lowered it to the ground. Now there was a gap. I slipped through and then beckoned Molly along.

She hesitated, then followed. I slowly pushed the fence section back into place. The hook wasn't connecting it to the other barrier, but nobody would notice unless they came close.

I gazed around the area. We were underneath one of the lower arches of the Colosseum's base. A tunnel led deeper into the structure, with felt ropes marking where tours were allowed to go and where they were prohibited.

"See?" I said. "We're in the normal walking area. We won't go in the areas where we could damage any of the—"

153

I cut off as I heard footsteps outside. Molly and I ducked under the arch and pressed ourselves flat against the stone. She looked up at me with confusion. Had I actually heard something, or was it my imagination? I was probably jumpy because of what we were doing. That's all.

Seconds later, the policeman walked into our view.

I held my breath. We were veiled in darkness, but there was nothing between us and the barrier. If the officer had heard something and took a closer look with his flashlight...

But the policeman continued walking along his patrol route, never taking his eyes off his phone. He disappeared out of view. Neither of us moved until his footsteps had faded away.

I took Molly's hand. "We'd better be quiet."

I expected her to protest, to say that we should go back before we got caught. But her eyes sparkled with mischief, and she nodded.

We walked deeper into the Colosseum, hand-in-hand. We stayed in the tourist sections, which led us through the dark concourse underneath the outer facade. It was eerie at night, but beautiful. We gazed in awe at the dark arches, and at the crumbling stones that had stood there for nearly two thousand years. The bones of a civilization that had fallen long ago.

The path led us up to the second level. From there we could see down into the Colosseum floor, which was open and full of vertical pillars.

"Those tunnels ran underneath the floor," Molly explained quietly. "The Romans used them to move gladiators and animals around. They could even fill it with water to simulate naval battles."

The sight was awe-inspiring. I was struck with *literal* awe as my brain processed what I was looking at. A shiver of understanding ran up my spine.

"It's so empty," Molly whispered. "So silent. So *peaceful*. I wonder how many tourists have seen the Colosseum like this." She squeezed my hand. "Thank you for making me come along."

"I just wanted an accomplice in case I got caught," I joked. "I figured they would go easy on a woman."

She smiled at me and pulled her mask down. Slowly, I did the same. No more teasing, no more games. There was just Molly and me, and the quiet darkness of the ancient place. She was beautiful, so beautiful, and I knew I couldn't resist any longer. I ached to finally know what it was like to kiss her.

Our faces drifted together softly, slowly, simultaneously.

Molly's lips were as soft and warm as I imagined. I folded my arms around her and held her against my body, shielding her from the dangers of the world, protecting her the way I had promised I would. Her fingers gripped me with need, clinging to me like I was the only thing she had ever wanted.

We kissed in the shadow of the ancient Colosseum, which tonight was ours alone.

Molly pulled away, rested her head against my chest, and then smiled up at me. Her dark eyes sparkled in the Roman moonlight.

"How many people have had their first kiss like this?" she whispered. "Breaking into the Colosseum during a pandemic?"

"Only you, and me," I said, caressing her cheek.

"I'm glad you made me wait. It was worth it."

"Yeah," I whispered. "It was. Want to head back now?"

She bit her lower lip. "No."

Before I could ask what she meant, she dropped to her knees and unzipped my pants.

"What are you..." I quickly looked around. We were underneath an archway on the second level, shielded from most angles. Nobody would see us unless they were *inside* the Colosseum.

Molly gazed up at me. "The only reason we're here is because you pulled me out of my comfort zone. I'm glad you did, and I want

155

to do this..."

She pulled me through the hole in my jeans. Her fingers gripped my shaft tenderly, and I could feel her hot breath on my skin. Then, while looking up at me through her long eyelashes, she wrapped her lips around the tip.

I sighed and leaned against the stone slab as she began sucking me off. She stroked me steadily and moved her lips back and forth. Her mouth was warm and wet and felt better than anything in the world.

I gazed out at the sight before me. It was a once-in-a-lifetime view, and I was enjoying it while getting a blowjob.

I didn't expect this when I signed up for cooking school, I thought.

Molly's lips were wrapped tightly around my shaft, and I moaned as she moved faster. Everything was perfect—the view, the speed at which she sucked, the hand she ran up my chest, the way she batted her eyelashes and looked up at me innocently. Molly herself was perfect—the perfect hotel neighbor, the perfect friend, the perfect *woman.* Soon I was running my fingers into her hair and pushing her along softly.

"Molly," I groaned softly. "I'm close. I'm so close."

I expected her to pull away so I could spill my seed all over the Roman stones, but she tightened her lips around my head and stroked my shaft rapidly.

"Oh my God," I gasped. "Molly..."

Tingling ecstasy ran up my legs as I realized what she intended, and then I just fell apart. She kept a tight grip on my shaft as I spasmed, and she hummed a moan into me as I filled her mouth with my come, rope after rope of it. The whole time she gazed up at me longingly, and when I was spent, my knees were so weak that I almost couldn't stand.

Molly stood up and grinned at me. She must have swallowed it already because she asked, "Did that feel good?"

"Are you kidding? I think I've died and gone to Roman heaven. Did the Romans believe in heaven? If so, that's where I am."

"They called it Elysium." She giggled and said, "I've never done that before. It wasn't as gross as I expected. And it was worth it to see you come so hard."

She rested her hands on my chest and leaned in to me, then stopped.

"You probably don't want to kiss me right now, do you?" she asked.

I pulled her closer and gave her a long, convincing kiss. "I'll *always* want to kiss you, Feisty."

"Know how many guys have gotten a blowjob inside the Roman Colosseum?" She pointed at me. "Only you."

"I'm sure plenty of Roman emperors got frisky here two millennia ago."

"You're the only one *this century,*" she said. "Okay, ready to leave?"

"Leave? Babe, I can barely walk right now. You sucked the life out of me."

We giggled, then quietly retraced our steps downstairs and out to the Colosseum barrier. We waited until the police officer walked by on his patrol, then sneaked through the metal barrier. I picked it up and threaded the metal hook back into the groove so nobody would know we had been here.

We ran across the road and into the safety of the dark alley. Molly clutched my arm and sighed happily.

"I'm going to eat *three* cookies when we get home," she said. "And I don't want you to judge me for it."

"We've already established that you're on vacation," I said. "You can do whatever—"

We rounded the corner and stopped as a blinding light hit us in the face. I held my hand up to block the light so I could see. A police officer was standing five feet away.

Oh fuck.

"Non muoverti," the officer said. I didn't know what that meant, but he said it with a warning tone.

"Shit," Molly whispered next to me, holding up her palms.

The officer barked a question that I didn't understand, but I assumed he was asking what we were doing out.

"Medicine," I said. I reached a hand toward my pocket. The officer struck out a hand to stop me, then gestured for me to do it slowly. I pulled the bottle of Italian cough syrup out of my pocket and held it up to the flashlight beam.

The officer grunted. "Home?" he said in halting English. "Where is?"

"The Residencia Al Gladiatore," Molly said, punctuating it with a cough.

The police officer finally lowered the flashlight. "Bene. Come." He waved for us to follow him.

We breathed a sigh of relief as we were escorted back to the hotel.

26

Molly

The Day We Got Caught

The cop escorted us back to the hotel in silence. When we got there, Donovan thanked him profusely and waved the bottle of cough syrup as if it were a shield. The officer nodded, then walked back the way he had come.

Donovan sighed and leaned against the front door. "Shit. That could have been bad."

"So *that's* why you brought the cough syrup. As an alibi."

"I'm kind of surprised it worked."

I peered out the window at the dark plaza. "You don't think he's going to report us, do you?"

"I hope not. But just in case, we should probably get out of the lobby."

I was still riding an adrenaline high from our excursion to the Colosseum. "Want to have a night cap in the lounge? There was a cabinet full of DVDs. I bet we can play them in English, too."

He let out a long, shuddering sigh. "I dunno. After getting caught, I think I'm done for the night. I'm going to go to my room and think about what I've done."

I snorted. "You sound like a grounded teenager."

"That's exactly how I feel! The cop letting us go feels like the pandemic version of *wait 'til your father gets home.* And in this case, dad is the long arm of the Italian judicial system."

We grabbed cookies from the kitchen and took the elevator upstairs. Outside our rooms, Donovan gave me a peck on the cheek.

"Sweet dreams, Feisty."

"Goodnight, Donovan."

I felt jittery with adrenaline as I went inside my room. I had never gotten in trouble with the police before. Heck, I had never received so much as a parking ticket. Breaking the law in a foreign country, during a nationwide lockdown, felt as serious as murder.

But everything was fine. They let us go. It was over.

I needed to take my mind off the police run-in. It was still the afternoon back home in Indiana, so I decided to call my best friend Sara. I had been having a *lot* of fun with Donovan, and I really wanted to tell someone about it.

I can't believe I gave Donovan a blowjob in the Colosseum, I thought while the phone rang. *She's never going to believe me.* Usually she was the one with the exciting sexual adventures. I had lived vicariously through her my entire life without doing anything fun myself. She would lose her mind when I told her.

But after five rings it went to voicemail.

I still wanted to hear someone else's voice, so I called the store next.

"*Nellie's Boutique, Andrea speaking.*"

"Hey, it's me. How is everything in Elkhart?"

"*It's weirdly normal,*" Andrea told me. "*I keep waiting for the other shoe to drop on this whole thing. How is Italy? It looks really bad there!*"

"Rome isn't too bad yet," I said while sinking into my bed. "I'm quarantined in my hotel. There's only one other person stuck in the hotel with me, a guy named Donovan. We're pretty bored, but we're finding things to do..."

My relationship with Andrea was professional. I had met her boyfriend twice, but she didn't share personal details. I wanted to talk to someone, though, and I was hoping she would ask about Donovan.

She didn't take the hint.

"*You could always get started on the fall order catalog!*" Andrea said. "*Your mom always tried to get that done by March, and you didn't finish it before leaving for your trip...*"

There was a lot of administrative work to be done at the boutique. I had been putting it off because I didn't want to do it. It was the kind of work my mom *loved* to do, but I didn't have the same passion for the boutique as she did.

"I don't have my laptop here, so I would need to do it all on my phone."

"*Yeah, good point. I guess it can wait until you get back... Oh! A customer just pulled up! I've got to go. Bye, Molly!*"

I sighed as I hung up the phone. I considered calling one of my other girlfriends, but it didn't seem worth the effort now. I didn't *really* want to talk to them.

The only person I want to talk to is Donovan.

I could hear him moving around over there. It didn't sound like he was getting ready for bed.

Molly: You still up?

It seemed kind of silly to text when we were only separated by a single wall, but he stopped moving around in his room and replied within seconds.

161

Donovan: I'm kind of wired. Adrenaline is a hell of a drug.

Donovan: I'm getting all my clothes together to run a load of laundry. This button-down is my last clean shirt.

Molly: I keep forgetting you've been here a week longer than me. I thought I was going crazy, but you must REALLY be getting impatient

Donovan: Honestly, I'm trying not to think about it. I've learned to focus on things within my control, and to ignore everything else

Molly: Right now NOTHING is in your control, though.

Donovan: Laundry is!

Donovan: And you, of course

Molly: I'm in your control?

Donovan: Oh yeah. You totally are.

Molly: My mouth had control over YOU about an hour ago

Donovan: That's just what I want you to think

I giggled at the memory from the Colosseum. With my exes, blowjobs were things done with reluctance after a *lot* of pestering. A chore that I tried to ignore until finally I couldn't put it off any longer. Like laundry.

But with Donovan...

Oh, it felt so *good* to be in control! Dropping to my knees and totally catching him off guard. Hearing his groans of surprise, feeling his fingers lace into my hair as he urged me along. And then the warm, salty explosion in my mouth that proved I had succeeded in my task. That I was better than Donovan expected.

What I liked most about Donovan was that he made me feel so sexy. Like I was a different woman when I was around him. The kind of woman who sneaks into the Colosseum to fool around.

Our first kiss was pretty good, too.

My phone buzzed.

Donovan: I'm about to run a load of colors. Got any laundry you want to toss in?

Molly: Yes!

I hopped out of bed and began collecting clothes. Most of my dresses would need to be washed on their own, but I could throw my shirts in with his laundry. I had an armful when I heard him knock. I opened the dividing door and he was standing there with a basket of clothes.

"Make sure you wash them on cold, please and thank you." I tossed the shirts in his basket.

"Molly," he said softly. There was a weird expression on his face.

"What's wrong?" I asked. "What is it?"

"Molly, I can't do this anymore."

My heart sank. "What do you mean?"

He blinked while searching for the words. "I can't do *this*. The stupid games and playful flirting."

In the space of a heartbeat, a dozen intrusive thoughts ran through my mind.

He doesn't want to fool around anymore.

I came on too strong at the Colosseum.

Our first kiss was so bad that he never wants to touch me again.

And then, the worst thought of all: *he was never really interested in me. He was only fooling around with me because I was literally the only other person in the hotel.*

The thoughts were crippling. I couldn't bear the thought of ending things now, not when we had come so far together, especially in the last day. I didn't know what I would do without Donovan at my side.

"Okay," I said, voice trembling. "If you want to stop then I respect that. We can stay in our separate rooms..."

"No," he said emphatically, dropping the basket of clothes to the floor. "I don't want to stay in my room. I don't want to sip wine by myself and text you from the other side of this *fucking* wall. I can't do it, Molly. It's not enough."

I held my breath. "What *do* you want, then?"

He stepped across the divider into my room.

"I want *this*."

27

Molly

The Day I Gave In

Donovan is in my room.

The thought flashed across my mind as he stepped across the invisible line. There was a look in his eyes that excited me, a look that said *fuck flirting, fuck the rules, we're doing this.*

He grabbed my face with his hands and lowered his lips to mine.

Our first kiss at the Colosseum was soft, tender. This was a completely different animal. He *took* me like I belonged to him, his tongue forcing its way into my mouth, conquering and claiming. Every part of us touched as he held me against him—forehead to forehead, chest to chest, mouth to mouth. The kiss deepened and Donovan swallowed the sounds I made, muffling me with his unrestrained lust.

He pulled back and gazed at me with raw desire. "No more games, Molly." His words were deep and dark.

Blood rushed in my ears and I didn't trust myself to speak, so I bit my lower lip and nodded.

Donovan kissed me again, pushing me backward with his lips

until I sat on the edge of the bed. He grabbed me by the waist and pushed me farther up the bed, pleasure pinging off his body as he followed me, setting me on fire with his torrid waves of arousal.

I hiked up my dress so he could sink in between my legs, aching for him to fill the hollow gap. The thick ridge of his cock pressed against my panties through his jeans, hard and warm and full of sexy potential, and my hips surged upward with need.

Are we really doing this? I thought as he claimed my body with his hands, clawing and squeezing. After days of teasing and flirting and touching...

Donovan's thin beard scratched my skin tantalizingly as he kissed a line down my shoulder. He ground his hard length against my panties, a wonderful pressure against my sex. He pulled back and I expected him to strip his clothes as quickly as possible, but he remained bent over me. His tongue licked a trail across my breasts, sliding my dress up so he could continue down my belly. I arched my back and preened for him as he reached my panties.

He paused to gaze up at me, destroying me with his storm-cloud eyes before he had even touched me.

He kissed the waistband of my panties, biting down on the elastic and pulling them down with his teeth.

I trembled with pleasure, both immediate and delayed. His teeth raked my skin as he tugged the panties a few inches down my left leg, then moved to the right leg to do the same. His beard rubbed my skin and he teased me with kisses in between pulls with his mouth, until I was *dying* for him.

"Now you're just showing off," I breathed.

He smirked up at me and continued his work. My body was on fire from my toes to my fingertips and *everything* in between. I was ready to explode, and the delay only made my desire grow in strength.

Finally he used his hands to pull my panties down over my ankles. He pulled me up into a sitting position so he could pull my dress over my head, then he tossed it aside like the fabric covering my

166

body offended him. I hastily unclipped my bra and let it fall to the bed.

Donovan pulled his shirt over his head, revealing the tapestry of chiseled muscle I was now accustomed to. But unlike the gym or the pool, now Donovan's bare skin was inches away from me, filling the space between us with radiating body heat. I traced the lines of muscle down to his navel.

He stepped off the bed, removing his belt while gazing down at me longingly. His gaze felt like a caress as he let his pants and boxer-briefs fall to the ground, revealing his hard length. I reached out because I couldn't *not* touch him, I needed to feel the heat of him between my fingers. He was as hard as a rock, even more than earlier tonight at the Colosseum. Donovan let out a sigh as I dragged my fingers along the underside, from base to tip.

Before I could do anything more, Donovan bent to get something out of his pocket. A condom—and not one of the *normal* sized ones.

He came prepared.

He tossed away the gold foil and then lowered his lips to my leg, tracing a line of kisses up my thigh. He flicked his tongue across my clit for just an instant, sending a single jolt of pleasure up my spine. His breath whispered across my core as he kissed me again, tenderly moving his lips against mine.

I moaned softly underneath him. I could feel his tip brushing against my wet heat, and I spread my legs for him, *opening* myself.

He hummed into my mouth, a deep rumble, while he kissed me. I loved the way he slid his tongue into my mouth, then nibbled on my lower lip. Like he could kiss me for *hours* and still wouldn't get enough.

He held himself over me while kissing me. His biceps bulged on either side of my body. I leaned over to kiss one of them, walking my fingers along the firm muscle.

I'm ready, I thought. *I'm ready for all of him.*

167

Donovan's tip suddenly found purchase between my lips. He buried it into me, filling me inch by glorious inch, until he had nothing left to give me and our bodies were joined. Both of us sighed and groaned and clung to each other.

I squeezed my legs around him, holding him inside of me. Donovan filled me so *completely*, every inch of him pressed against my tight walls. I needed to savor the feeling a little bit longer, because there was nothing like it. That wonderful moment where our bodies were connected, and everything felt perfect, and none of the problems of the world could reach us.

His eyes were wide and searching as he drank me in. I caressed his cheek, thumb brushing across his lips. He gave it a playful little bite, then leaned down to kiss me with more passion and hunger than before.

I loosened the vice-like grip of my legs around his waist, spreading myself wide. Donovan pulled his hips back and gave me a little thrust. I sighed as he filled me, stretched me, sending new pleasure spreading through my body. He nibbled at my neck and gave another pump, pulling back farther this time.

"Yes," I breathed.

He let out a shuddering exhale as he began fucking me steadily, surrendering to the restraint he had shown for so long. I closed my eyes and moaned softly.

This is really happening.

Donovan slid a hand underneath my body, grabbing my ass in his palm and *pulling* me toward him. The new angle hit a different part of my wet heat and I moaned deeper, raking my fingernails over his back and down to his muscular ass, squeezing him with both hands as he ravaged me.

The two of us rocked and crashed together on the bed. Donovan bottomed out with every motion, and I arched my hips to take more of him with every thrust. He rumbled a moan into my neck as he pushed deeper, his tip caressing my G-spot each time in a way that made me surge upward with need.

"Molly," he breathed my name like a blessing and a curse. "*Molly...*"

And then my orgasm overwhelmed me, powerful waves of pleasure that squeezed my eyes shut and made my pussy tighten around him. Then his own roar filled the room and he strengthened his grip on me, one hand clinging to my ass for dear life while the other held the back of my neck, crushing me against him as a new light filled his eyes, full of ache and ecstasy as his cock throbbed inside me.

Our cries echoed off the walls as we came together, with all of Rome lit up outside the window.

28

Donovan

The Day I Gave In, Too

I cleaned up in the bathroom and returned to the bed. Molly was waiting for me with lidded eyes, and as soon as I lay in bed she threw a leg over my body and rested her cheek against my chest. Her nipples were hard against my ribs.

"You're warm," she said happily while closing her eyes.

I gently stroked her hair while gazing out at the city. There still wasn't any sign of life out there. No movement, no sounds, no flashes of cameras as tourists took photographs. But the Colosseum was a magnificent sight in the distance, all lit up against the night sky. Beyond it, in the distance to the right, I could see the lights of The Vatican.

Despite the grim reason for the lack of people, the silence gave the city a romantic feel. It was *our* city tonight, as if the doors had been closed and only we were allowed in. A private experience that no amount of money in the world could pay for.

"You were right," Molly whispered against my chest. "That was worth the wait."

"Was it worth breaking the rules?"

"Fuck the rules," she murmured into my skin. Her eyelashes tickled me as she blinked. "It's pretty at night. All lit up like that."

I followed her gaze to the ancient Roman structure in the distance. "I was just thinking that."

"How many girls have you fucked in view of the Colosseum?"

"Are you interrogating me, Feisty?"

"Well," she said softly, "you *did* have condoms ready to go. Who knows how many you used before the lockdown?"

"Only you," I replied. "That's who I've fucked in view of the Colosseum." After a short pause I added, "So far."

I grunted as she poked me in the ribs.

We cuddled a little longer, and then Molly stretched her legs across my body. She frowned and said, "It's been a few minutes."

"What do you mean?"

"You're already hard again."

"Hard *again?*" I chuckled. "Molly, I never went soft. Since I walked into your room I haven't dropped below *diamond* on the hardness scale."

She let out a little giggle, vibrating her tits against my chest. "I'm kind of impressed."

I walked my fingers down her back until I felt her smooth ass. I gave it a squeeze and said, "With you in my arms, I'll always be hard enough to pound nails."

"Is that my new nickname?" she asked with a giggle. "Nails?"

Goddamn this girl was cute. Sexy as hell, sure, but fucking *adorable* too. I couldn't help but smile at her.

"I still prefer Feisty," I said, "but that doesn't mean I can't still give you a good hammering."

She yelped as I kissed her neck, then took a hold of her breast in my hand. I rubbed my thumb over her hard little nipple, then bent down to give it a lick. She responded with a shiver and a sigh, so I gently wrapped my mouth around it and nibbled on it with my lips.

Molly responded the way I hoped she would: she arched her back and moaned. "Ohh, that feels *good.*"

"You taste even better," I insisted.

As I enveloped her nipple with my mouth, I reached over the side of the bed to my jeans. After some fumbling around I found the pocket I needed, and the contents within.

Molly leaned forward and said, "You brought *two* condoms over here?"

"You said it yourself: I came prepared."

I rolled it on and sank into her again. She was still soaked with desire and made a soft noise deep in her throat as I began fucking her. She practically sang every time I filled her to the base, bottoming out inside of her and then pushing even deeper, like I was desperate to give her more than I had.

She spread her legs wide for me, and I obliged by fucking her harder. I planted my arms and practically did push-ups on her pussy. Normally there was some loss of sensitivity when a guy went for round two so quickly—or round *three,* if you counted the Colosseum blowjob —but Molly felt every bit as good as she had the first time. Maybe even better.

I squeezed her in my arms and kissed her fiercely, and she responded by pushing up into my kiss. Her lips were heady and addictive, more than I expected in all the times I had imagined kissing her, a powerful sensation as she tried to devour me with her tongue. My body was on fire as I surged against her, groaning with barely-formed words.

I'm glad I'm stuck in Rome, I thought as we lost ourselves in the mindless drive of our bodies.

29

Molly

The Day We Danced Again

Maybe being stuck in Rome isn't so bad, I thought as we cuddled again, Donovan on his back and me resting on his broad chest. We had kicked the sheets aside because our bodies were on fire and damp with sweat. I felt my body rise and fall every time he breathed. For a long time, I counted his breaths and filled my nostrils with his wonderful, masculine scent.

"So," Donovan said after awhile. "Want me to put on a mask?"

My laughter filled the room. "We're *way* beyond that, now."

I felt him nod. "That may have been safe sex, but it *definitely* wasn't pandemic safe."

I giggled despite the grim nature of the joke. "This was worth the risk," I muttered into his skin.

Donovan took my hand and gently kissed my fingertips. "Now that I've gotten a closer look at you, you're feistier than I thought. Check out these tattoos."

"Are you serious right now, mister butterfly-tattoo-on-his-hip? Yeah, that's right. I noticed it when you got in the hot tub."

173

"I thought you were checking out my junk."

"Also yes."

He looked down at the colorful ink on his upper thigh. "I lost a bet with another cook," he said simply. "What's your story?"

I held out my fingers and examined the tattoos. "I'm not much of a rule breaker..."

"That's been established," he interrupted.

"...but these small tattoos were the only wild side I had when I was younger. A little rebellion. My girlfriends and I would go out and get drunk, and instead of making mistakes at the bar, we would make mistakes in the ink chair."

"You all got the same tattoo?"

I nodded and held up my fingers. "The moon was at Amy's bachelorette party. We were walking back to our hotel and the crescent moon was shining *incredibly* bright, so we hopped into the first tattoo parlor we saw and got it tattooed on our middle fingers. The heart was after she got back from the honeymoon. She was wearing a wedding ring, and the rest of us said our ring fingers were lonely, so we got the heart tattoo."

"My knowledge of breakfast cereal is outdated, but that's two of the Lucky Charms marshmallows," Donovan said. "Now you need a horseshoe, a clover, a red balloon..."

I gave him a playful little shove.

"What about this one?" He kissed the last knuckle of my pinky finger.

"I don't know what that one is."

He blinked with confusion. "You have a tattoo on your finger and you don't even know what it means?"

"Don't judge me! We literally just opened the tattoo book to a random page and pointed at the first thing we saw. The tattoo itself doesn't matter—it's about remembering the night with the girls. I think it's a symbol for electrical current or something."

He gently stroked my hair. "You should come up with a better story than that. Like how you got struck by lightning and it left a scar there, so you got a tattoo to cover it up."

I laughed. "I'm not interesting enough to pull off a fake story like that."

"I think you're interesting as hell." He reached down and gave my ass a firm squeeze. "What's more interesting than giving a guy a blowjob *inside* the Colosseum? This whole trip is going to make one hell of a story years from now, when all of this is over."

My smile slowly faded. "Just so you know, I'm not normally like this."

"Like what?"

"I'm not... promiscuous. I've never had a one-night stand before."

"Is that what this is?" he rumbled softly. "Just a one-night stand?"

"Yes. No. Maybe? I don't know. That's kind of my point: I'm not used to this kind of thing."

He arched a dark eyebrow. "Are you implying I am?"

"No, I—"

"You're totally calling me a man-slut, aren't you?" He wrapped his arms around me and squeezed me against his body. "I've never been insulted like this before. I'm going to hug you to death."

I giggled as he squeezed me tighter.

"Don't fight it," he said. "It will all be over soon."

"There are worse ways to go," I squeaked.

He let me go and then brushed his lips against mine. "You can't call this a one-night stand because it's our seventh or eighth night together. Plus, we've fooled around a lot before finally banging."

"Good point." I drummed my fingers nervously on his bicep. "I've only had three serious boyfriends in my life, and one of them wanted to wait until marriage, so I've only slept with two guys before. And, we didn't get very creative in bed."

Donovan smirked. "They sound lame as hell."

"They were!" I said with a laugh. "But I'm trying to say that I'm not very exciting. I've never pushed my boundaries the way I did in the Colosseum, or on the pool table..."

He pressed a finger over my lips to shush me. "Don't care how you normally are, Feisty. Only care how you feel right now. We're stuck together until the lockdown ends. And I intend to have a *lot* of fun with you until then."

Donovan cradled my head in his hand and pulled my lips up to his. It was the kind of kiss that stirred me inside and made me wonder if he had a *third* condom in his jeans.

But then he sat up. "How about some dessert from the vending machine? I always crave chocolate after sex."

"You sound like a girl."

"Guys can like chocolate too." Donovan stood and stretched his arms over his head. "Back in a flash."

He walked across the room without putting any clothes on.

"What are you doing!"

He paused by the front door. "Getting you a bag of cookies."

"Naked?"

"Why not?" he smirked. "We've got the whole place to ourselves, Feisty. Might as well make ourselves at home."

I smiled to myself as he propped the door open and went into the hall.

One thing he said still stuck out in my head. He said he intended to have a lot of fun with me until the lockdown ended. But what about after that? Would we fly home and go our separate ways?

That's what made this feel like a one-night stand rather than something serious. It had an expiration date.

It gave me the freedom to be bold with him, to push my boundaries in a way I wouldn't do with a *normal* date, but it also made me wish we had a chance for more.

"Shortbread, or lemon?" Donovan said when he returned, holding out two bags. He was magnificent in the dim light, all of his muscles standing out in wonderful nude contrast.

"Lemon. If I close my eyes I can pretend it's orange." I lowered my gaze down his body, then back up to his face. "I would like to formally request that you remain nude for the rest of the lockdown."

"For you? I think that can be arranged. Especially since I'm out of clean clothes."

"Your laundry is still on the floor," I pointed. "Where you dropped it."

"I don't want to do laundry now. Doing laundry means leaving this room, and leaving this room means leaving you." His eyes suddenly widened as he thought of something. "Hey, get dressed."

"What did I just say about you staying nude?"

Donovan pulled his underwear on, then his pants. "Let's finish our dance."

"What dance?"

"The dance from the other night. When I heroically hopped the balcony."

"It wasn't *that* heroic," I said, even though it had seemed pretty damn charming at the time. "I'm very unhappy that you're wearing pants now. I was enjoying our cuddling session. I thought you were too."

"Believe me, I was." He threw on his shirt. "We can cuddle more later. Right now I want to dance with you, and not just as a gateway to *other* physical activities."

177

I pulled my dress on and followed him out to the balcony. Donovan put some music on his phone and took me in his arms the way he had a few nights earlier, holding me close against his body as we began to sway in a slow dance.

"I haven't met a lot of guys who want to dance with a woman *after* they've slept together," I said.

He tilted my chin up. "I'm not like most guys."

I can see that, I thought as we danced in front of the silent, still city.

30

Molly

The Day After

For a few minutes after I woke up, I forgot everything that had happened. I blinked at the bright light streaming through the window. I had slept in.

Then I felt the body next to me.

We had slept in.

All the events from last night came back to me in a rush. The Colosseum, the police, the sizzling sex in my hotel room, and then dancing on the balcony. I didn't remember coming to bed after that.

Yet here Donovan was, asleep in bed next to me.

I gently rolled over to face him. He was on his side facing me, but his eyes were closed. A few strands of his dark hair had fallen across his face. His leg was perfect and warm against mine.

I can't believe we did that last night.

I watched Donovan sleep for awhile, his body rising and falling with every breath. I studied his face: the strong nose, Mediterranean skin, and black eyebrows. The thin beard that covered his cheeks and jaw. I had been looking at him for over a week now, but never from this close. It was like zooming in on a map and suddenly seeing beautiful new features.

I couldn't get over how sexy he was. I could stare at him for hours.

What was someone supposed to do in a situation like this? Did we act like we were together, with cuddles and kisses and—dare I say it—morning sex? I *wanted* to cuddle and kiss him, but I was afraid our passionate behavior was limited to the evening.

I didn't know how to act.

Suddenly his eyes blinked open, unfocused for a moment before locking onto me. He smiled.

"Watching me sleep?" he asked, voice thick with sleep. "Kinda creepy, Feisty."

"I just woke up," I whispered back.

"What time is it?"

"Ten."

"Wow," he said. "Been a long time since I've slept this late. But waking up next to you, I can see why."

He leaned over and kissed me, which answered my question about how we should act. I kissed him back and then said, "I probably have morning breath."

"You totally do," he replied, "but I don't care."

He grinned and pulled me into a longer kiss. I laughed and forgot all about what my breath smelled like.

There was a sound outside in the hallway. Footsteps. Both of us froze in bed and listened as something bulky was dropped on the ground, then another item. The footsteps disappeared and we heard the *ding* of the elevator.

Donovan tip-toed to the door, peeked outside, then brought my box of daily supplies inside. "He delivered them early. Usually it's in the afternoon. Huh, there's a letter with it today." He glanced at me.

180

"It's signed by the concierge of the Residencia Al Gladiatore hotel."

"What's it say? Maybe we can go home!"

"If you are not comfortable remaining in the hotel," Donovan read out loud, "you are invited to move to our partner location, the Express Hilton Roma. You will still be confined to your rooms there, but you will find a greater number of amenities, such as a fully-operational kitchen and maid staff."

He lowered the letter and looked at me. I searched his face to gauge his reaction. We had an opportunity to go somewhere else. Did he want to leave?

"I don't need maid service," he finally said.

My heart swelled with happiness. *He doesn't want to leave. He wants to stay here with me.*

"We already have a fully-operational kitchen," I said. "Switching to whatever chefs they have will probably be a downgrade."

"Not to mention there are more people there," Donovan agreed. "And we would be stuck in our rooms."

"Other people *suck*. Present company excluded, of course."

"So you're cool staying here?" Donovan asked.

"Are you kidding? I have a private chef who I also get to have sex with whenever I want."

Donovan sat on the bed and kissed my shoulder. "Is that what I am to you? A sex robot who can also make pancakes?"

"Oh, pancakes! I'll have those, please. Chop chop, sex robot chef." I clapped my hands together.

He stood up and made mechanical, robotic movements across the room. He stopped at the divider door and said, "Ah, fuck."

"What?"

He pointed at the door. "It must have blown closed when we opened the balcony door. I don't have my room key."

181

"Then how are you going to get back in?"

He looked at the balcony.

I quickly slid out of bed and got dressed so I could watch him climb over to his balcony. It felt far more dangerous in the bright light of morning, but he jumped the gap easily and then disappeared into his room. A few minutes later I let him through the dividing door to my room.

"Let's prop these open so that doesn't happen again," he said. "Grab the door stopper..."

Sliding the jammer under each door felt like taking a step forward in a relationship. Our two separate rooms were now one *big* room that we were sharing.

I showered, and Donovan brought me breakfast in bed. While we ate, we watched Italian news with English subtitles. The number of infected Italians had increased, as well as the death count. Both numbers seemed to be climbing with alarming speed.

France had finally closed their borders and implemented a nationwide shutdown. The first cases in South America were reported in Rio de Janeiro. North Korea claimed they had zero cases due to the quick response from The Glorious Leader.

"I can't watch this anymore," Donovan finally said. "I'm going to the gym."

"Want me to walk around the hall and distract you with my ass?"

He grinned. "Don't you dare. I might break my neck this time."

I stayed glued to the TV while he exercised. The footage of grocery store lines and empty shelves was like something you typically saw in a developing country. New York City had implemented a stay-at-home order. It was jarring seeing Times Square completely empty. It felt like the apocalypse.

Donovan returned to my room shirtless and sweaty. "There's a rumor they'll start opening up travel again to the United States," he said while drying off with a towel. "Well, it's not a rumor. It's one person on Twitter who says so. Have you gotten an update yet?"

"Let me check…" I logged into the portal where we had registered. "Nope. It says my flight request is still pending."

"Me, too," Donovan said gloomily.

"What's your estimate? Mine says April fifteenth. That's three weeks from now!"

He frowned at his phone before answering. "April twelfth."

I gave him a playful shove. "We're both in Rome. Why are *you* ahead of me in line? You would think we would get put on the same plane!"

"No idea," he said, staring off in thought. He shook his head and glanced at the TV. "You're still watching the news?"

"I can't look away," I whined. "It feels like nine-eleven, but in slow-motion."

He took me by the hand. "Come on. I have something that will help distract you."

"What's that?"

He grinned. "Me."

I squealed as he led me into the shower and made me forget about all the problems outside the hotel.

31

Molly

The Day Without The Condom

Time passed lazily in our private hotel. Donovan made me breakfast in the kitchen every morning, and then spent much of the day experimenting with recipes. Apparently he had learned a lot of new food techniques in his cooking school but needed a better kitchen to try them out. He was totally at home in the hotel's spacious kitchen, moving pans from one burner to another, tossing the food in the air with skillful flare.

There's nothing sexier than a man who is good at what he does, I thought while watching him.

One afternoon, while helping him try a chocolate shortbread cookie recipe, our playful flirting escalated. Donovan's fingertips ran down my leg and up my dress, digging into my lips in just the right way. He lifted me into his arms while we kissed and placed me on the counter like I was a sack of potatoes.

Then his fingers danced deeper up my dress and yanked my panties down.

"I'm pretty sure this is a health code violation," I said while he nuzzled my neck and unbuckled his belt.

"I won't tell the health inspector if you won't," he said.

He dropped his pants, revealing a dick that was long and as stiff as could be. I reached out and caressed the soft skin, feeling the heat radiating off of it, wrapping my fingers around him and stroking while he groaned.

An alarmed expression crossed his sexy face. "I didn't bring a condom with me," he said.

"I don't care," I breathed, pulling his hard length toward me. "I want you now."

His eyes widened with lust, but he hesitated. "Are you sure..."

"I'm on birth control," I said. "And I'm clean. I know I don't have anything. As long as you..."

It was an awkward thing to ask a guy, especially in the throes of passion. Hey, do you have any weird sex diseases? But Donovan didn't take offense, and he shook his head.

"I've never had sex without a condom," he said.

I pulled him toward me. "There's no better time than now. I don't want anything between us."

His cock throbbed in agreement in my hand.

He kissed me so passionately, so deeply, that it took my breath away. I continued stroking him, pulling him toward my wet, waiting lips. I rubbed the crown against my entrance, coating him in my juices. Then Donovan put a hand on my hip for support and pushed deep inside me, taking over.

I leaned back on my elbows on the kitchen counter and moaned as he finally filled me. I didn't notice much of a difference without a condom, but Donovan let out a rumbling groan of pleasure that told me just how amazing it felt for him. His fingers dug into my hip as he held himself inside me.

"How does it feel?" I asked.

He leaned over me, dark hair falling across his face. "You felt

185

amazing before..."

"But?" I breathed.

"But it's so much better this way."

The visible nature of his pleasure enhanced my own, and I moaned as he began thrusting with nothing between our skin.

"I wish. I could show you. How *good* you feel," he breathed.

I leaned toward his lips. "I can tell."

Donovan pumped into me for a few seconds, then suddenly looked to his left. He grabbed one of the electric beaters that we had just used to mix cookie dough. He removed the metal beater from the end, then flipped the switch. The whole thing hummed, but nothing on the outside moved without the attachment.

"What are you—"

I cut off as he pressed the beater against my mound. The vibrations from the electric machine cascaded into my clit, stimulating me in a way I had never experienced before.

"Ohh!" I cried out.

He removed the makeshift vibrator. "Was that too much?"

I grabbed his hand and pulled it back against my clit. Immediately I was overwhelmed with powerful waves of ecstasy, like the volume on the radio station was finally cranked *way* up.

Donovan responded to my moans by fucking me urgently, slamming his dick into me hard enough to shake the entire countertop against the wall with dull, muted *thumps*. I came within seconds, an overpowering orgasm that hit me like a freight train and then carried me along the tracks for miles, and miles, and *miles* of bliss.

"Oh, Molly." Donovan moaned my name like a prayer.

"Come inside me," I begged, still on the tail end of my own climax. "Come in me, please!"

He grabbed the back of my neck and pulled me into a kiss. I clamped myself around him and he exploded inside me at that moment, a shuddering spasm as he filled me with his hot, sticky seed. He gasped and clung to me until neither of us could move.

"I've... never..." he breathed as we cleaned up, "come inside. Someone before."

"Never?"

"Only with you."

"You're my first too," I said. "But the vibrating beater? That was a game-changer. What made you think of it?"

"I don't know," he said, fingers digging into my thigh lovingly. "You felt so good without anything separating us. Like everything was black and white before, and suddenly I could see in *color*. I wanted to make you feel the same way. It was good?"

"You heard the noises I made," I replied. "What do you think?"

He used a towel to wipe down the counter. We both paused to laugh at the butt-shaped imprint in the flour where I had been sitting.

"The next time I go out, I'll look for a sex shop. Then we can get you a *real* vibrator."

"I doubt those are considered essential businesses," I replied.

He smiled sideways at me. "Sex is totally essential. What's the point of surviving a global pandemic if you can't get your rocks off?"

We giggled together while cleaning up the kitchen. One thing that surprised me was how *easy* everything was with Donovan. We just sort of meshed together without any problems. Maybe it was the circumstances, being stuck together without a choice. It probably forced us to accept each other the way we were.

Or maybe we're perfect for each other, I thought while admiring him in the kitchen.

32

Molly

The Day He Wasn't Nice

The days ticked by. We stayed in bed late into the mornings since there was no rush to get up. Neither of us wanted to leave each other's arms, anyway. We snuggled together and watched the Roman sunrise stream through the window, a jumble of tangled sheets and tangled legs.

Donovan exercised in the gym every day. I started going with him, walking on the treadmill next to him while listening to my daily news podcast. It kept me updated on the state of affairs with the virus, and it got my blood flowing a little bit. That was better than sitting in bed and doom-scrolling all day. At least this way I felt like I was doing something productive with my time.

We started watching movies in the lounge after dinner. They had hundreds of DVDs to choose from, and although they were somewhat out of date, it was better than Italian Seinfeld on the hotel channel.

One night, after watching *Mission Impossible*, neither of us were ready to go to bed. So Donovan made Negronis behind the bar and we played another game of pool.

"Same game we played the other night?" I asked. "Winner gets to make the other person do whatever they want?"

Donovan leaned on his pool stick and smirked. "You're not mad at me for hustling you?"

"Hah! So you *were* hustling me!"

"I don't know why you're complaining. It resulted in my tongue inside that pretty pink pussy of yours."

"Ohh, alliteration," I said while sipping my drink. "Poetic for a line cook."

He scoffed. "Line cook? I got promoted, Feisty. In case you didn't notice, I'm the chef of my own hotel kitchen."

"Damn right you are. And almost all your reviews are five stars."

"Almost?"

"The cookies you baked the other day were dry," I teased. "Four stars."

"They were shortbread. They're supposed to be dry."

I pulled out my phone and pretended to type with my thumbs. "*Poor customer service. One star.*"

"Forget the game," he said, tossing aside his stick. "I'll show you customer service."

He cradled my head in both hands and kissed me so hard that I was instantly wet. I leaned against the pool table and savored the way his lips felt, with a hint of licorice taste from the drink.

The way he held me, the way he kissed me, made it clear he had been thinking about this for a while.

Donovan ripped away from the kiss and unbuttoned my jeans, then pulled them down along with my panties. I kicked them off and he lifted me onto the edge of the pool table, then kissed me again while removing his own pants. I heard them fall to the ground.

"Good thing we turned off the security cameras," I breathed.

189

He guided himself into my waiting lips, burying himself deep into my pussy without hesitation. Both of us exhaled together as the pleasure of our intimate contact took over. Donovan rested his forehead against mine and caressed my cheek with his hand while I squeezed him with my wet heat.

The felt from the edge of the pool table was soft against my bare ass cheeks as Donovan began making love to me. His tongue massaged its way into my mouth and I met it with my own, moving wetly together while his hips gyrated between my legs. For several minutes we were a jumble of grunts and groans and kisses.

"Was this what you wanted?" he rumbled into my neck. "If we had played the game and you won?"

I draped my arms over his shoulders and said, "It's kind of what I wanted."

He bent down to kiss my neck. "Kind of?"

I bit my lip. "I was hoping you wouldn't be so *nice* to me."

Donovan slowed down. "Not so nice?"

I nodded while looking up at him.

I didn't know any other way to ask. In fact, I wasn't used to asking for what I wanted in bed—or on a *pool table*, as it were. But with Donovan, I felt like I could tell him what I wanted. Like he wouldn't judge me.

He grinned lustily, then gripped my waist in his hands. He pulled himself back, then *slammed* forward as hard as he could.

I moaned as new elation spread through my body.

"Is this what you wanted?" he asked in his deep voice.

I nodded, and as soon as I did he pounded me again.

"Oh God yes." I leaned back on my elbows as he fucked me harder.

Donovan pawed at my breasts while jack-hammering into me, rougher and rougher. All the while he kept his eyes locked onto mine, drinking in my desire like it was as intoxicating as the Negroni.

After a few minutes he said, "I know what you *really* want."

He pulled me down from the table and kissed my neck, dragging his teeth across my skin. Then he spun me around. He planted a strong hand on my back and bent me over the pool table, then filled me from behind without hesitation.

I cried out with pleasure as he took control. The new angle was intense, but in *just* the right way. I gazed over my shoulder at him as he grabbed my waist and began slamming into me, holding nothing back.

Donovan moaned loudly, and I opened my lips to join my cries of ecstasy to his. I rolled my head back and caught a glimpse of our reflection in the mirror behind the bar. I was bent over the pool table, back arched and ass in the air. Donovan's gorgeous body gripped mine tightly, arms bulging with taut strength as he refused to let go.

We looked *hot*.

As new pleasure overwhelmed me, I clenched my eyes shut and let my moan echo through the empty lounge.

33

Donovan

The Day She Got Adventurous

There was a very long list of ways I wanted to make love to Molly. In every room, in every position possible. So when she told me not to be nice with her, I knew *exactly* what she meant. And I knew exactly what I was going to do to her. I'd known since the moment she teased me by bending over during our *first* pool game, over a week ago.

You want to show off your ass? Well then I'm going to make it mine.

She reacted just how I hoped as I bent her over the table and buried myself into her. She was already soaking wet, but now she was *drenched.* My length slid in and out of her with ease, despite how tight she was.

Molly's ass was a masterpiece. I don't want to overstate it, but the sight of it alone was enough to make any man cry with joy. The smooth, round globes of her ass pressed together, then tapering off at a narrow waist. I clutched one of her cheeks in my hand, squeezing her flesh beneath my fingers and letting it fill my palm. I savored the sight of my cock disappearing between those orbs, devoured by the lushness of her pussy within.

I've never been into a person this much, I realized.

I grabbed a handful of her hair and gave it a testing squeeze. She arched her back and moaned loudly, just like I hoped.

The sounds she made grew louder as I slammed into her. Harder and harder I fucked her, giving her exactly what she wanted. I needed her to come, both to hear her scream with elation and because *I* wanted to come, and I wouldn't let myself do it until she had. But the way her slit was gripping me, tight like a vice...

Molly twisted to look back at me, surprise and bliss in her dark eyes, and then she completely fell apart. Her cry of ecstasy was music to my ears. I fisted her hair and finally surrendered to the sweet release of her body, and as I came I pushed into her as deep as I could, bottoming out inside her wet heat while it clamped around me tightly.

When I came down from my eye-watering, toe-curling orgasm, I wrapped my arms around Molly and pulled her up into a standing position, her pale ass cheeks pressed warmly against my skin while I was still inside of her. I twisted her face around so I could taste her lips, and we stayed like that until I finally went soft.

Yeah, I thought, *I'm so into you, Molly.*

She excused herself to the lounge bathroom, and then I did the same to clean up. When I returned, Molly was jiggling her empty glass in the air behind the bar.

"Excuse me, bartender line cook sex robot? I need another Negroni. Don't you know I'm on *vacation?*"

I grinned and took her glass. "Right away, ma'am."

She giggled and leaned on the bar top. "I've never done that before."

"I've never had sex on a pool table either." I gave her a wink and added, "I've eaten a girl out on one, but not sex. The only girls I ever saw at the bar back home were biker chicks older than my mom. And they had a *lot* more tattoos than you."

Molly didn't laugh at my joke. "No," she said. "I meant... I've never done that position. Like, bent over."

"You've never had doggy style sex," I said skeptically.

She bit her lip.

"Wait, really?" I asked.

"Don't judge me!"

"I'm not, I'm just surprised."

"I told you, I've only had sex with two guys before. And they were both really boring. We never got a chance to do anything adventurous."

Personally I didn't consider fucking someone from behind to be *adventurous*, but hey, I didn't want to seem judgmental.

I grabbed the bottle of gin and poured some into each glass. "I didn't realize I was corrupting you so much. First the Colosseum blowjob, now this..."

"Now you know." She leaned across the bar to kiss me. "I love it. I guess what I'm trying to say is, I'm open to new things."

"Yeah?"

"Yeah," she said. "It feels like the world is ending. I want to have some fun while I'm here."

Molly was speaking my language. I wanted all kinds of sex with her: sweet, rough, gentle, hard, and everything in between. If she wanted to try new things, then I was all too happy to oblige her.

I handed her a drink. "See? I knew you were feisty."

She was absolutely adorable as she glared at me, then took a sip.

Yeah. I was definitely going to corrupt this girl. And I was going to enjoy every sweaty moment of it.

34

Molly
The Day We Ran Out

Being in the hotel started to feel like our own little honeymoon. Donovan and I cooked together during the day, then made love at night. We fell asleep in each other's arms, slept in until sunlight streamed into our bedroom, and then made love again before getting out of bed.

Everything was perfect. Despite the horrors of the pandemic raging throughout the world, we were in our own romantic bubble.

But after another week, we ran into a new problem.

We were in the gym when I told him. "You enjoy having sex with me, right?" I asked.

He jogged on the treadmill, sweat glistening in his hair and on his bare chest. "With you? I hate it. It's worse than doing laundry."

I rolled my eyes at him, and he grinned back at me. "What kind of a question is that, Feisty?"

"Here's the thing," I explained. "I didn't expect to be here more than a week. I thought I would be home long before now."

Donovan turned the speed down so he could walk. "What's

wrong? Tell me."

"My birth control runs out in two days," I said.

"Ah, damn," Donovan said. "I knew things were too good to be true."

"We have to go back to using condoms," I said. "You don't mind, do you?"

I steeled myself for his response. I knew how much better it felt for him without a condom, and I expected him to resist.

But he laughed and shook his head. "Yeah, I've gotten used to feeling you and *only* you. But I don't mind wrapping it up again. If that's the only hardship we have to face during the quarantine, then we're pretty fucking lucky. When do we need to make the switch?"

"We should go back to condoms *today*," I said. "Just to be safe. We're already kind of taking a risk, since we had sex this morning. If your little swimmers can survive a few days..."

He grinned over at me and said, "I'll do whatever it takes to keep making love to you, Feisty." He increased the speed and began jogging again.

I beamed for the rest of my workout. Donovan wasn't just amazing in the kitchen and bedroom. He was also a good guy.

Way better than my asshole exes, I thought.

When we returned to the room later, Donovan checked his stash. "Shit. I've only got one left."

"One condom?"

He held it up like it was Willy Wonka's golden ticket. "The sole survivor."

I crossed my arms over my breasts. "How many did you use before the lockdown?"

He furrowed his brow and stared off. "Let me think. There was Heather. Then Maria. Then the twins, whose names I never learned..."

I smacked him playfully on the chest. "Ha ha. Very funny."

"I'll get more tomorrow. I saw them at the grocery store the last time I was there."

I stood on my toes to brush my lips against his. "In the meantime, we'd better make this one count."

I stripped out of my workout clothes and got in the shower. I left the bathroom door open, and Donovan took the hint and joined me.

When I checked into the Residencia Al Gladiatore—which felt like years ago—the concierge warned me that the hotel building was old and hot water was scarce. That wasn't a problem now that Donovan and I were the only two guests, and we took our time in the shower. Donovan hugged me from behind while we let the scalding water run over our bodies. I felt him stiffen against my ass, slick and soapy.

Slowly, Donovan began kissing my neck. I squirted body wash onto a washcloth and rubbed it together until it was covered with bubbles. Before I could wash myself, Donovan took the cloth and began cleaning my body for me. He scrubbed it over my neck, across my shoulders, then down around my breasts. My nipples were instantly hard as he carefully guided the washcloth in a circle around one breast, then the other.

"I think you're enjoying this too much."

"I'm enjoying it exactly the right amount," he growled into my ear, giving it a playful nibble.

He continued scrubbing my body, covering it with soapy suds, then he handed the washcloth back to me. He ducked out of the shower, not even bothering to towel off.

"Was it something I said?" I asked while standing there in shock.

He returned with a piece of gold foil in his hand. He jumped back in the shower, placed the condom on the soap rack, and then took me in his strong arms. I let the washcloth fall to the shower floor as he kissed me, lips soft and seeking.

Donovan lowered himself to my chest, gently sucking on my diamond-hard nipple. I craned my head back and moaned, the sound echoing in the acoustics of the shower. Donovan didn't stay there long, and continued downward until he was on his knees on the wet tile. He kissed my mound of pubic hair, then slid his tongue up between my legs.

My knees buckled as he went down on me in the shower, licking around my clit and up into my slit. The water ran over his black hair as he buried his face into my sex, devouring me. I loved the way he tasted me, tongue flashing across every surface, painting me with his saliva.

"I want you," I breathed.

He grinned up at me, his chiseled face glistening from the water. "Not as much as I want you."

He hastily grabbed the condom from the soap rack. I wrapped my fingers around the ridge of his cock and stroked him while he opened the condom, then rolled it on.

Suddenly he flinched. "Fuck!"

"What?"

He held up the condom. "It ripped."

"Oh *no*," I groaned. "Why is your dick so big!"

He rested back against the shower wall and let the water run over his chest. "You have got to be kidding me."

"We can fool around in other ways," I said, allowing my fingernails to brush across his still-hard shaft. It pulsed underneath my touch. "Once I rinse off, let's get out of the shower and see how *creative* we can get."

I stood in front of the water stream to wash the rest of the soap off my body. Donovan hugged me from behind, squeezing his entire body against mine while kissing my neck.

I ground against him. He felt so good between my cheeks, hot and hard and full of potential. I hated the thought of *not* being able to feel him inside of me.

Donovan gently guided himself lower, pressing his hard length between my thighs. Slowly he began thrusting back and forth, grinding the shaft against my lips.

"You feel good," he breathed into my ear. One arm squeezed around my chest, and the other hand slid down between my legs. I relaxed into his embrace as his fingertips made love to my clit.

We stayed like that for a few minutes, grinding and rubbing together while the shower filled with steam.

"I want you inside me so bad," I breathed. The words came out of me without thought.

"I know," he whispered into my ear. "But you said we can't risk it."

"It's not fair," I said with a laugh. "You woke something in me, and now I can't have it!"

He nuzzled at my neck, tongue flashing against my skin. "I told you I'll get condoms tomorrow."

"Tomorrow is too far away. I need you *now*."

Donovan made a rumbling noise in his throat and he began humping me a little faster. Between his shaft grinding up against my pussy lips and his fingers on my clit, I was feeling good. *Really* good. But it still wasn't what I wanted.

I bent forward, reached down between me, and took hold of him. I guided him up into my dripping-wet lips.

"Just the tip."

He hesitated like he was going to resist, fingers clawing into the flesh of my ass. "Just the tip," he agreed.

Both of us sighed together as his crown pushed apart my waiting lips. My pussy *ached* for him, to feel all of him, but he was a man of his word. He kept only the tip inside me, moving it back and forth no more than an inch.

It was torture.

I pushed my hips back, taking more of him inside me. His hand tightened on my waist as he tried to stop me.

"You said..."

"Just a little more," I begged with barely formed words of desire.

"That's your pussy talking," he replied in a deep, calm voice. "I know, because my cock is screaming the same thing."

I moaned as he continued fucking me with just the tip, the smallest amount of movement a man could possible give a woman. His fingers curled around my hip and rubbed my clit, driving the pleasure —and the torture—even higher.

I kept pushing my hips back to take more of him, but he wouldn't let me. His willpower was stronger.

"You're. Killing. Me," I moaned.

His fingers danced faster around my clit, pushing it inward with the perfect amount of pressure. I felt my climax nearing, but it wasn't enough, it wasn't *nearly* as strong as I wanted. I needed Donovan inside me, all of him, every throbbing inch.

And then, when I thought I was going to die from withdrawal, he gave me what I wanted. He gripped my waist with powerful fingers and *thrust* up inside of me, filling me to the brim with all of him.

My world went to pieces. I cried out in the shower as I shook and shivered with release.

"Oh God," he sang as he slammed inside of me, making up for lost time. "Molly. *Molly!*"

Donovan suddenly pulled out, then thrust forward so that his length rested between my cheeks. He groaned and I felt him explode, twitching and trembling against my skin as he came all over my back.

He wrapped me in another bear hug from behind, clinging to me in the shower like he never wanted to let go.

35

Molly

The Day We Went Out Again

"As amazing as that felt," Donovan said while pouring sugar into a big mixing bowl, "we shouldn't risk it again."

I was sitting on the counter next to him, watching him cook. "I know. We're already being extra careful by switching to condoms two days *before* my birth control runs out, but I promise I won't coerce you with my feminine wiles again."

He leaned over and kissed me. "Deep down, I *wanted* to be coerced."

I giggled and reached into the mixing bowl. Donovan was making cookies, and the raw dough smelled too delicious not to grab a piece of.

"It's better cooked, you know," he said.

"Not true!" I replied cheerfully.

Donovan pulled the bowl away and glared at me. "You can get sick from eating raw flour."

"Don't care!" I said. "Since I can't have oranges, I might as well indulge my sweet tooth in other ways."

"You miss oranges that much, huh?"

I nodded emphatically. "I told you. I normally eat one every day with lunch."

"I know a lot of orange dessert recipes," he said casually. "Iced orange cookies. Cinnamon rolls with orange frosting. Sunshine orange pie. It's like key-lime pie, but with oranges."

I bounced up and down on the counter. "Stop it! You're killing me!"

"Just letting you know there are more ways to eat them than just sliced up."

"I'm a simple girl." I sighed. "When I get home I'm going to sit down and eat an entire bag in one sitting."

"Is there such a thing as Vitamin-C poisoning?" Donovan wondered out loud. "If so, I bet that's how you get it."

I rolled my eyes. "What do you want to do tonight? We've got the fourth *Mission Impossible* movie next on our DVD list."

Donovan dumped the cookie dough onto the counter and began flattening it with a rolling pin. "I was thinking of sneaking out and exploring the city some more. It's been a while since we got caught. I think we're safe."

"You sure? There are rumors that the lockdown might be lifted in a few days. Maybe we should wait until then."

"Fuck that," he said. "I want to see more of Rome *tonight*, with you. That's so much better than seeing it with a bunch of other tourists in the way. Isn't there some place on your list you really want to see?"

"You just want to get another ancient Roman blowjob, don't you?"

"I'll be honest. The thought crossed my mind."

I pulled out my phone. "Actually, the Oppian Hill is high on my list. It's in the park right across from the Colosseum. There are a bunch of ruins there, like Nero's Golden House and Trajan's Bath."

"I'm sold," Donovan said. "We'll head out after dinner."

As soon as the sun set, we put on our masks and exited the hotel. It was fun to sneak through the city, hand-in-hand like a couple of outlaws. It was dangerous, but not *too* dangerous. Especially now that we knew the worst they would do to us was send us back to the hotel.

We took the same route we had the other day, but when we reached the Colosseum plaza we stayed in the alleys and skirted around it. Oppian Hill was across the road, a squat hill that rose above the Colosseum itself. There was a ticket booth and a small barrier at the entrance. We climbed over it and scurried into the park.

The path zigged and zagged up the hill, stopping at various pillars or ruins, but Donovan took me by the hand and led me straight up the hill without stopping. When I asked what he was doing, he put his finger over his lips.

We climbed until we reached the ruins of a little amphitheater at the top. Donovan put his arm around me and turned me around. We were high enough that we could look down on the Colosseum, which was illuminated with exterior lights. The sight took my breath away.

Donovan put his masked mouth next to my ear and whispered, "I wanted to get up high, to see if there are any cops patrolling. The view is just a bonus."

We held hands while admiring the view of the Colosseum and the rest of the city beyond. We were veiled in darkness here, which allowed us to easily spot the flashlight cones of two police officers down at the base of the hill. They moved slowly, in predictable paths around the grounds. None of them came up into the Oppian Hill park.

"Okay," Donovan said. "Let's look at some ruins."

It turned out that the small amphitheater ruin we were standing next to wasn't an amphitheater at all: it was the remains of Trajan's

203

Bath. I held up my phone to the sign so I could read it.

"We don't want any light..." Donovan warned.

"That's why I'm using the screen, and not the flashlight," I replied. "Now shush, I'm trying to read about history."

"Nerd."

We wandered through the park, stopping at each ruin area when there was a sign to read. Even though it was night and we couldn't see the ruins clearly, I devoured everything I read. A column that had been part of Nero's original house stood alone, a pale pillar clawing at the night sky. Another section of stone blocks was the remains of the emperor's stables.

After being stuck in my hotel for weeks, I couldn't get enough.

"Okay, we should probably head back," Donovan said after ten minutes.

"I want to see what's on the north side of the park," I insisted. "There's another exit there."

Donovan's face glowed as he looked at his phone. "But then we'll need to circle around to the east to get back to the hotel. We haven't seen what kind of patrols are over there..."

"It'll be worth it to see what's on the other side," I insisted. "Come on. You're the one who convinced me to sneak out here. Don't chicken out on me now!"

He wrapped an arm around me and kissed my hair. "You've gotten braver in the past ten minutes."

"I'm enraptured by all this history!" I whispered excitedly.

"Yeah, you're definitely a nerd."

"You say it like it's a bad thing."

We wound our way along the path to the north side of the park, which then sloped down toward the city. Donovan waited patiently while I read every single information sign along the way. When we finally reached the north exit, I felt a pang of disappointment.

"Okay," I said. "Now we can go."

"I wonder if there's a pharmacy on the way back," he whispered. "We can break in and grab some condoms."

I giggled in the darkness. "Minutes ago you were afraid we would get caught, and now you're casually suggesting we commit burglary?"

"If it means putting my penis inside of you tonight," he replied, "then yes!"

We hopped the barrier at the north exit and hurried down an alley. "Since you waited patiently while I read all those signs," I said, "I'll make it up to you when we get back."

"You have my attention," he replied.

"I'm going to slowly take your pants off."

"Go on."

"Then I'm going to wrap my fingers around—"

I cut off as a figure stepped into the alley ahead of us, blinding us with light. They shouted something in Italian.

Oh no.

Donovan grabbed my hand and turned us around. But then a flashlight beam hit us from a second person, who was behind us. Blocking our route out of the alley.

"*Fuck*," Donovan muttered under his breath.

"American," the person behind us said in a thick Italian accent. As soon as my eyes adjusted to the blinding light, I saw that it was the same police officer who had caught us by the Colosseum the other night.

Donovan pulled out the bottle of cough syrup and held it up. "Medicine! Medicinale. Si?"

The officer's bitter laugh was recognizable in any language.

"No. Lies. Home, now."

We complied as the two cops escorted us back to the hotel. Before letting us go inside, one of them snapped our photos with his cell phone.

"Stay," the officer commanded in his halting English, patting the door to the Residencia Al Gladiatore. He pointed to our photo on his phone. "Leave again? Jail."

"We understand," Donovan said. "It won't happen again."

The cops watched us go inside. I felt their eyes on us as we walked through the lobby to the elevator.

"I wonder if they'll barricade us inside," I said with a nervous laugh. "Like those crazy videos from China. Right?"

Donovan clenched his jaw and stared straight ahead. "That was a mistake."

"Yeah," I agreed. "We probably shouldn't have left..."

"I meant taking a different route home." He thumbed the elevator button harder than it deserved. "From the top of the hill I knew where every officer was around the Colosseum, but we didn't know how many were patrolling on the other side. You shouldn't have insisted on going that way."

"I'm sorry," I said as the elevator door opened. "At least we didn't get thrown in jail."

He rounded on me. "We will the next time we try to sneak out! We could have explored the city a bunch more times, but now we're on our final warning. Now we're stuck in here." He mashed the button for the third floor. "We should have stuck with the plan."

His frustration took me by surprise. In our three weeks together, we'd been perfectly happy and content. This was the first time I'd seen him upset about something.

And it stung extra because he was right.

"I'm sorry," I said in a small voice. "We should have stuck with your plan."

He nodded and stared at the door.

"Want me to make it up to you?" I slid my arm around him. "What I talked about earlier..."

"Let's just go to bed," he said.

Disappointed in how the night had gone, I followed him down the hall to our rooms.

36

Donovan

The Day I Fucked Up

I was so fucking stupid.

I knew we were running a risk by going out. I had taken every precaution to make sure we wouldn't get caught: moving slowly, pausing every couple of minutes to listen for cops, not using the light on our phones. But as soon as Molly insisted on seeing more of the Oppian Hill, I folded like a cheap table. I let her take her phone out to illuminate the information signs. And then I let her convince me to go out a different way, even though it meant a longer walk home in an area we didn't know.

As I lay in bed that night, staring at the ceiling and listening to Molly's breathing next to me, my anger faded. Now I was mad at myself for yelling at her. Okay, maybe I didn't *yell* at her. But I definitely took out my frustration on her. That wasn't fair. Hell, going out into the city was my idea in the first place. She originally wanted to stay in and watch a movie. So if anyone was to blame for getting caught, it was me.

It feels like our first fight.

That thought conjured new emotions in my chest. *Firsts* were for people in a relationship. But what were we? Two people killing time with each other while waiting for a ticket home?

When all of this had started, I didn't have much of a plan. There was a cute girl staying in the hotel room next to mine, and she was willing to trade wine for pasta. When we hooked up, I figured it would be a good way to spend the quarantine. Some no-strings-attached fun while we waited out the lockdown.

But Molly was so much more than that. I was certain of it now. She was beautiful, and smart, and constantly found new ways to make me laugh. I knew all of her little quirks, including the way she hummed to herself while brushing her teeth, and how she always tapped her feet happily when she took the first bite of dinner.

Molly was special, and I was falling head-over-heels for her.

But how did she feel about me? Was I just a stranger she was sharing her bed with until she could go back to her life in Elkhart, Indiana? Had I ruined my chance for something more by snapping at her?

I tossed and turned all night thinking about it.

At six in the morning I gave up on trying to get any sleep. I quietly slipped out of bed and got dressed. Molly was a dark shape under the covers, rising and falling slowly with each breath. Once again I was struck by just how gorgeous she was, even asleep. Like an angel that had found her way into my bed.

I slipped out the front door of the hotel while it was still dark out. Civilians were permitted to go to the grocery store between six and ten in the morning. Would the cops that had caught us last night still let me leave? I hoped I wouldn't have to find out.

I walked down the middle of the street like I wasn't doing anything wrong. The store was about two miles away—*three kilometers,* I corrected in my head—and I got to enjoy the gorgeous Italian sunrise on the way, filling the sky with streaks of pink above the red-tiled roofs.

A cop nodded to me on the way, but didn't say anything. I

walked a little bit faster.

I got to the grocery store early, before a line had formed. It was a relief to walk around inside without having to dodge people in every aisle. I retrieved a box of condoms from the pharmacy section and then headed to the check-out line. We didn't need any food since the kitchen at the hotel was still stocked, but I swung by the produce section just in case.

The fresh fruits were wiped out. There was only a single orange in the bin, bruised and pitiful looking. If I brought that home to Molly it would probably make her cry.

"Excuse me," I said to a passing employee. I pointed at the orange. "More? Um, quando?"

He looked at the stand and shook his head.

Oh well. I tried.

The check-out guy scanned my condoms and made a comment in Italian. He chuckled, so he was probably joking about how I was having a better quarantine than he was. I laughed as if I understood, then left the store.

I was tempted to go home, but it was still early. I checked the map on my phone. There was another grocery store three kilometers to the east, deeper into the city. It made a triangle with my current location and our hotel, which meant it wouldn't be *that* much farther to go home if I swung by there.

I decided it was worth a try. I needed to make up for being a dick last night. Plus I wanted to see the smile on her face if I came bearing gifts.

As the sun climbed above the tiled Roman roofs, the streets narrowed and became more crowded with people. The morning rush of people going to the store while they were allowed.

Soon it became difficult to keep two meters of space between myself and everyone else. One woman behind me kept coughing into her sleeve, like she had something in her throat that she couldn't get out. I glanced back at her nervously—everyone was giving her a wide berth.

It's probably a normal cough because of allergies, I told myself. It felt like a comforting lie.

I hurried along as best as I could to the next store. It was about the same size as the previous one, but this one had a long line out the front. After walking this far, I figured I might as well wait. I would wait an hour for Molly, if I had to.

I read the news on my phone while the line slowly crept forward. Cases were spiking in the big coastal cities back home: New York, San Francisco, Los Angeles. Boston wasn't as bad as those, but cases were still rising steadily. Hospitals would be at capacity soon, a Boston Globe article predicted.

As I reached the front of the line, I noticed a woman standing by the entrance. She had a baby in one arm, and a cardboard sign in the other. I translated the sign on my phone: *Need money for diapers.*

Fuck. I couldn't imagine going through this sort of global event with a baby. It was a reminder that in the grand scheme of things, I was lucky as hell. Camping out in a four-star hotel wasn't so bad.

I fished around in my pocket for Euros, but then a police officer ran up to the woman and started yelling. He gestured, and she quickly scurried away from the front door. When she was across the street, she resumed bouncing the baby and holding up her sign.

"Signore? Mi scusi?" the man at the front of the store called to me.

I apologized and let him scan my forehead temperature.

Even though the stores looked similar in size on the exterior, this one was *much* smaller on the inside. The ceiling was lower and the aisles were more narrow. But they were allowing the same number of people inside, crammed into a smaller space.

I stood in the entranceway and debated what to do. This

definitely felt more risky than my other grocery trip. Every instinct was telling me to turn around and go home. But I could see the produce section to my right, and it was stocked.

For Molly, I thought stubbornly.

I weaved through the displays in the open produce section. One woman had a face shield covering her entire head like a plastic welding mask. Another couple hastily grabbed avocados while scanning their surroundings, eyes wide and fearful behind their masks. The butcher was next to the produce, and there was a long line that snaked through the entire section. I had to backtrack and circle around to avoid getting close to anyone.

As I picked my way through the building, I felt my anxiety rise. My pulse throbbed in my temple like a drum. I got caught between two people by the onion display and had to wait for one of them to move. A man nearby suddenly sneezed, which made me jump and then squeeze past the woman blocking my way.

Finally I reached the orange display. And oh baby, it was worth it. There were individual Valencia oranges stacked high, and big bags full of them underneath the display. I grabbed one bag, then grabbed a second one. If Molly was serious about how much she loved oranges, then one bag wouldn't last very long.

Time to make a break for it. The checkout lines were short right now, if I could get through the crowd in time.

I started that way, then stopped.

There's one more thing I need to do.

I made a detour deeper into the store. It was crowded, and I couldn't avoid getting within one meter of several customers, however I found what I was looking for near the back. When I returned to the front of the store, the checkout lines were longer than before. I decided it was still worth it.

I exited the store and walked across the street. The woman with the baby and cardboard sign looked longingly at the box under my arm. I could see the desperation in her eyes, and the pride she was

212

swallowing just to be outside, begging.

"Mi scusi," she said in a shuddering voice.

With my hand holding the bags of oranges, I pointed at her sign. Then I held out the big box of diapers I had purchased. Her eyes jumped from the box, to my face, then back to the box. She babbled a question to me in Italian.

"Um, per te, I think?" I said. "These are for you. That's what I'm trying to say. Per te?"

Tears ran down her cheeks and the cardboard sign fell to the ground. She took the box of diapers with one hand, placed it on the ground, and then lunged at me, hugging me tightly with her free hand while clutching the baby in the other.

"Grazie," she whispered through her mask. "Grazie, grazie, grazie..." The baby was pressed between us, and he looked up at me with big blue eyes, wondering who this strange man was.

Alarm bells went off in my head. Aside from Molly, this was the first physical contact I'd had with anyone in *weeks*. In terms of pandemic safety, it was the worst thing I could have done.

But she clung to me like I was her savior, and I couldn't bring myself to push her away. "You're welcome." I patted her on the back with my free hand.

I didn't like praise. It felt immodest taking credit for a good deed, or bragging about an accomplishment. I did it to help her, not to give myself a pat on the back. If there had been a way to give her the diapers anonymously, I totally would have done that.

She finally let go of me, then scooped up the box under one arm. Even though most of her face was covered by her mask, the look in her eyes was unmistakable.

Happiness. And hope.

I waved goodbye and slung my oranges over a shoulder.

It's just a hug, I thought while walking home. *It was worth it to help her.*

37

Molly

The Day With ORANGES!

It was bad enough that I slept terribly, with nightmares about getting caught by the police, and about upsetting Donovan, and about going to bed without saying a word to each other.

Then I woke up alone.

For a few moments it felt like I had been abandoned. My bed was *empty*. I had messed up last night and now he was gone. Our fun adventure had come to an end. I was alone again, just like I had been the first few days of the lockdown.

But of course that wasn't true. For one thing, I was in *his* bed. His suitcase was on the table to my right, and his shirts were hanging up in the closet.

For another thing, there was a folded note on the pillow next to me.

Out running errands. If I don't come back, it's because the zombies got me.

I smiled at the joke. It meant things were okay between us, despite what had happened last night. But I still felt guilty about everything.

I brewed a cup of coffee and walked out to the balcony. The sun was shining brightly and there was a cool morning breeze that stirred my Residencia Al Gladiatore bathrobe. I pulled it tighter around myself and watched the plaza below. A woman was hurrying along with a bag of groceries, making use of the four hours when she was allowed to be out for non-emergency reasons.

She was the first person I had seen in the plaza in a long time. It made things feel somewhat normal as I sipped my coffee.

By nine I started getting worried.

Molly: Did the zombies get you?

Donovan: They tried, but I escaped. I'm 100% unbitten.

Molly: That's exactly what a zombie would say. Where are you?

Donovan: At the airport

Molly: ???

Donovan: I finally got a ticket home. I'm in first class as we speak. They're serving champagne. Should I get the chicken, or steak?

Molly: Not funny!

Molly: You had better not be!

Donovan: I'm out running an errand. I'll be home soon.

I typed out my next message, then waited several minutes before working up the courage to hit *send.*

Molly: I'm really sorry about last night. You were trying to be careful, and I got reckless. I shouldn't have been using my phone to read the info signs, and we should have gone back the way we came. It's my fault we got caught. I hope you can forgive me.

Donovan: Shit, it's not your fault. And even if it was, I overreacted about it. Sorry for being a dick when we got home. I guess I was flustered after our run-in with the po-po.

Molly: You weren't a dick about it! I deserved it! I'm the one trying to apologize here. You have nothing to be sorry for.

Donovan: That's a relief. I picked up a surprise for you, but since I have nothing to be sorry for, I guess I'll take it back.

Molly: Ohh

Molly: A surprise?

Molly: What is it?

Molly: Did you charter a private plane for us to take home?

Donovan: Line cooks can't afford private planes, Feisty. My surprise is cheap.

Donovan: But I promise it's worth more than all the

216

art in the Pope's house down the street.

I knew the surprise was condoms. He was right: that *was* worth more than all the wealth in the Vatican. As exciting as our shower sex was, teasing and rubbing and then pulling out like a couple of teenagers, I didn't want to take the risk again.

And I planned on having a *lot* more sex with Donovan.

Just then I saw Donovan on the other side of the plaza. He was tall in his jeans and a grey T-shirt. Once again I was struck by just how well he fit in, with his Mediterranean features and dark hair. Even with his mask on, I could tell he was grinning widely.

When he got close, I leaned over the balcony and in my best Shakespeare impression said, "Donovan, oh Donovan, wherefore art thou Donovan!"

He laughed and unslung something from his shoulder. Two big bags, orange in color, which he held up like the prize-winning salmon at a fishing competition.

I gasped. "OH MY GOD!"

His smile disappeared. "Don't scream too loud," he shouted up at me. "Someone's going to think you're being murdered."

I threw on some clothes and ran downstairs. Donovan had dumped the oranges in the lobby cleaning station we had built, and he was already running into the pool room to scrub himself clean. I poked my head in there in time to see his cute naked butt jumping into the hot tub.

"When you're safe to touch," I said, "I'm going to *smother* you with kisses." I tossed him a change of clothes.

He lathered his chest with soap and grinned widely. "Don't eat all the oranges in one sitting. There are some recipes I want to try."

I went back into the lobby, put gloves on, and began wiping down every orange with a disinfectant cloth. It felt like overkill, but I didn't care! I was too excited!

There was a box of condoms under the orange bags, too. I squealed happily when I saw that.

As I collected the clean oranges in a cardboard box from the kitchen, I noticed the receipt. Five Euros for the oranges was cheap indeed.

Donovan came out of the pool room in his new clothes. He dried his hair with a towel and said, "So you like the surprise?"

"I love it! The grocery store finally restocked?"

"Actually, I had to walk across town to the other store. I walked like six kilometers today."

"You did that for little old me?" I batted my eyelashes at him.

"Only you," he replied. "If it was anyone else, I'd let them get scurvy."

His lips tasted like soap as I kissed him, but I didn't mind. I held up the receipt and said, "Did you get diapers?"

"Must be a mistake on the receipt," he replied after a short pause. "Things were crazy at the store. Come on, let's get cooking. I have an orange-iced cookie recipe I want to try."

I glanced at the box. "Do we have enough oranges?"

"My recipe only calls for one."

"In about ten minutes, there might not be one left!"

He laughed. "Thankfully I only need to zest the peel. The inside is all yours."

I sat on the counter in the kitchen while he prepared his cookies. I had sliced open an orange and was slowly eating the pieces, savoring them to make them last longer. The tangy, sweet fruit tasted better than I remembered and juice ran over my chin.

Donovan used a zesting grater to flavor a bowl full of icing he had made from scratch. The smell of oranges hung in the air, putting a permanent smile on my face.

"Mom always included orange slices in my lunchbox," I said.

218

"She thought oranges cured everything. Sleepy? Have an orange. Headache? Time for an orange. Scraped knee? Squeeze some orange juice on it—the stinging means it's working! If she were alive to see the pandemic, she would probably claim oranges cure the virus. Or at least reduce your likelihood of catching it."

Donovan laughed while mixing the icing with a whisk. A strand of black hair fell across his face, and he blew a puff of air to brush it away.

"I'm sorry it's not a plane ride home," he said. "But it's the next best thing."

"Oranges make me *feel* like I'm home. That's good enough." I swallowed a bite and then said, "I really am sorry about last night."

He pursed his lips together. "Me too. At least we're not in jail."

"Yeah, but it still sucks we can't go anywhere now," I insisted. "And that's my fault."

Donovan stopped stirring his bowl. "That just means we have to find more things to do *inside*. So really, it's a good problem to have."

"Especially now that we have *oranges!*"

"Taste this." He stuck his finger in the bowl and came out with a little blob of frosting. He aimed it at my face, and I leaned forward to suck it off his finger, giving it a little swirl with my tongue.

"Oh my God," I said. "That tastes *amazing.*"

"Wait until you taste it *on* the cookies."

"Forget the cookies—give me the bowl!"

I tried to steal the bowl from him while he pushed me away, laughing and play-fighting in the hotel kitchen without a care in the world.

38

Molly
The Day He Cheated

We put the new box of condoms to good use. Part of me missed the few weeks where we'd been able to have sex without anything between us, and I could tell Donovan missed it too, but that didn't diminish the fun we had together.

Donovan came up with creative new ways to fill the time. One afternoon we played hide and seek in the entire hotel. Whoever hid the longest got to do whatever they wanted with the other person. I hid first, choosing the dry-goods pantry. There was an enormous bag of jasmine rice that I hid behind, and it took Donovan almost twenty minutes to find me.

Then it was his turn. I closed my eyes behind the concierge desk and counted to one hundred. "Ready or not, here I come!" I shouted, even though he probably couldn't hear me.

I had a hunch as to where he was. I took the elevator to the second floor and walked into the lounge. The lights were off, and natural sunlight streamed through the glass dome above. I tip-toed over to the bar and opened one of the cabinets underneath the taps.

Donovan was hidden inside, with his knees folded up to his

chin. "What the hell!" he exclaimed.

I looked at my phone. "Three minutes. I win!"

"You must have cheated." He crawled out of the cabinet and brushed himself off. "There's no way you found me that quickly without cheating."

"You commented on this cabinet the other day!" I said smugly. "You opened it and said, *wow, you could hide a dead body in here!*"

He crossed his arms over his chest. "I don't believe you."

"Too bad! I win! Which means I get to decide what you have to do. Let's see. How about..."

I leaned forward and whispered in his ear, "*I want you to eat me out on this bar until I come all over your face.*"

Donovan's sexy mouth curled in a half-smile. "You sure?"

I bit my lip and nodded.

He suddenly spun me around and bent me over the bar. I gasped with surprise.

"This isn't what I—"

"You weren't specific enough," he said, throwing my dress up and pulling aside my panties. "I'm doing it my way."

My protests turned to cries of pleasure as he buried his face in my sex from behind. His tongue flicked up and down my lips, then began focusing lower on my clit. From this angle, his nose was pressed deep into my wet heat while he enveloped my clit with his lips.

His voice rumbled into me, "Still want me to do it a different way?"

"No," I sighed. "Don't stop. Don't you *dare* stop now."

Within minutes he had me screaming *here I come* in a context totally unrelated to hide and seek.

"Your turn to hide," he said afterward. "If you can still walk."

"That remains to be seen," I said.

221

He gave me a firm slap on the ass. "I'll go downstairs to count."

As soon as I heard the elevator door close, I ran up the stairs to the fifth floor, then climbed the ladder to the roof. I closed the hatch silently, then laid on my back next to it, staring up at the perfect blue sky. As if on cue, a V-shaped flock of birds drifted across my vision, heading west toward the Mediterranean Sea.

I sighed and enjoyed the sun's warmth on my face. I had been here over three weeks, and yet it felt like only a few days. It was weird how time could feel so different depending on your circumstances. If I didn't have Donovan, the lockdown would have dragged on.

This is turning into the best vacation ever, I thought as I closed my eyes.

I was just settling in for a long nap on the roof when I heard a noise below me. The clang of metal ladder rungs, followed by the creaking sound of rusty hinges. The hatch flew open and Donovan's gorgeous face appeared next to me.

"Two minutes and eighteen seconds!" He thrust a victorious fist into the air. "I win!"

"How on earth did you find me so quickly?" I asked, sitting up. "I thought I was going to get at least twenty minutes alone up here."

"It's suspicious how quickly I found you, isn't it?" he said, narrowing his eyes. "There's no way I could have found you without help..."

"Wait a minute. Did *you* cheat?" I demanded.

"Of course I cheated!" he replied. "I plugged in the security system and watched where you hid, just like you did to me!"

I gasped. "I didn't cheat! You mentioned that hiding place to me the other day! But *you* totally cheated! You ruined my best hiding spot!"

He rested an elbow on the roof. "We agreed only to hide *inside* the hotel. So technically you're still cheating by hiding here."

"I... but... The roof is totally part of the hotel!" I argued.

Donovan shook his head and disappeared down the ladder. "I'm gonna start calling you Cheater instead of Feisty. This is really disappointing. Don't you follow the *rules?*"

"Oh come on," I said while following him down the ladder. "The roof is part of the hotel."

"Nope."

"So, using your logic, the balcony would be an illegal hiding place, too?"

"Yep."

"Fine, this round is a draw," I said as we took the stairs down to the ground floor. "You go hide, and I'll find you. And I *promise* I won't need to cheat to beat you."

"A likely story," he said.

I went behind the counter and counted to one hundred. "Ready or not, here I come!" I called. "And unlike some people, I'm not looking at the security system!"

I walked across the lobby and wondered where to search first. Then I heard a noise in the pool room.

What's that?

I tip-toed through the lobby. The noise grew louder as I approached the door, and when I peeked inside, I saw Donovan doing the backstroke across the pool.

I threw open the door and said, "You know you're supposed to *hide* during hide and seek, right?"

"I guess you win," he said while continuing to swim.

"Did you lose on purpose?"

"I had a lot of fun the last time you won," he said, "So I figured I would let you win again."

"You don't have to let me win. I would have won regardless,

223

because I'm better than you at hiding. And I don't cheat."

"Forget the game. Join me for a swim."

"I didn't bring a swimsuit."

"Neither did I!" Donovan reached the end of the pool, then rolled over onto his belly in the water. His bare ass cheeks broke the surface of the water for a split second before he dove underwater.

I giggled, then decided what the hell. I stripped down until I was naked and ran across the tile floor, doing a cannonball next to his swimming form.

The pool was heated to the perfect temperature. I casually swam laps next to Donovan while he did the backstroke across the pool. Occasionally I splashed water at his face, causing him to sputter and choke.

"Okay, now you've done it," he said when I did it one too many times.

I squealed as he swam over to me and play-wrestled with me in the water. Bear-hugging me to his chest, then spinning me around in a circle like some sort of amusement park ride, spraying water in all directions. Then he lifted me up onto his shoulders and walked across the pool, tilting me this way and that. I slid off his shoulders and hugged him like a jetpack while he playfully tried to throw me off.

It was silly fun, and for a few minutes we forgot all about the pandemic raging outside the hotel.

"Okay, I'm spent," he said after half an hour. "I forgot how exhausting swimming is. Hot tub time."

I rested my chin on the edge of the pool. "You first. Give mama a show."

Donovan grabbed the ladder to exit the pool. When he was halfway up the ladder he paused, tossing his head back like he was on Baywatch and sending water spiraling through the air. I giggled as he walked up the ladder slowly, swaying his bare ass like Pamela Anderson. I quickly swam over and gave his butt a wet smack.

We both hurried over to the hot tub and jumped inside. It was a good deal hotter than the pool, but after a few seconds it felt great. Donovan turned the jets on, and soon we were both sighing and relaxing under the water.

"You didn't tell me what you want," he said after a few minutes. "For winning this round of hide and seek."

"Did I win, or did you stop playing?"

"Does it matter?"

I looked sideways at him. "I think you know what I want."

He slid over to me, planted his arms on either side of my head, and kissed me wetly. I sighed and wrapped my legs around his body as he sank into me, his body hot and hard and *mine.*

I moaned as he took me in the pool room, our cries echoing off the tile.

39

Donovan

The Day We Made A Sex Tape

After our fun in the pool room, I baked a loaf of Italian bread for lunch. When it was done, I sliced it into thin pieces and used it for sandwiches with the leftover ham from last night.

"I've never had bread this fresh," Molly said around a mouthful of her sandwich. We were eating them in the restaurant with bottles of Coke. Her dark hair hung damply down to her shoulders, like a beautiful mermaid who had just come ashore.

"Yeah?" I said.

"It makes for a better sandwich. So much tastier than store-bought."

"Mine needs more mustard," I said as I grabbed the bottle. "I could barely taste it on my first bite. It must be this European brand."

"My sandwich has plenty," she said while chowing down. "And the ham is thick and salty."

I raised an eyebrow while spreading mustard on my sandwich. "Is that how you like it? Thick and salty?"

She tossed a stray piece of bread at me.

"This is the first loaf of bread I've ever baked," I revealed. "Not bad for my first try, huh?"

"I think you should bake another loaf tomorrow, and the day after that," Molly said with a full mouth. "Just to practice, of course."

I bit into my sandwich and sighed happily. "It's nice to get all this practice in. A real kitchen is much better than the single stove burner in my hotel room. I'm going to miss it when we go home. The kitchen in my apartment sucks."

"*I'm* going to miss having my own private chef cooking for me every day."

"What do you eat normally?" I asked. "Lots of take-out?"

Molly shook her head. "I signed up for one of those meal services, where you get dinners shipped to you once a week."

"The kind with all the raw ingredients?" I asked. "That you prepare yourself?"

Her pretty face twisted with annoyance. "No, I *hate* those. Way too much work. Mine are pre-made. I just throw them in the microwave."

I groaned. "That's a crime against cooking. The food police should lock you up and throw away the key."

She leaned across the table and grinned at me. "Sometimes, when I'm feeling *really* fancy, instead of microwaving the meals I *bake* them."

"That's not much better."

She waved a dismissive hand at me. "I don't want to think about those. For now, the only thing I want in my mouth is whatever you feed me."

I started to respond with a joke, but then I thought about something she had just said.

For now.

It was yet another reminder of the fact we had both been trying

227

to avoid: all of this was temporary. Our cutesy hotel relationship had an expiration date, just like the food in the fridge. Eventually it would have to be thrown out.

I pushed the thought away. I didn't want to think about it right now. Instead, I pulled out my phone. I had another email update about my status on the flight waiting list. They were sending me reminders every day now.

I felt a flash of annoyance. *It's like they're taunting me.*

"Have you gotten an update on your status?" I asked. "For the flight waiting list."

"I haven't gotten one since last week," she mumbled around a mouthful of sandwich. "Let me login and check. Let's see, status update, name..." She swallowed. "Nope. It still says *pending.*"

I exhaled out my nose. "Why is it still pending? It's been too long. It doesn't make any sense."

"Relax," she said, putting her hand on mine. "Look on the bright side: we've been here so long that we can probably claim Italian citizenship."

I smiled and replied, "Rome is nicer than Boston. I bet the winters are better, too."

"I've decided to accept that this is our home now," Molly said firmly. "We're never going back to America. We're Romans now. Buongiorno!"

"You need to learn more Italian if we end up staying here forever," I pointed out.

"I know plenty of phrases. Pasta primavera! E pluribus unum! Carpe diem!"

"Those last two are Latin. You do know the difference between Latin and Italian, right?"

Molly glared at me. "Gelato, risotto. Focaccia Americana? Lasagna!"

She said the garbling of Italian words with such a ridiculous accent and extravagant hand gestures that I couldn't help but laugh. She grinned at me like she had proved her point.

Christ, this woman makes me happy.

I plopped the last piece of my sandwich in my mouth and said, "Now that lunch is over, I have a surprise for you."

"Is it dessert?"

"It's not something you can eat."

"My interest is rapidly disappearing," she said.

I got up and took her hand. "Trust me, you're going to want to see this."

I led her out of the restaurant and across the lobby to the office behind the concierge desk. The computer monitors for the security station were all on.

"The security system," Molly said. "You left it on?"

"I forgot to turn it off. Then, when I remembered... I found something."

I used the mouse to navigate through the program on the main screen. The windows were sorted by camera, with a listing of the previous recordings. I re-sorted them by date, then clicked on one of the newer ones. A video maximized on the screen and began playing. It showed the kitchen, with the wall of stoves to the left and the pantry to the right. Molly came into view and opened the pantry, then disappeared inside.

Next to me, she gasped. "You turned this on and cheated in the very first round!"

"Uh..." I quickly closed the video. "That wasn't the one I meant to open."

"We're coming back to this later, you big fat cheater," she promised.

"Here's the one I wanted." I maximized the next video. It

showed the two of us in the lounge, standing behind the bar. There was no sound, but it was obvious we were arguing.

"This is when you accused *me* of cheating," Molly said. "Typical projection. You think you know a guy..."

"Keep watching."

On the screen, I spun Molly around and bent her over the bar. Then I raised her dress and buried my face in her pussy from behind. Molly arched her back and opened her mouth in a silent moan.

"Oh my God," Molly gasped. "You made a sex tape of us!"

"*We* made it," I corrected her.

Her eyes were wide and shocked. "I didn't know about it!"

My heart sank. She wasn't as excited as I thought she would be.

"I was going to delete it," I quickly said, "but I wanted to show you first."

Molly leaned closer to the screen. "Damn, we look *good*."

I caressed my fingers up her back. "*You* look good."

"So do you. The way your face is all up in there..." She bit her lip. "Mmm."

We continued watching the video. Molly put an arm around me, then slowly slid her hand down to my butt. I responded by pulling her in front of me, my hands on her hips while grinding against her ass. I pulled aside her still-damp hair and kissed her neck.

"Did you get the pool video?" she breathed.

I leaned over her and switched videos, then fast-forwarded a bit. We were in the hot tub together, making out like there was no tomorrow.

Neither of us took our eyes off the screen as we undressed. Molly pulled her panties down and gently hiked her dress up, revealing the perfectly-smooth skin of her ass. I unbuckled my belt and let my pants drop to the floor.

In the hot tub, I grabbed a condom from my pants and quickly rolled it on. Molly climbed on top of me, holding onto the edge of the tub for support. She reached under the water, and then both of us let out silent cries of pleasure. Molly craned her head back while I held her in my lap.

Molly reached between her legs and began rubbing herself in the security room. I tore the edge off the condom wrapper and rolled it on, then guided my thickness up into her. She was already soaked from watching the video, and I slid inside with wonderful ease. Molly planted her hands on the table and arched her back, pushing her hips against me to take as much as she could.

It was weird watching a video of ourselves, but it was exciting, too. And hot as hell. Both of us were transfixed by what we saw on the computer screen: I climbed out of the hot tub, bringing Molly with me in my arms. I lowered her to a nearby bench and pulled her legs up over my shoulders to give myself a better angle to fuck her.

"Ohh," Molly moaned as we watched. I pawed at her ass and matched my movements to the video of me fucking her on the pool bench, a steady rhythm that had both of us panting and gasping until we came together, matching the cries of pleasure that hadn't been recorded on the video as we shook and shivered with sweet release.

"That..." Molly breathed as I paused the video. "That was *hot*."

"I know, right?"

She draped her arms around my neck and kissed me deeply. "How many women have you made a sex tape with?"

"Only you."

She grinned. "Good. Now delete it forever."

"With pleasure."

I copied the filename in the program before deleting it and the other files. Then I ran a search on the filesystem for that filename, and found a backup copy on another drive. I deleted all of those too.

"Doesn't look like there's any cloud backup," I said. "It's

deleted. Nobody will ever see it."

Molly climbed under the desk and unplugged the power cable again. "You going to workout in the gym now?"

"Feisty, I just had my workout."

She gave me a silly grin that brightened up her entire face.

"After we do the dishes, I think I'm going to skip my workout," I said while we went back to the restaurant. "I'm kind of worn out from swimming laps. That's a full-body workout."

"*You're* a full-body workout," she teased.

She tried to pinch my ass, but I dodged out of the way. I snatched her arm before she could run away, then threw her over my shoulder and carried her back into the restaurant while she pounded on my back with her fists and squealed happily.

40

Molly
The Day We Split Up

The next morning I woke up alone.

I stretched my arms out and didn't feel Donovan next to me. Sunlight streamed through the window as I imagined the breakfast he was probably making for me in the kitchen. Or maybe he went to get something at the market. More condoms, probably. We'd been going through a lot of them lately.

Which, of course, was a good problem to have.

I lazily grabbed my phone from the nightstand and checked my email. I had a new one from Andrea at the boutique.

Hey Molly, just checking in. Everything is still closed. I went ahead and took care of the monthly inventory, even though it hasn't changed much from last month. There's not much else for me to do until things open up again.

I heard there's a way for small businesses to get

interest-free loans. Maybe that will help the store get by? Just until things are normal? Everything is in your name so I can't do it for you.

Hope you're still eating lots of yummy pasta in Rome!

-Andrea

I replied back and told her the loans were a good idea, and that I would take care of it soon. But as soon as I sent the email, my motivation disappeared like steam after a shower. I didn't feel like doing anything related to the boutique. I was very much enjoying being *away* from my problems.

I hadn't realized just how much I needed a vacation from everything, even though it turned out totally different than I expected. The previous six months had been a whirlwind of stress: dealing with my parents' death, planning the funeral, taking care of their estate, and then immediately jumping into management of mom's store. I had been in fifth gear non-stop before coming to Rome.

Now that I was relaxing? I didn't want to go back to the way things were.

The problem, I knew, was that owning your own business was a lot of work. You had to love the business, and be driven enough to give it all your blood, sweat, and tears. But the boutique wasn't mine. It was mom's. And even though I was holding onto it out of guilt, deep down I knew I couldn't do that forever.

What am I going to do?

I could sell the business, although I didn't know who would want to buy it in the middle of a pandemic. I owned the building the boutique was in, so I could always sell that too. Or close the boutique down and rent the space to another retailer. I didn't know how much income that would provide.

I sat up in bed and decided to stop thinking about it. I knew I was avoiding my problems, but I just wasn't ready to deal with them yet. Instead, I decided to text the sexy man who wasn't in my bed.

Molly: You had better be downstairs making me breakfast. That's the only excuse I'll accept as to why you're not spooning me right now.

Molly: Unless you're getting more condoms and oranges. That is also an acceptable reason.

Moments after I hit send, I heard a high-pitched *chime* sound. It was the sound Donovan's phone made when he received a text. Had he left his phone here?

I searched under the covers and next to the bed. Then I sent him another text. This time I heard the chime more clearly: it was coming next door, from Donovan's room.

And the door connecting our rooms was closed.

That's weird.

I frowned at the door, then knocked. "Donovan? Are you over there?"

I heard the rustling of his down comforter, and then the squeak of mattress springs. "I'm here."

I opened my door, but came face-to-face with the door leading into his room. I tried the knob but it was locked.

"What are you doing over there? Let me in."

I heard footsteps walking across the floor. "I can't do that."

"What?" I said with a nervous laugh. "Why not? Do you have another surprise for me?"

"Molly," he said from the other side of the door, "I think I'm sick."

235

I tensed. Was this a joke? I waited for the punchline but it never came. I realized I was holding my breath, so I let it out, then took a step away from the door.

"What are your symptoms?" I asked slowly. My mind was cloudy without coffee. "How do you feel? Do you have a dry cough?"

"One question at a time," he said. His voice was soft, but not hoarse. "My throat is a little sore, but I don't have a cough. Mostly I'm just exhausted. Like, *really* tired. Fatigued worse than after pulling a triple-shift at the diner."

"Okay, okay, that's not bad," I said. "Maybe you're just tired! You only had one cup of coffee yesterday, because then we played hide and seek. And you were swimming! Yeah, the swimming! You're not used to doing that type of workout. You said so yourself."

There was a long pause. "Molly, this feels different."

"You don't know that. You might just be tired."

"I hope you're right. But until I know for sure, I can't be around you."

I blinked. "We've already been around each other non-stop. If you're sick..."

Then I probably am too. The thought slammed into place like a deadbolt and I started analyzing my own body. I didn't feel tired, aside from normal morning sleepiness. I didn't have a cough. My throat wasn't sore. I ran over to the desk and took a sip of cold leftover coffee. It was bitter. I still had my sense of taste.

"We can't be together right now," Donovan said through the door. "I can't risk it. You know it's for your own good."

No, I thought. *Please don't make me be alone again.*

"I can go in there and snuggle with you," I said enticingly. "That will make you feel better. I don't care if I'm risking myself."

"Molly..."

I sighed. "You're not budging on this, are you?"

"You can't see me, but I'm shaking my head right now."

I glanced at the sunlight streaming through the glass balcony door. A thought came to me...

"I locked my balcony door," Donovan said, as if he could read my mind through the wall. "You can't hop across and get in that way."

"I have the keys to the hotel." I grabbed them from the desk and gave them an audible jangle. "I bet one of them is the master key that will open your door."

"If you open my door," Donovan warned, "I'll never forgive you."

"Fine." He wasn't going to let me in, even if he was just tired.

I changed mindsets. Donovan, my quarantine boyfriend, was sick. I needed to take care of him. Hopefully it was just a cold or something, and I could help. Because if it really was the virus...

Stop it, I told myself. *Focus on what you can do.*

"What do you want for breakfast?" I asked.

"I'm not hungry."

"Do you need medicine? That cough syrup downstairs is good for more than just fooling Italian police officers."

"I already got what I needed downstairs. Cough syrup, a bottle of aspirin, and a thermometer."

I tensed. "Are you running a fever?"

"No."

"You hesitated before answering. Are you lying?"

"I wouldn't lie to you, Molly."

"You lied during hide and seek. What's your temperature? Take it again and send me a text message photo."

"It was thirty-seven point two."

I blinked. "What the hell does that mean!"

"The thermometer is Celsius. That's like ninety-nine degrees Fahrenheit."

"So you have a fever!"

"Barely," he insisted. "I'm fine. I'll take my temperature every hour and let you know if it gets higher."

"Fine," I said stubbornly, "but the next time you take it, I want photographic proof. What do you want for breakfast?"

"I told you I'm not hungry."

"You need to eat. I'm not a master chef like the famous Donovan Russo, but I can manage eggs and toast."

"I'll eat lunch in a few hours," he said. His voice sounded weak. "Right now I just want to go back to sleep. Is that okay, Doctor Feisty?"

I chewed my lip. "Okay. Sleep is good. Do you need anything from the store while it's open? I don't mind going."

He chuckled and said, "I've got everything I need. I'm going to sleep now, okay?"

"Okay." I sighed and said, "I don't like being on the other side of a wall from you."

I felt a thump, like he was leaning against the door. "It's killing me too."

I rested my forehead on the door and imagined I could feel his warmth on the other side.

"Good night," he said. I heard his footsteps walking back to the bed.

"Donovan?"

The footsteps stopped. "Yes?"

I wanted to say something more to him. It felt like my heart had been torn open and a whole bunch of new emotions were pouring out. There were words I wanted to say to him, words that scared me.

238

I held them back and said, "You'll be okay. I know you will."

"Hope so."

41

Molly

The Day I Made Soup

I wasn't sure what to do without Donovan. It was like someone had reached inside my brain and turned a switch off. Was this how co-dependent girls felt without their boyfriends?

I walked on the treadmill for a few minutes, but I didn't enjoy doing it alone. I only tolerated it because it was an excuse to watch Donovan jogging shirtless on the treadmill next to me.

I left the gym and walked the loop around my floor, just like I had done before Donovan and I had hooked up. But every time I walked by his door I began worrying about him all over again. I changed my route and walked down the stairs to the first floor, around the pool, up the elevator to the second floor, into the lounge, then back up the stairs to the third floor. That route kept me from having to pass his door.

But it didn't stop me from thinking about him.

My news podcast was focused on the pandemic, because *of course* it was. I'd been listening to updates every day for the last three weeks, but now it was no longer an abstract idea. The descriptions of helpless patients hooked up to ventilators now carried a grim reality.

I turned off the podcast and listened to music instead. That worked for ten minutes before my mind drifted back to what Donovan had told me. He didn't have a dry cough or a high fever. His only real symptom was that he was tired.

"He's going to be fine," I said out loud, just to hear someone's voice. "He has to be fine."

After spending the last three weeks together, being without him was excruciating. It was a taste of what things would have been like if I had been stuck in the hotel alone. It made me realize how lucky I was to have found him.

Mom would have called it fate, if she were still here.

At exactly noon, I knocked on the dividing door. "Rise and shine. What do you want for lunch? And don't you dare tell me you're not hungry."

"Soup is fine," came the muffled reply. He sounded even more tired than before.

"Do they have, like, cans of Campbell's downstairs?" I asked. "The kind you dump in a bowl and microwave?"

He laughed weakly and said, "I'll text you directions. I promise it will be easy."

I went downstairs and followed his instructions. I diced up a carrot with one of the kitchen knives. Donovan had a fancy way of chopping veggies, but my way was slow and clumsy. Then I boiled dry spaghetti in a pot of chicken stock. I chopped up some of the leftover chicken Donovan had cooked for dinner last night and dumped it in the pot with the carrots.

"How much of these spices do I add?" I asked him on the phone.

"*A pinch or two of each.*"

I stared at a ring of measuring spoons. "What's a pinch?"

"*How much you can grab between two fingers. You know. A pinch.*"

"But the thyme is fresh," I replied. "It's not like pinching a bunch of salt."

I heard him laugh on the other line. *"Maybe I should come down and finish it..."*

"No!" I insisted. "I can do it for you. I'll figure it out."

I hung up and added a little bit of ground pepper, oregano, thyme, and basil. I stirred it together then tasted it on the spoon. I winced—I had used too much of something, but I wasn't sure of what.

I tinkered with the soup for ten minutes, adding more broth and salt, before deciding it was as good as it was going to get. I filled a bowl with the steaming soup, placed it on a plate, and carried it upstairs.

I knocked on the partition door between our rooms and said, "It's not as good as what you make, but it will have to do. I added some crackers. These aren't your normal saltines. These are fancy Italian crackers I found in the pantry. I went the extra mile."

"Put it in the partition," he replied.

"I'm wearing a mask. I can bring it in to you."

"Molly," he said, "this is how it has to be. If you want me to eat..."

"Fine," I grumbled. I opened the door, placed the plate and bowl inside, then closed it.

"You aren't going to wait until I open my door," he said slowly, "and then try to jump through, are you?"

"No..."

"I don't believe you."

I went over to the bed and sat down. "Hear those springs? Squeak squeak squeak?"

"Do they squeak that much when we're having sex?" he asked.

"I don't know," I replied. "I'm usually distracted."

I heard the dividing door open, then close a second later. I got off the bed and sat next to the door.

"How are you feeling?"

I heard a slurp of soup. "I'm still really tired. My nose is congested."

"That's good! Maybe it's just a cold or something."

"Wow, these crackers *are* fancy."

"Only the best for my quarantine boyfriend," I replied.

"Quarantine boyfriend. I like that."

I listened to him eat for awhile.

"When was the last time you took your temperature?"

"Before you got back." Another slurp. "Thirty-seven Celsius. Totally normal."

"And still no dry cough?"

"Nope."

I nodded to myself. "See? This is just a cold, nothing to worry about."

"You sound like you're trying to convince yourself, not me."

"Maybe I am." I rested my head against the partition door. "We'll laugh about this when it's all over. How you got a cold during the pandemic and we panicked over nothing."

"You're bored without me, aren't you?" he asked.

"Oh my God, *so bored.* I was tempted to take another inventory of all the food in the kitchen."

"Wow, you've got it bad. You don't have any work you can do for your store? Accounting or something?"

"The store has been closed because of the lockdown," I said. "There's nothing for me to do but accounting work, and I do *not* want to look at the sales numbers."

"Better than my situation. I don't have a job to go home to."

"Hey, that's a good idea." I pulled out my phone. "I can help you look for a job. I still have the jobs app on my phone from when Andrea and I hired a new restocking girl. Let's see. Boston and the surrounding area, twenty-mile radius because I don't want you to have to commute very far, restaurant services..."

I trailed off when I saw the results on the screen.

"There's nothing out there, right?" Another slurp of soup. "Nobody's hiring. Every restaurant is running on reduced staff. It's kind of a good thing I'm stuck in Rome, because if I was back in Boston I wouldn't have a job. At least here, the room and food are free."

The hot soup must have been invigorating him, because he sounded a little more energetic now. That made me smile.

"Things will open up eventually," I said. "I have a friend back home named Sara."

"The one whose number you were going to give me?"

"You're lucky I can't smack you right now. As I was saying, Sara knows *everyone* in town. She can definitely help you find a job when we get back."

Donovan's spoon clinked on the side of the bowl. "Molly? Are you asking me to go back to Elkhart with you?"

I cringed. I had been speaking in a rush because I was worried, babbling on since talking was literally the only thing I could do with Donovan. I hadn't realized what I suggested.

What do I do? Take it back? Make a joke about Sara?

"I was just babbling," I said with a nervous laugh. "I wasn't trying to... That is to say, I wasn't necessarily... You know what I mean."

A long silence stretched.

"How's the soup?" I asked.

"It's... fine."

"Ouch," I said with a chuckle. "I know I'm not a very good cook. Tell me what I should have done differently."

"I don't really know," he replied in a strange tone.

"Come on. You know that the best way to improve is to get constructive feedback. I'm sure they gave you plenty of criticism at your cooking school. Does the soup need more salt? Is the broth too thin?"

"No, Molly, that's what I'm trying to tell you," he insisted. "I can't taste the soup at all. I just realized I can't taste *anything*."

42

Molly

The Day I Committed Theft

I jumped up from the floor. "No."

"Molly..."

"You're just congested," I insisted. "That's why you can't taste anything."

"That's not it," he said. He sounded resigned. "My taste is definitely gone."

There was no denying it now. All of my bargaining and excuses felt useless on my tongue.

Donovan has the virus.

And then, a moment later, another thought slashed across my consciousness: *I've been around him constantly before today.* If he had it...

I shook my head. There was no time to worry about that now. I felt fine, and Donovan was my primary concern. He *needed* me.

"You need to get tested," I said. "To confirm it."

"What's the point, Molly? They can't *do* anything about it."

"You don't know that!" I argued. "They might have some treatment or medication they're not telling people about. Or put you on a monitoring list. They can do *something.*"

"Molly. Listen to me." His voice was firm and strong. "The hospitals in Rome are nearly full. They need the beds for people who are *really* sick. That's not me. Not yet."

Not yet. I shook my head to make the words disappear.

"I feel fine," he went on, "except for my fatigue and lack of taste. Neither of those are life threatening."

"You should still get tested. That way if things *do* get worse, they'll already know you have it. They won't have to waste time testing you."

A sigh. "Molly..."

"What if they come up with a cure?" I was panicking now, but I couldn't stop myself from talking out loud because it was better than acceptance. "If they have a cure they'll give it to everyone they know is infected, and if they don't *know* you have it they'll leave you here, and you won't get better..."

"They won't have a vaccine for at least a year," he said calmly. "And that doesn't matter since I already have it. Molly, you need to relax."

"Don't tell me to relax!" I snapped. "I've been stuck in this hotel for weeks, and now my boyfriend is infected."

There was a pause. "Your *quarantine* boyfriend."

"That's what I said."

I heard the *tip-tap* of fingers typing on his phone. "I'm reading the ECDC guidelines now. For people with mild symptoms, they recommend sheltering in place. See? That's what I should be doing."

I frowned. "ECDC?"

"That's the European Centre for Disease Control. They even spelled *centre* the funky way, so you know it's legit."

I sat back down and rested my head against the door. "I don't like sitting around doing nothing. It makes me feel helpless."

"You're not doing nothing. You made me soup. It was hot and filling. And I'm sure it was perfectly delicious."

Tears began welling in my eyes. I wiped them away angrily. "Do you want anything else? I can try baking cookies."

"I've got everything I need right now," he replied. "I know you want to help more, but you've done enough, Feisty."

"Okay," I finally said.

"I'm going to lay back down. I wish I was cuddling with you, believe me I do."

"Me too."

I heard him walk across the room, and then springs squeaked as he got in bed. For ten minutes I rested my head against the dividing door, straining my ears to hear if he coughed or wheezed or made any other concerning noise.

I paced in my room and tried to think of other ways I could help. I looked up the ECDC guidelines myself, then checked the American CDC website too. Donovan was right: both organizations recommended sheltering in place until symptoms grew severe.

But I couldn't just sit around. I had to do something.

I found a map with the location of all the testing sites in Rome. One of them was half a kilometer away, next to the Celio Military Hospital. I got dressed, put on a mask, and left the hotel.

Medical care was one of the only exemptions to the lockdown guidelines, but I silently prayed that I wouldn't run into the same police officers who had caught us before. My prayer was answered and I didn't see anyone on the way to the testing site. It was in a sprawling plaza, which normally would have been filled with tourists visiting shops and eating at restaurants, just like the plaza outside our hotel. Now it was filled with drab military tents and medical personnel decked in full-body protective suits, like hazmat suits that were white instead of yellow.

There was a line of people waiting to be tested. I got in the back of the line, and a few minutes later, a volunteer handed out clipboards with forms for everyone to fill out. It looked like a typical medical form, asking for my name, age, address, and other information. But it was in Italian, so I had to use my phone to translate. It wasn't easy juggling my phone in one hand and the clipboard and pen in the other, but somehow I managed before I got to the front of the line.

A nurse took my clipboard and asked me a question in rapid-fire Italian.

"I'm sorry, I do not speak Italian. English?" I asked with an embarrassed smile.

She babbled at me in Italian and led me over to a table underneath the largest tent. She held her palm out to indicate *stay here*, and then she went back to the line of people.

I sat there and watched the volunteers scurry around the plaza for half an hour. Nobody came up to me, and when I tried to get someone's attention in passing they totally ignored me. It was beginning to feel like I had been forgotten.

Finally a nurse came up to me and said, "You need English?" in a slight accent.

"Yes! I'm so sorry, I'm an American who has been stuck here during the lockdown, and..."

"What symptoms?" she asked, scanning the medical document I had filled out.

"None."

"You have been in contact with an infected?"

"Yes, my... boyfriend. He has fatigue, a slight fever, and this morning he lost his sense of taste."

I searched her face for any kind of reaction, but she only nodded and tore open the seal on a big plastic bag. She removed a device that looked like a long Q-tip, then opened a plastic vial on the table next to me.

"I must take sample in nose," she said. "It will be, ah, unpleasant."

"Okay," I said, pulling my mask down so she could access my nostril.

She gently tilted my head back, then inserted the Q-tip. The tip hit the back of my nose, near my sinuses... and then *kept going*. My eyes watered and I let out a little whimper as it went deeper into my skull. It felt like it was touching my brain.

She removed the Q-tip and nodded at me. "See? Unpleasant."

"You weren't kidding," I muttered. My eyes were still watering.

She broke the long Q-tip in half, then stuck the cotton part into the vial on the table. Then she screwed the cap on, taped a red sticker over it, and dropped it in a big bin on the ground with all the other tests.

"Results in three days," she said. "Maybe sooner."

"Thank you so much," I said. "What about my boyfriend?"

She looked around. "He is where?"

"He's back at our hotel. He didn't want to come, but I was thinking you could give me the testing kit to take to him..."

"He comes here," she said while throwing away the remaining parts of the test kit. "Go now. Be healthy." She nodded at me and hurried off to the next testing table where a man had been coughing for several minutes.

I stood and prepared to leave, but the bin to my right caught my eye. It was full of fresh testing kits, hundreds of them in identical plastic bags. I looked around the tent. There was a bin just like it next to every testing chair. They had plenty.

I snatched a plastic bag, tucked it under my arm, and hurried away from the site before anyone could see me.

43

Molly
The Day I Panicked

"I can't believe you stole a test for me," Donovan said through the door. "What happened to the cute girl who was afraid to disobey a *closed* sign?"

"The test is easy," I said, ignoring his jests. "I had it done on me. I can walk you through it."

"You didn't have to do this," he replied on the other side. I heard the crumple of plastic as he examined the kit. "You shouldn't have gone out and risked yourself."

"I wanted to get myself tested," I replied. "Getting you a kit was a secondary benefit. If you test yourself now, I'll take it back to the testing site."

"I'll take it later, I promise," he said. "I just want to rest now."

He sounded much more tired than this morning. That worried me.

"You don't want dinner?" I asked. "It's five-thirty."

"I'm not hungry." The words came out as an exhale, like he could barely summon the energy to say them.

"You need to eat. I'm going to go make dinner for myself, and I'll bring you something."

I went down to the kitchen and gathered supplies. Dry fettuccine noodles, creamy alfredo sauce from a jar, and more leftover chicken. I boiled the pasta and then mixed everything in a bowl, topping it with freshly-grated Parmesan cheese.

"Knock knock," I said when I got back. "I've got fettuccine alfredo. Made from scratch."

He laughed softly. "*You* made pasta from scratch?"

"I'm going to pretend you don't sound so dubious." I opened the door and placed his bowl in the partition, then closed it. "I even grated fresh Parmesan cheese on it."

Donovan's door opened and closed. I heard a fork clinking against a bowl. "Even without my taste buds, I can tell the difference between fresh pasta and dry stuff. The consistency is different."

"Maybe I'm just really bad at making fresh pasta," I suggested.

I heard him eating, so I took my own bowl and started chowing down. After being spoiled by Donovan's cooking for so long, mine was definitely mediocre. But it was better than nothing.

"Thanks for making me eat," he said through the door.

"You need your strength."

After we ate, I looked up a video on how to self-administer the test. I sent him the link and then explained the process through the door.

"It's a tough test," I said. "It would be easier if I did it for you."

"No."

"You can open the door a sliver and let me do it through the crack. It'll be safe! Just like when I gave you a hand-job through the door..."

"I won't let you risk it. I'll do it to myself."

I heard the rustling of plastic as he prepared.

"I have to stick this all the way up my nose? To the marked line?" he asked incredulously.

"Told you it was tough. If you want me to do it for you..."

"Okay. No problem. Here I go. Three, two, one..."

He groaned on the other side of the door. I counted down fifteen seconds on my phone. "Make sure it's deep enough."

Instead of making a sex joke, Donovan replied with another muffled groan. He gasped and coughed when he pulled it out after fifteen seconds. "That was awful. I think I'd rather die of the virus."

"If you think that's bad, let me tell you about gynecologists."

"You've got me there."

I instructed him to break the tip off and place it in the plastic vial. Then he wiped it all down with the disinfectant wipe included in the test.

"Okay, it's in the partition," he said.

I opened the door and pulled it out. I gave it another wipe-down with my own disinfectant wipe, then pulled out the included forms.

"Full name?"

"Donovan Mark Russo."

"Mark. Boring middle name. It's a good thing you're sexy. Age?"

"Twenty-nine."

"Uh oh, the big three-oh is coming up. You're practically ancient. Birthday?"

I filled in the form with his answers: sex, nationality, phone number. For the address I put the Residencia Al Gladiatore.

"Now I need your weight and height."

"One ninety-five," he said. "Six-foot-one. These questions are getting personal."

"Now I need your favorite color. And your celebrity crush."

"Blue. And Salma Hayek."

"Salma Hayek? Really?"

"Yeah, why?"

"You just like her because she has *enormous* tits."

There was a pause, and then Donovan said, "Well, yeah?"

"I want you to know that I'm rolling my eyes at you," I said with a laugh. "I kind of like asking you questions like this. You're too sick to lie."

"Disease is nature's truth serum."

I frowned at the next entry. "Codice fiscale? What's that mean?"

"I think it's their equivalent to a social security number," he said. "Mine is two-four-zero..."

After he rattled the numbers off, I said, "Perfect. I have everything I need to steal your identity. Now if you'll excuse me, I'm going to go order ten credit cards in your name."

I heard him laughing on the other side of the door. "This was a long con the entire time. I knew it!"

"Hope the sex was worth it," I replied.

It felt good to laugh about everything. For a few moments it didn't feel like there was a barrier between us.

I stuck the filled-out forms in the plastic bag with the test, then sealed it with the included red tape. I changed clothes and put on my shoes.

"I'm taking this to the testing site. I'll be back in ten minutes."

"Can you bring me dessert on the way back?"

"Sure. What flavor of gelato do you want from the creamery down the street?"

"Actually, I was craving some cookie dough from the kitchen."

I blinked with surprise. "You want cookie dough? I thought you said it was better baked."

"I'm taking a page out of the Molly Carter playbook," he replied. "I'm sick and I want comfort food."

"Your wish is my command."

"Molly?"

I paused. "Yeah?"

"Be safe out there."

"I will." I rested my hand on the dividing door, then left.

Even though the sun had set over an hour ago, the night was pleasantly warm. But there was no time to enjoy it: I was on a mission. I clutched the test bag in my hand and hurried across the plaza, then down an alley toward the test site.

During the walk, I thought about what I would tell the people there. I had stolen the test. They might know that I shouldn't have it, that there was no way I could have administered it away from the testing site.

Then again, I doubted they would ask any questions. They were swamped earlier today and probably wouldn't have time to worry about the details. They would take the plastic bag and toss it in the pile with the other tests that had been administered.

I was a block away from the testing plaza when I came across two police officers, chatting quietly while looking at their phones.

I stopped out of instinct, and considered hiding. But one of them had already seen me. He said something to his partner, who also looked down the street in my direction. A flashlight clicked on and they approached me.

"Test," I said, holding up the bag. "I have to take this to the testing site."

One of the cops shook his head and pointed back the way I had come. I recognized him as the same cop who had caught us twice already. And based on the look in his eyes, he recognized me too.

"This isn't like the other times," I said with a nervous laugh. "I'm just dropping this off at the test site. It's right over there, around the corner. It will only take me a minute..."

The other cop barked an order at me in Italian. His hand drifted down to his hip, unclipping something from his belt. His handcuffs.

The other cop said something, and the only word I caught was *stazione*. It sounded like station.

Police station.

They're going to arrest me, I realized in horror.

My legs moved without thought.

I darted between the cops and sprinted toward the testing site. Shouts followed me but I could barely hear them over the sound of my breathing, constricted by the mask. My feet pounded on the cobblestones and the plastic bag swung at my side as I ran down the street, turned left, then ran some more.

The drab tents of the site were up ahead. There was a line, but if I could run around it and drop the bag off at the front...

A body slammed into me from behind, knocking the wind out of me as arms wrapped around my chest and dragged me to the ground, sending Donovan's test flying. I cried out as the bag slid across the cobblestones and came to a stop underneath a bench.

"The test!" I cried out. "Please, just give me the test, I need to turn it in, they're waiting for it *right there!*"

I felt cold metal snap onto my wrist behind my back. One of the cops growled something like a curse.

"Stop," I begged as he dragged me to my feet. Tears ran down my cheeks and were absorbed by the fabric of my mask, the mask I had borrowed from Donovan, the man waiting for me at home. "Please stop, just let me turn in the test. I need to turn it in for Donovan. He's *sick.*"

I let out a wail of anguish as they dragged me away, leaving the test underneath the bench.

44

Donovan

The Day Without Molly

Everything was a blur.

I slept, and woke, and drank some Gatorade, and then slept again.

I didn't want to get out of bed. I was more fatigued than I had ever been in my life. I barely had enough energy to walk to the bathroom. Even the simple motion of bending over to wash my hands in the sink left me feeling lightheaded and weak.

My dreams were vivid. First Molly and I were in a big empty room, tearing walls down with sledgehammers and then painting the remains green. She leaped high into the air and clung to a chandelier while spaghetti sauce dripped out of her pockets onto a big plate of pasta.

Then Molly and I were carrying trays full of white dishes, more dishes than I had ever seen in my life, a *cartoonish* amount of dishes stacked high and wobbling this way and that like the Leaning Tower of Pisa. Molly weaved between tables and chairs while balancing the tray of dishes, and then she tripped and fell! But as she crashed to the ground, the dishes flew in all directions and landed at all the tables in the room, one in front of every person who was seated and waiting. None of them broke, and everyone clapped like it was some sort of magic trick.

Then I was sick again, lying in bed and too nauseous to eat. Molly took my plate and wolfed food into her mouth and made a joke about how if I couldn't eat, then she would have to eat enough for two.

I woke to sunlight streaming into the room. My brain felt fuzzy, but I knew the sunlight didn't make sense. It had just been nighttime, when Molly was walking me through the self-test.

I winced and touched my nose at the memory. That sucked.

After using the bathroom and drinking a big glass of water, I felt a little better. Molly hadn't checked on me in a while. Maybe it was a good thing she was leaving me alone. I didn't want her to worry about me.

There was an empty pit in my stomach, so I reheated the pasta from last night and ate it slowly. It wasn't great, but I'd had worse before. And I appreciated the effort she had made to keep me fed. Her care meant more to me than any entree at a five-star restaurant.

I took my temperature. Thirty-eight point one. I didn't bother converting it to Fahrenheit—I knew it was a slight fever. That explained why it felt so *cold* in my hotel room.

I closed my eyes and imagined soaking in the hot tub. Allowing the scalding heat to absorb into my skin, my muscles, and my bones. That would feel really good right about now.

But I could barely stand up, let alone walk all the way downstairs to the pool. If I tried, I'd probably slip on the tile and crack my skull open. That would be a really stupid way to go.

I guzzled the remains of a bottle of Gatorade from my mini-fridge. Even though it was lemon-lime, I could barely register any flavor. When all of this was over, I had better be able to taste food again. A chef without his sense of taste was like a deaf musician. Or a blind painter. Or one of those fancy French guys who sniffed perfume for a living losing his sense of smell.

Okay, too many metaphors. I needed to sit down.

I was still thirsty, but I didn't want to bother Molly to get more Gatorade from downstairs. She hadn't heard me moving around, which meant she was still asleep. The poor thing had probably sat up all night worrying about me. She had gone into caregiver mode as soon as I told her I was sick. It was endearing seeing Molly do her best to take care of me. She deserved to sleep in.

I went back to sleep, and woke sometime in the afternoon. Molly still hadn't checked in on me. *That* was weird.

Donovan: Morning, Feisty. I had a sex dream about you. If you bring me a Gatorade I'll tell you all about it.

She didn't respond. Maybe she was going for one of her walks around the hotel. If she was listening to a podcast she might not hear the text. Or maybe she was watching a movie in the lounge, or going for a swim. She was probably bored without me.

Because that's what I felt right now: alone. I missed my quarantine girlfriend.

Cuddling with her.

Sleeping with her.

Holding her in my arms while staring into her eyes.

So far, being away from her was the worst part about this virus. But there was one silver lining: it gave me a strange sense of clarity about this trip, and about what would happen when it was over.

I didn't want to go back to Boston. Not without Molly. I knew it with a certainty in my chest, more than anything I had ever known before.

But does Molly feel the same way?

260

I shook my head. We would boil that pasta when we came to it. If she ever got a response from the flight standby list. While I had slept, I'd received another email about my own status. It sat in my inbox, taunting me.

I left it unread and closed my phone before it could taunt me.

"Molly?" I knocked on the dividing door between our rooms. "You in there?"

When there was no response, I went out to my balcony. My brain was still fuzzy from all the sleeping, and it took me a few moments to remember what happened last night. She had made me pasta. Then I took the brain-violating test. What had happened after that?

I snapped my fingers. Molly took the test back to the site. To turn it in.

That was the last I had heard from her.

Adrenaline hit my body like a jolt of electricity. Molly had left, and she hadn't returned.

"Molly!" I banged on the door. "Molly, answer me!" Panic surged through my brain and spots floated in my vision.

I put on some clothes and went searching for her. I checked the gym, then the lounge on the second floor. I used my shoulder to open doors so I wouldn't have to touch the handles. She wasn't in the pool room, nor the kitchen. In fact, the kitchen looked like it hadn't been used since she made dinner last night.

I went to the front door. It was still unlocked. The sun was setting above the plaza buildings. I could barely see the top section of the Colosseum from here.

Molly had been gone for almost a full day. She was out there somewhere.

I took a step outside before realizing I was barefoot. I went back upstairs to put shoes on, and when I got back up I felt even more tired than before. I longed to lay back down in bed and close my eyes. To wait until the morning.

Molly is gone, I thought, seizing on the idea like a splash of cold water to the face. *I have to find her.*

I took the elevator back downstairs and walked across the lobby. My legs were exhausted by the time I reached the front door, so I sat in the chair to collect myself.

It was the same chair I had been sitting in when we met. When she yelled at me.

I smiled at the memory and closed my eyes. After I rested for a few minutes, I would go looking for her. And I wouldn't stop until I found her.

Even if it was the last thing I did.

45

Molly
The Day I Spent In Jail

I sat in the Italian jail all night, tapping my foot and waiting to be released. The sun came up the next morning, then drifted across the sky outside my cell window. Occasionally a police officer walked by with another prisoner. There were four cells, each full of benches and big enough for a soccer team, but they were keeping everyone separated because of the virus.

That was a small miracle, I guess.

It was almost night again when a police officer unlocked my cell. I jumped up and asked, "Where are you taking me? Where am I going?"

"You are free to go," he replied in surprisingly-good English. "Please come with me."

I followed him through the police station numbly.

"Here are your belongings," he told me at the front desk. "Cell phone, passport, and keys. You are receiving a formal warning for breaking the quarantine."

"I told you I was turning in a test to the—"

"We have taken your passport information, and have reported your behavior to the American Embassy. If you are detained again, we will have no choice but to remove you from the European Union."

"Is that a promise?" I muttered. The cop gave me an impatient look.

I left the station and pulled my belongings out of the bag. My phone battery was dead. Damn.

I hope Donovan is okay.

Without a phone I was kind of lost. I walked down a street for awhile until I saw the Colosseum in the distance. Based on the sun setting over *there,* that meant my hotel should be *that way.*

I followed the road, picking up speed as I went. Within a few minutes I was practically jogging. If Donovan's condition had gotten worse and I wasn't there to help him...

The front door to the hotel was still unlocked. I threw it open and rushed inside, turning toward the elevator, until something in the lobby caught my attention.

I gave a start. Donovan was sprawled out in the chair by the door, snoring softly behind his mask.

"Donovan!"

He blinked awake, then pulled himself to his feet. His dark hair was messy, and there was pasta sauce on his mask. His belt was only threaded through three of his jeans loops. He looked like a toddler who had tried to dress himself for the first time.

"You're okay," he said with a sigh of relief. "Molly..."

He stepped toward me, arms outstretched. I wanted nothing more than to hug him, to fall into his comforting arms and cry away my worries.

But I made myself step back behind the concierge desk, turning away as if the mere sight of him could infect me.

"You're still sick," I said.

"Shit," he said. "I almost forgot. I came down here to go looking for you, and I needed to rest because I was so tired…"

He sounded so weak. Instantly I snapped back into my role as caregiver.

"Go back upstairs," I told him. "I'll make dinner."

"Okey dokey," he said. "I'm kind of hungry. You didn't bring me cookie dough last night!"

I waited until he was in the elevator, then counted to a hundred like we were playing hide and seek. Then I took the stairs to the third floor. I held my breath as I walked to my room, knowing that Donovan had been walking and breathing in this space just minutes before. I slipped inside and closed the door with a deep exhale.

I took a shower to wash the damp, mildewy feeling of jail from my skin. Then I went downstairs and reheated the leftover soup from the other night.

"I can't believe you got arrested for me," Donovan said while we ate, chatting between the dividing door.

"Want to know the crazy thing? The food they gave me in jail wasn't bad! It was definitely better than the pasta I made last night. What I'm trying to say is that if my food drives you crazy, you can get yourself arrested."

"Yeah, but the company is better here," he replied.

"How do you feel?"

"Tired. After running around looking for you… I was so worried about you, Molly. I'm glad you're okay."

"I'm glad *you're* okay," I said. "While I was in jail, all I could think about was how I wasn't taking care of you."

"You can make it up to me with cookie dough, please and thank you. Then I'm going to crash."

It was great to not be in jail, but the next day was boring. I brought Donovan some Gatorade in the morning, and then he went back to sleep.

I went to the lounge and played three games of pool by myself. After that I watched some TV on the projector, but that just made me miss him even more. The couch was too big for just one person; I was used to snuggling up with him on it.

I walked around the hotel, but my back was kind of sore from sitting on the bench in jail.

Eventually I decided to try my hand at making pasta from scratch. I looked up directions online, and copied the technique I had learned from Donovan. I cracked an egg on the counter and rolled it around a pile of flour with my fingers, allowing it to coalesce into a doughy consistency.

Somehow, I was doing it wrong. The result turned out all messy and crumbly, rather than the smooth dough Donovan had made.

"Good thing I can't taste anything," Donovan said at lunch. "This might be the ugliest pasta I've ever seen."

"You're eating for *fuel,* not for comfort," I shot back.

"What I'm doing is fantasizing about eating jail food." He chuckled at his own joke, then said, "Oh, I got an email from the testing site. My results came back positive."

"Oh, thank God!" I said.

"Uh, what am I missing?" he replied. "Why are you happy about my positive test?"

"I'm happy the police turned in the test!" I said. "I was afraid they would throw it away to get back at me for breaking quarantine. I'm not happy you tested positive. We already knew you had it, anyway."

"Did you hear back about your test?" Donovan asked.

"Nope! I'm assuming that's a good sign. I still feel fine. Speaking of that, it's time for a temperature check."

I listened on the other side of the door as Donovan collected the thermometer. It beeped, and he said, "Thirty-seven Celsius."

"Send me a photo," I said.

"Molly..."

"I'm serious," I insisted. "Proof, please."

He sighed. "It's actually thirty-eight."

I quickly converted it on my phone. "That's a hundred degrees!"

"I'll take an aspirin." I heard the rattle of a pill bottle. "My throat is sore, but I feel fine otherwise. No breathing problems at all."

I chewed my lip. "If it gets worse, I'm going to make you go to the hospital."

"I promise I'll go if it gets worse," he said.

All day I felt helpless. Donovan was sick and there was almost nothing I could do. Bringing him Gatorade felt like too little.

For a distraction, I threw myself into my new pasta-making endeavor. I spent an hour cracking eggs and rolling dough on the counter in the kitchen. The next batch of spaghetti that night was better than before, but there was something off about it.

At lunch the next day I tried ravioli. I assumed it would be easier to make since it didn't need to be extruded like spaghetti, but it was much harder than I anticipated. I made the ravioli just fine, pressing down on the ends with a fork, but as soon as I dipped them in the pot of boiling water they fell apart.

That night I tried penne noodles. The dough felt *right* in my hands this time, and the noodles themselves looked downright normal when I dumped them in a strainer. I made a creamy vodka sauce to go with them, starting with a mixture from a jar and tweaking the amount of garlic and spices. I had to add three times as much salt as the recipe recommended because it didn't taste salty enough, but eventually I got it right.

"I *really* hope this batch turned out okay," I said after placing his bowl in the partition between our rooms. "But I want you to be brutally honest."

While waiting for him to try it, I had an idea. I went out to the balcony and eyed the gap. I couldn't carry pasta across, so I climbed over without it. I could eat it later.

I knocked on the glass door and waved. Donovan came over with a huge grin on his face. "You're a sight for sore eyes. I know I saw you yesterday, but I was too tired to *really* look at you."

I got a good look at him again. He was still ruggedly handsome, but his dark beard hadn't been trimmed in several days. There was a sunken look in his eyes. They were bloodshot, too.

"I'm happy to see you too," I said, "but you look like you need a shower."

"I'm trying a new tactic," he replied with a lopsided grin. "I figure if I get nice and stinky, it will scare the virus away. Where's your food?"

"I couldn't bring it over. I'll eat later. I just wanted to see you. Go on! Try yours."

He took a bite, chewed, and swallowed. "Holy shit. This is *good.*"

"You're just saying that."

"No, I mean it. The pasta is the perfect consistency."

"Are you sure there's enough salt?" I asked. "I kept adding salt and adding salt, but it didn't taste salty enough."

"I can't really taste the sauce," he admitted. "I'm going based off mouth feel. And it feels like something I made myself."

I squealed happily and did a little dance on the balcony. Donovan grinned at me and sat on the ground next to the glass.

"God I've missed you, Feisty."

"I've missed you! It's good to talk to *you*, and not to a wooden door."

I watched him eat as the sun drifted below the Colosseum to the west. There were a smattering of clouds in the sky, which made the sunset extra colorful. Like a Renaissance painter had swished his brush across the sky.

"This is like our first night together," Donovan said on the other side of the glass. "Remember?"

"I do. It feels like it was just yesterday... But it also feels like it was a year ago. Does that make sense?"

"Totally. The last month has felt like the longest of my life, but also the shortest."

I smiled while watching him finish his entire bowl. That was a good sign. He even sounded like he had more energy. Maybe he was starting to recover, fever be damned.

"Want some cookie dough?" I asked.

He put the empty bowl down and covered his belly with his hand. "I'm full. Couldn't possibly stomach another bite."

Donovan kissed his hand, then touched the glass. I copied the motion and pressed my fingers against his. My food was getting cold on the other balcony, but I didn't want the moment to end so I rested my back against the glass door. A moment later I felt him do the same thing. It was probably just my imagination, but I thought I could feel his warmth.

"Do you think we'll ever go home?" I asked.

"I don't know, Molly." There was a pause, and he said, "I have a confession to make."

I tensed. "Okay."

"I cheated at hide and seek."

I snorted. "I *know* you cheated. I saw the footage!"

"Yeah, but, like, I still get points for admitting it. Right?"

"We may only be a stone's throw from the Pope," I said, "but this isn't a Catholic confessional. You don't get points for admitting your hide-and-seek sins *after* you got caught."

"Aww."

My phone buzzed in my pocket. "Maybe that's my flight standby status. Fingers crossed..."

He turned around to look at me. "Yeah? What's it say?"

But it wasn't an email about a flight home. It was from an Italian address I didn't recognize. I opened it and scanned the body of the email. It was written in Italian, with an English translation below.

I gasped when I came across the important line:

TEST RESULT: POSITIVE

46

Molly
The Day I Got It, Too

"Molly?" Donovan asked. He stood up and pressed his hands against the glass door. "What is it? Molly? Talk to me."

"No, no, no," I moaned, shaking my head like I could dispel the news with sheer will alone. "I knew I couldn't taste the salt in the pasta, but I thought it was nothing. I didn't think it was because of *this...*"

"*Molly,*" Donovan said forcefully. "Talk."

I held up my phone with quivering fingers. "My test came back. I'm positive."

His mouth hung open. "Are you sure?"

"Yes."

"You're not translating it wrong or anything?"

"It's in Italian and English. There's a list of precautions for me to take, just like in the email you got. I have it, Donovan. I have the virus."

Saying it out loud made it more real. My bowels turned to liquid and my knees trembled. I felt lightheaded.

Suddenly the balcony door slid open, and Donovan's strong arms were surrounding me and holding me close. I exhaled into his broad chest as he hugged me fiercely.

"We can be together now," he whispered. "That's one silver lining."

"Once you shower," I said.

His chest rumbled with laughter. "That bad, huh?"

I looked up into his eyes and gave him a pitiful smile.

"I can manage that. Why don't you go eat your dinner? You need your strength."

We opened the dividing doors between our rooms and I slowly ate my pasta while the shower ran. Now that I knew I was infected, I couldn't stop analyzing my body's feelings. My throat wasn't sore at all. My eyes were achy, I guess. I was tired, but I assumed that was because I didn't get much sleep at the police station.

I ate half the bowl of pasta before I decided I needed to do something, *anything*, to take my mind off things.

Donovan's room was messy with clothes and dishes from the meals I had been sending him. I picked up his clothes, tossed them on the bed, then stripped the sheets. I carried that bundle downstairs to the laundry room and started a load, then brought back fresh sheets for the bed. After that, I began cleaning up the dishes.

While I tidied up, I thought about everything I had learned about the virus. Some people who contracted it only had mild symptoms. Others reacted *really* badly. There seemed to be no rhyme or reason to it, aside from age. Donovan and I had that on our side, at least.

But what if my symptoms weren't mild? Who would take care of Donovan if I was bedridden?

While putting fresh sheets on the bed, Donovan stepped out of the bathroom wearing only a towel. "You don't have to do that."

"I need to do something to feel in control." I smiled at him.

"It's hard not to jump your bones right now, you know."

He smiled weakly. "I don't have much energy, but I'll see what I can manage."

"That would be an embarrassing message on your tombstone. Here lies Donovan Russo. Rather than fighting off a deadly virus, he wasted his last energy having sex."

"I wouldn't say it would be a *waste*. There are worse ways to go, Feisty."

I went back downstairs to move the laundry to the dryer. This was an emergency, and I needed to prepare. What would my mom do if she were here? What would she tell me if I could call her on the phone, like I so desperately wished I could do?

I went into the kitchen and cooked the rest of the raw pasta I had made. Then I packed it into six plastic to-go containers and brought them back upstairs to store in Donovan's mini-fridge along with a few other supplies.

"We used to get blizzards back home, thanks to lake-effect snow rolling south," I explained when he asked what I was doing. "Mom would make a dozen peanut butter and jelly sandwiches, just in case we lost power. That's what I'm doing: making food in case we get too sick to leave the room. I brought oranges, too. We have seven left. Those are for me, but I *could* be convinced to share if you ask nicely."

"Molly..."

"Oh! I forgot to tell you: I made a Russo Pie earlier today! It was supposed to be a surprise after dinner, but I kind of forgot about it when I got my test results. It's downstairs if you want some. I think I nailed the recipe, but I want your opinion."

"That's great, but Molly..."

"I need to bring a bunch of Gatorades up here too. There are only eight bottles left downstairs, and we might as well keep them close."

"*Molly.*" Donovan grabbed me by the arms. "You need to slow down."

"I need to *do* something," I insisted. "Because if I'm not being productive, then I'm just... I'm just..."

He pulled me into another hug. "It's okay to feel things," he said softly. "You don't have to put on a strong face for me."

I realized that's what I had been doing. Running around in caregiver mode, putting on a strong face to keep Donovan from worrying. And to keep *myself* from accepting what was happening.

Once I let my guard down, the reality of the situation sank in. I was far from home. I was infected. I might get sick.

I might *die.*

I fell apart in his arms and wept. He held me close, stroking my hair and telling me it would be okay. His skin was warm from his fever, which made me cry even harder.

What if it isn't going to be okay?

We crawled into bed and fell asleep together. After a few days sleeping alone, I realized just how much I *needed* to be in his arms. It felt right.

I woke up the next morning with a sore throat, and a dry cough. I was also tired, like I hadn't slept well—even though I knew I had.

Donovan was still fast asleep. I felt his forehead to make sure his fever wasn't alarming, and then went downstairs to get the Gatorade that I hadn't retrieved last night. Hydrating was important. Most of the medical recommendations emphasized that. There wasn't a lot I could do about the virus, but drinking plenty of fluids was something.

I came back upstairs and put the Gatorade away. Donovan was still asleep in bed, sprawled out on his belly with the sheets tangled around his waist. Sunlight from the window reflected off his olive skin. Even while sick, it was impossible to ignore just how sexy this man was.

His phone vibrated on the kitchen counter. I glanced at it out of habit, and saw the beginning of an email notification.

STANDBY LIST REMINDER: Your flight from FCO to BOS is awaiting confirmation...

"That's not what my emails have said," I muttered. I picked up the phone and swiped it open. There was no passcode, and it opened straight to the relevant email.

I was only half-awake before, but as I scanned the email I quickly woke up. My eyes flew back and forth as the details sank in.

"Donovan," I said. "You got a flight back?"

He rolled over and rubbed his eye with a fist. "Huh?"

I sat on the edge of the bed. "You got an email from the standby list. You have a flight back to Boston!"

"I..." He sat up in bed and blinked away the sleep from his eyes. "What? That's, uh, awesome."

"It says you were selected from the waiting list _two weeks ago._"

"Oh." I saw the panic in his eyes as he tried to think of an excuse. He looked like he'd been caught.

"You could have gone home," I said, "but you chose not to?"

He let out a long sigh. "I got the email a while ago, yeah. And I was excited because I assumed you would be selected too. We're in the same city, so if there's a return flight for us to take, it only makes sense that both of us could go. But for some reason you weren't selected. They're processing applications slowly back home, for whatever reason. And I couldn't... I couldn't leave you here, Molly."

"That's sweet," I said, "but I can't believe you didn't take the flight! You can't just stay in Rome because of me."

"Sure I can," he said simply. "I don't have a job waiting for me

275

back home. It'll be a while before a chef position opens up. There's no point to me going home and doing nothing for months." He squeezed my thigh. "I want to be wherever you are, Feisty. Even if we're stuck in a hotel together. This feels more like home than my empty apartment, and it's because *you're* here."

We hugged, and tears welled in my eyes. I was feeling vulnerable and scared because of my positive test, and everything he had told me was exactly what I needed to hear. It mirrored how I felt about him. If I had gotten a return flight, I wasn't sure I would have left him.

"Hey. You don't feel hot anymore." I rested my cheek against his shoulder. "You feel normal."

"My fever must have broken," he said. "I feel okay, I guess. Still tired, but okay."

"If you had left two weeks ago," I pointed out, "you wouldn't have gotten infected."

"I don't care. I would suffer the worst virus in the world for you, Molly."

"Easy to say once you're feeling better."

He laughed and squeezed me tighter, and for a few moments I stopped worrying about everything. As long as I had Donovan, I felt safe.

47

Donovan
The Day I Took Care Of Her

I let Molly relax in bed and I went downstairs to make breakfast for us. I was still tired, but it felt good to walk around and stretch my legs. Maybe I was on the other side of the sickness.

"Knock on wood," I said to myself, rapping my knuckles on a wooden table in the restaurant on the way to the kitchen.

When I went inside, I frowned at what I saw. The kitchen was a *mess*. All the pasta machines were used and covered with flour. Bits of pasta dough were scattered on the counters, and there was a pile of used pots and pans in the sink.

Rather than get annoyed, I realized what this was evidence of. Molly had been working hard to make fresh pasta for me. She had tried, over and over again, until she made something halfway decent. And all for someone who had lost his sense of taste.

She did all of this for *me*.

"God, I love this woman," I said out loud. I decided then and there that I would go to the ends of the earth for her.

While making breakfast, I thought about my flight back. I was glad Molly had found out about it. Everything was out in the open now. No more secrets between us.

After breakfast, we napped some more. By the afternoon we found the energy to go down to the lounge and watch a movie. I brought the comforter from my bed so we could cuddle together on the couch.

We may have been sick, but at least we were sick *together*.

"I have a theory," she said in a raspy voice during the movie. "You intentionally got me sick so you wouldn't be alone."

"I'm the one who quarantined myself away," I pointed out. "You wanted to come take care of me, and I wouldn't let you."

"That was all a cover, for appearances," she replied. "You secretly wanted to infect me all along."

I sighed. "Okay, you caught me. While you were sleeping I breathed underneath your door, blowing all the infected particles into your room."

"I knew it!" she said weakly.

Molly's symptoms were worse than mine. In addition to fatigue and loss of taste, she had a sore throat that made it hard to talk. Then she developed a cough. At first it was like she was trying to clear her throat, but by nightfall it sounded like she was coughing up a lung.

The next morning she started throwing up.

She had two bites of buttered toast and one bite of scrambled eggs, then abruptly got up and ran to the bathroom. I followed her and held her hair while she vomited in the toilet.

"I don't know what came over me," she said while washing out her mouth in the sink. "I didn't even know vomiting was a symptom."

"Nausea is," I said. "I guess I was lucky I didn't get any of that."

Since she couldn't keep her breakfast down, at lunch I made her some tomato soup. I couldn't make it from scratch since we didn't

278

have fresh tomatoes, which annoyed me to no end, but Molly didn't seem to mind as she gently sipped on the soup.

"I actually can't taste anything," she said when I commented on it. "It tastes like thick water to me."

I was beginning to really worry about her, but I patted her leg and made myself smile. "I think you just found the secret to becoming a great chef. Only make food for sick people."

"You can start a restaurant with that as the... the..." She turned her head and coughed for ten seconds.

My smile wavered as I helped her eat.

I woke up in the middle of the night to use the bathroom, and when I crawled back in bed I realized Molly was shivering. Her forehead was on fire, so I covered her with spare blankets from the other room and then cuddled with her underneath them. I was sweating from the blankets and her furnace-like body, but Molly clung to me for dear life while whimpering in her sleep. I didn't dare leave her.

"I'm here," I whispered. "I'm not leaving your side until you get better."

The next day she got worse.

48

Donovan

The Day Things Got Worse

Molly was able to drink chicken broth without throwing it back up, but that was about it. She stayed in bed, shivering and coughing. Her temperature was thirty-eight Celsius, just over a hundred Fahrenheit.

"I... just... need... to sleep," she whispered after taking a few sips of Gatorade. "I'm so tired."

Even just getting those words out drained the remains of her energy, and she quickly fell back asleep.

I began doing research on what to do. Hospitals were still close to capacity, so they would only take people who were in *very* bad shape. Despite her fever and coughing, she still had no trouble breathing. She was a borderline case.

For my own part, I was recovering. My sense of taste was still gone, but my temperature was totally normal. I even had some of my energy back, although I was still more tired than usual. Compared to how I was a few days ago, I called that a win.

Throughout the day I sat next to the bed and listened to Molly sleep. Was that a wheeze I heard? Or a rasp? I couldn't be certain. It might have just been her arm moving under the covers.

Every few hours I made her sit up and drink something. "I had... a sexy dream... about you," she mumbled during one such break.

"Is that so?" I asked.

She sipped warm broth and nodded. "It was sexy. You were there. So was your penis."

"Me *and* my penis were there?" I asked. "Sounds like a party."

Molly nodded softly. Her eyes were bloodshot and watery. "I was there too. So was my vagina. You were *doing stuff* to it."

"Yeah?"

She handed me the bowl of broth and sighed back into the pillows. "It was nice. I'm going back there now. Bye bye."

I stroked her hair and said, "Sweet dreams, Feisty."

"Not... feisty... right now," she mumbled as sleep took her.

I did everything that was recommended. I kept her hydrated and gave her aspirin. Her fever broke and she tossed the covers off, then slept on the bare bed. Hours later the fever returned and she was shivering again.

I tried feeding her toast and jam that night. That was a mistake. It stayed down for about twenty seconds before she scrambled to the bathroom.

The next day, her fever was the highest it had been: thirty-eight point nine. That was the equivalent of one hundred and two Fahrenheit.

"That's it," I said while looking up the emergency number. "You're not getting better, Molly. It's time to take you to the hospital."

I dialed the number. When someone answered, I recited the words I had memorized from Google Translate: "Emergenza. Malata di virus." *Emergency. Sick with virus.*

My accent must have been terrible, because I was transferred to someone who spoke English.

281

"*Hello? What is emergency?*" they asked in a thick accent.

"My... Girlfriend is sick," I said. "She tested positive for the virus four days ago, and her symptoms are getting worse. She's coughing non-stop, her breathing is getting raspy, and she has a fever of a hundred—I mean, a fever of thirty-nine Celsius."

"*What is your location?*" she asked.

"We're at the Residencia Al Gladiatore hotel. In the Piazza del Colosseo. Her name is Molly Carter. She should be in the testing registry."

I heard typing on the other side. "*Yes. Very good. She is able to walk, yes?*"

I glanced at the bed. "The last time I fed her, she barely had enough strength to sit up in bed. Can you send an ambulance?"

"*Yes, ambulance, of course,*" she replied. "*Ambulance can arrive... Nine o'clock.*"

I glanced at my watch. "Ten minutes from now? Perfect. I can bring her downstairs if..."

"*No, no, no,*" the operator replied. "*Nine o'clock tonight.*"

"What?"

"*Very busy. Many sick.*"

After confirming her information and hanging up, I paced around the room. Molly's shivering was worse, and the aspirin wasn't breaking the fever. Her coughs were rougher and rougher, too.

I filled a bucket from the ice machine, soaked washcloths in it, then placed them on Molly's head. She seemed to relax more when I did that, so I swapped them out every ten minutes. The next time I took her temperature, the fever was a *little* bit lower.

But by noon her breathing was labored. I put my ear to her chest and listened. Her lungs made a crumpling sound with every breath, like a paper bag being rolled into a ball.

"I can't let you sit here any longer," I said to her. "You're getting worse. I don't know if we can wait until nine o'clock tonight, Molly."

Her eyes fluttered behind her closed lids, but she didn't respond otherwise. She hadn't been responsive in hours.

I got dressed and tried helping Molly out of bed. She didn't have enough strength to sit upright, and kept clinging to me while breathing heavily. There was no way she could walk on her own.

I pulled up a map on my phone. Celio Military Hospital, the one Molly had told me about when she took the test, was half a kilometer away. That was a long way to go with Molly, but I thought I could do it.

I *had* to. For her.

It took ten minutes to pull a pair of sweatpants and a fresh shirt onto Molly, and another five minutes to put her shoes on. Then I lifted her in my arms and carried her out of my room, down the hall, and into the elevator.

When I reached the lobby, I lowered Molly into a chair and paused to catch my breath. Even though I was feeling better than the other day, I still wasn't at a hundred percent.

"Half a kilometer," I said out loud. "No problem."

I checked the map on my phone to orient myself, since I wouldn't be able to check it when I was carrying Molly. Out the plaza, around to the right, then a straight shot down the road to the hospital.

Then I unlocked the front door and propped it open with a chair. I put a mask on Molly, then on myself. Finally I collected Molly in my arms, walked out the door, and kicked the chair behind me so the door would close.

Molly wrapped her arms around my neck while I walked. Despite how weak she was, and despite being barely conscious, she clung to me fiercely. Like she trusted me.

Like I'm her only hope, I thought.

The sun was high in the sky and the air was warm and pleasant.

In another context, it would have been a gorgeous day. But while carrying Molly, the woman I was quickly falling in love with, I couldn't enjoy the weather. All I felt was fear. Fear that I should have taken her to the hospital sooner. Fear that it might be too late.

I walked steadily, putting one foot in front of the other. Molly wasn't very heavy, but even carrying groceries was tough when you had to walk half a kilometer. My legs grew heavier with every step. Soon it felt like I was wearing lead boots.

My thighs burned painfully by the time I reached a plaza filled with tan-colored tents. This must be the testing site Molly had mentioned, which meant the hospital was the building just beyond it.

I trudged along, holding her in my arms, until a nurse or volunteer or other testing person came jogging up to me.

"Virus," I breathed. "Lei malata. She's sick."

She waved for another volunteer, a grey-haired woman with a pointed chin behind her face shield. "I speak English. How long has she been this way?"

"She had a fever and cough for several days. Today her breathing got bad. Can I take her to the hospital?" I nodded across the plaza.

The grey-haired woman shook her head. "Hospital full. Closed. No beds. She must go to Ospedale Britannico."

"How far is that?"

She pointed. "Too far. I will call for an ambulance."

I sat on a bench outside of what used to be a coffee shop, back when things were normal. The woman spoke with another volunteer. It looked like an argument. Finally the grey-haired woman threw up her hands and returned to me.

"An ambulance... It will take some time."

"How long?"

She shrugged. "I am not sure. Many ahead in line."

284

"What about a taxi? Or an Uber? Do you guys have Uber here?"

She winced. "Yes, for some. But if she is positive for virus..." She shook her head. "One moment. We have bed we can put her on."

"A bed inside the hospital?" I asked. "Where she can get treatment?"

"A bed outside. In plaza. Until ambulance arrives. Wait here please. I will bring it."

She went back to the tents.

I gazed down at Molly in my arms. She looked so pitiful and weak from this angle. Every breath she took came with a ghastly rasp. Like her soul was struggling to breathe.

Since we were sitting down, I shifted Molly in my lap and retrieved my phone. Ospedale Britannico was half a kilometer farther to the south-east. It was on the same road that was next to this plaza. All I had to do was follow it.

"I can't wait for an ambulance, Molly," I said. "I need to get you there sooner. Even if it kills me. Now's your chance to tell me not to."

She let out a little whimper and rested her head against my chest.

"Good. I wasn't going to listen anyway."

Standing back up took a lot more strength than I expected, and I damn near fell over. My legs were dead from the walk here. It was already the most activity I had done since I got sick. The urge to sit back on the bench and rest was overwhelming.

I made myself take one step toward the alley, then another. By the time I reached the main road I had some momentum.

Other pedestrians passed me on the street. Most gave me a wide berth. I couldn't blame them. One Italian man walked ahead of me, looked back at me, and stopped. Underneath his mask, he had the longest nose I had ever seen. It made his mask look like a tent.

285

He said something that sounded like he was asking if I needed help. I shook my head and said, "She's sick. Virus."

He gave me a pitying look, like he wished he could help me anyway, but then hurried along.

My legs grew numb from exhaustion. Sweat poured down my neck, and my arms began to ache too. I looked longingly at every bench I passed, but I knew if I sat down to take a break I wouldn't be able to stand up again. Besides, I didn't want to delay Molly's treatment. I could suffer a little longer if it meant getting her to the hospital.

She rolled her head to the side and her eyes opened a crack. "... playing... hide... seek," she muttered.

"Yeah, we're playing hide and seek," I said. "Ready or not, here I come."

Molly closed her eyes and smiled faintly, and mumbled something about cheating, and then fell back to sleep.

My legs burned. It felt like acid was pumping through my veins, not blood. I was winded, and couldn't catch my breath. Every step I took was a miracle.

The Ospedale Britannico came into view, surrounded by trees and gardens. That gave me a burst of energy, and I walked faster. My legs were numb and it felt like I was walking in someone else's body, but I kept pushing forward. Molly slumped in my arms. I could barely hold her anymore.

I reached the sliding glass doors of the entrance. As soon as the doors opened, I fell to my knees with exhaustion, but I managed to keep Molly from hitting the ground.

"Help!" I shouted. "She has the virus! Help me!"

Darkness crept around the edges of my vision. Nurses in full PPE ran toward me. It looked like they were running in slow-motion. That was strange. I lifted Molly higher in my arms, and they took her from me like she was precious cargo.

Then everything went black.

49

Molly

The Day I Woke Up

I dreamed that Donovan and I were playing hide and seek. First I hid in the walk-in freezer downstairs, and I shivered and turned into a block of ice before he found me. Then I blinked my eyes and I was suddenly standing over a pot of boiling water in the kitchen, holding my face over the steam like I was in a sauna. The steam was so hot it made my skin break out in sweat, so I stripped my clothes until I was comfortable.

Then, suddenly, I was in the freezer again. The sweat turned to ice on my arms and chest and my teeth chattered so loudly that it made my ears ache.

Then we were playing hide and seek outside, with the warm sun shining high above. Donovan told me I was cheating by being outside, but then I told him that *he* was the real cheater. He laughed, but it felt forced. He looked worried.

I remembered that he was sick, that I should be taking care of *him,* but I couldn't control my legs to get up and help him. I thrashed and screamed but it was like I was paralyzed, unable to move.

Then Donovan disappeared and I was being handled by lots of

different people, some with bright lights and some veiled in darkness. I tried to tell them that hide and seek was a solo sport, that they weren't allowed to help me or Donovan would call me a cheater again, but when I opened my mouth I couldn't seem to find my voice to say the words.

Then I slept, but I was in a different bed than the one in the hotel, and I hated it because Donovan's warm body wasn't cuddled against me.

I opened my eyes.

The first thing I noticed were the ceiling tiles. They were different than the ones I had memorized at the Residencia Al Gladiatore. There was a whiteboard on the wall across from me. Most of the words were Italian, but I recognized my name.

To my left, the window showed a dark sky. It was night.

To my right, Donovan was sitting in a chair that had been pulled over to the hospital bed. His head was slumped onto the edge of the bed, and he snored softly.

"Don..." I tried to speak but my throat was raw. I coughed a few times, which was even *more* painful.

Donovan leaped to his feet. "Molly! Let me get you some water..."

He filled a cup from a pitcher and placed it in front of me. There was a straw, which made it easy to sip. The water was cold and soothed my throat.

"More?"

He refilled the cup and I drank all of it again. I opened my mouth and this time it didn't hurt as much to speak.

"Donovan."

He leaned over me and caressed my cheek with his thumb. His dark hair was messy, and his beard was fuller than I remembered. His steel eyes were sunken into his handsome face with exhaustion, but he smiled broadly at me.

"Where am I?"

"Your condition got worse," he explained softly, still caressing my cheek. "Your fever got high, and you couldn't keep fluids down. Which is weird since vomiting isn't listed as a symptom anywhere. But it made things worse for you since you couldn't eat, and you started sleeping more. When your breathing started getting raspy... I had to do something. I brought you here. It's been a day and a half."

I smiled weakly. He looked so worried that I quickly tried to think of a joke. "It's a good thing Italy has universal healthcare. Otherwise I would hate to get the bill for an ambulance."

He smiled wryly. "The wait was too long for an ambulance. I brought you here."

I blinked in confusion. "But how..."

"I carried you."

"You carried me? All the way to the hospital by the testing site?"

"Well... It turns out that hospital was full. I had to carry you twice as far. We're at the Ospedale Britannico."

"Twice as... You carried me a kilometer?" I said groggily. "That's, like, a bunch of meters."

"A thousand of them, to be exact."

"How did you not pass out."

"I kind of did!" he said cheerfully. "I made it to the door before nurses took you. Then I woke up in the bed next to you, with an IV drip in my arm. They said I was dehydrated. I guess I was so worried about taking care of you at the hotel that I neglected myself."

I closed my eyes and chuckled softly. "You passed out from carrying me to the hospital. All I did was make you crappy pasta you couldn't taste."

He picked up my hand and kissed it softly. "Molly, it's all my fault. I must have gotten infected on my trip to the store. Then I got *you* infected. Carrying you here was the least I could do. If it wasn't for me, you wouldn't even be sick."

I found the remote control that operated the bed, and used it to raise the back until I was in an upright position. Then I took one of his wide hands in both of mine and squeezed it to my chest.

"Oh, Donovan. It's not your fault. You did everything you could to keep me safe. And you took amazing care of me. It's fuzzy, but I remember you making me drink Gatorade, and trying to feed me..."

I frowned as another memory came back to me.

"You got an email. From the wait list. You can go home. You can't stay here for me. No, don't shake your head, I don't want to hear it. You should get out of Rome while you can. If they'll let you."

He continued shaking his head, and a smile touched his lips. "That's the thing, Molly. Look." He picked up my phone from the table. "You got an email from the wait list yesterday. Your request was finally processed. You can book a flight home anytime! Well, not *any* time. We have to wait until it's been forty-eight hours after a negative virus test. But that should be soon. We're going home, Molly. We're finally going home."

It took several heartbeats for the words to sink in. Then cool, calming relief washed over me. The day we had been waiting for had finally come.

We could leave.

But my relief was quickly replaced by sadness. Leaving Rome meant leaving *him*, Donovan, the man who looked absolutely gorgeous even though he probably hadn't showered in several days. What was originally supposed to be a one-week trip had lasted almost two months, and yet I wasn't ready for it to be over.

I wasn't ready for *us* to be over.

"What's wrong?" he asked. He was still all smiles.

"Donovan..." I said. I struggled to think of the words to express

291

how I felt. "I..."

There was a courtesy knock on the open door, and then a white-coated doctor strode into the room. She was wearing a plastic face shield and a mask, and she had a big smile for me.

"She's awake!" the doctor said in very good English. "At long last, sleeping beauty has returned to us. It was a kiss from her prince, was it not?"

"The first nineteen kisses on her forehead didn't work, but I guess the twentieth did," Donovan replied.

"You are a lucky woman," the doctor told me, "to have such a devoted man. He did not leave your side since you arrived, I swear it. How are you feeling, Molly?"

"I feel... pretty good," I said. "My throat is really sore, and it hurts to talk. And I'm still exhausted."

The doctor read the numbers on one of the machines next to my bed, and nodded to herself. "You were fortunate. Your oxygen levels never became too low, so we did not need to connect you to a respirator. The intravenous drip was sufficient, and your body did the rest."

"That's good," I said.

"We drew additional blood this morning, and I hope you are no longer positive for the virus. If that is the case, and your condition continues improving, you may leave the hospital in two days time."

Donovan squeezed my hand and grinned. I smiled back at him.

The doctor flipped through two pages on her clipboard. "We do not think the fetus was affected by your respiratory issues or fever, but when you return home we recommend you begin taking a higher dose of prenatal vitamins."

Donovan suddenly stood up a little straighter.

"I'm sorry," I said to the doctor. "The what?"

The doctor blinked at me in confusion. "The fetus. This is the word in English, yes? You are with child. You are pregnant."

50

Molly

The Day I Learned I Was Pregnant

"Based on the hCG hormone in your bloodwork," the doctor explained, "you are quite pregnant! It is early, of course, and we have been too busy to perform any of the relevant tests, but at this time we have no reason to believe the virus has any effect on the gestation of a child. I will leave you to your doctor in America to take additional steps, although—as I said—a stronger dose of prenatal vitamins is a good first step. Do you have any questions for me?"

I stared at the doctor without really hearing her. A switch had flipped in my brain as soon as she said the word *fetus.*

I was pregnant.

My mind raced. It must have happened when my birth control ran out. We switched to condoms two days before the last pill, which was already a slight risk, but there was also the time we fooled around without a condom and Donovan pulled out...

My eyes swung to Donovan. His mouth hung open, and he was blinking rapidly. He looked like he was in shock.

Then he looked down at me. Our eyes met, and I held my breath while waiting for his reaction.

He gave me a huge face-splitting grin. The pure joy in his steel eyes was as genuine as could be. He wasn't just faking it for me.

My heart swelled with love. I squeezed his hand.

The doctor sighed. "My goodness. You were not aware. Of course. I, ah... I will give you two a moment alone." She dipped her head and left the room.

"That explains all the vomiting," Donovan said with a chuckle. "It wasn't the virus. It was morning sickness."

I folded my hands in my lap. "How do you feel about... I mean, do you really want... I don't know what I'm trying to ask."

Donovan sat on the edge of the bed and smiled down at me. "I'll be honest. I didn't expect for *this* to happen so soon. I always thought I'd be older. But when the doctor said those words just now? Something blossomed in my chest. I feel *happy*, Molly. Happier than I ever expected to be. As long as you do too, I mean. Maybe you..."

"I want this," I quickly said. "I really, really want this, and I didn't realize I did until just now."

"You're sure?" he insisted. "We're not rushing into things? We've only known each other like seven weeks..."

I shook my head and allowed my heart to speak for me. "We're not rushing into anything, Donovan. I've spent more time with you in the last two months than I've ever spent with anyone else. I feel like I've known you for *years*."

I reached up and caressed his hair, smoothing out the parts that were sticking up.

"Whatever else happens with us," I said, "I know that I want you to be the father of this child. I'm lucky, Donovan. I'm so, so, *so* lucky."

There were tears in his eyes as he hugged me, and kissed me on the forehead.

"Were you serious when you mentioned your friend finding me a job in Elkhart?" he asked.

"Yes!" I said. "I mean, I was serious at the time. Are you sure you want to come with me, though? We can try long-distance at first. And maybe I can move to Boston..."

"I want to come with you," he said. "My parents retired in Florida. There's nothing in Boston waiting for me. And even if there was, it wouldn't matter. I want to be where you are."

I rested my hand on my belly. "You're just saying that because you know I'm carrying your child."

"Nope. I swear."

"I don't believe you," I teased. "You cheat at hide-and-seek, after all."

Donovan took out his phone and swiped on the screen. "I booked my return flight on the waiting list. I'm not flying back to Logan. I'm flying to O'Hare."

He held out the screen so I could see.

"You did *what?*"

He frowned in confusion. "Was that not the right airport? I looked online and it said the easiest way to get to Elkhart is to fly into Chicago and drive to Indiana from there..."

"No, that's the right airport. I'm just surprised."

He rested his hand on top of mine on my belly. "See? This proves I want to be with you, regardless of the situation. You're stuck with me, Feisty. As long as your friend can get me a job, that is. I don't want to be a bum all day."

"You can be a bum as long as you make me breakfast, lunch, and dinner!" I said. "I'm eating for two now."

He kissed me and said, "Molly, I have something to tell you."

"Uh oh. First you knock me up, then you tell me your deep dark secret..."

He laughed and waved a hand. "I was going to say that... I love you. I love you, Molly. I know, it's nuts. We've been together less than

296

two months, but I know how I feel and I can't deny it—"

"I love you too!" I blurted out.

Donovan hesitated. "You don't have to say it just because I did."

"The last year has been really tough for me," I explained softly. "Since my parents died, I haven't felt like I have a home. I sold my parents' house. My apartment is big and lonely. I visit my friends, and they're supportive and loving, but it's all just temporary. But when I'm with you? I feel like I'm home again, no matter where we are. Whether it's the hospital, or Elkhart, or the Residencia Al Gladiatore hotel, I'm home whenever I'm with you."

"Damn, Feisty. That speech definitely trumps my *I love you*."

"Expressing our love isn't a competition," I said. "Although if it were, I'm sure you'd find a way to cheat."

He narrowed his eyes at me. "I'm never going to live that down, am I?"

"Nope!"

The doctors kept me in the hospital for two more days, just in case. Now that my condition wasn't as dire, I was moved to a larger room that I shared with about fifty other patients. It was cramped, but I still considered myself lucky. It could have been worse.

It could have been *so much* worse.

I replied to the standby email and got myself added to the same flight as Donovan. The timing worked out perfectly: the flight was scheduled for the evening when I was released, which was forty-eight hours since I'd had a negative test. Donovan and I were safe to fly.

"It feels so good to walk around!" I said when we finally left the hospital. "It's beautiful out. Rome really is gorgeous. Maybe we should stay longer."

"You're babbling," Donovan said while wrapping an arm around me.

"I can't help it. I'm excited! We should have sex."

Donovan laughed.

"I'm serious," I insisted. "I can't wait until we get back to the hotel. Let's find an alley to hide in so I can jump your bones."

"As appealing as that sounds, we're on a tight schedule," Donovan replied. "Our flight leaves in three hours. And we have to pack."

"Plenty of time!" I said.

He grinned over at me. "Well, I was sort of hoping you would use that time to take a shower. You've, uh, been in the hospital for a few days. And before that you were bedridden."

I pretended like I had been stabbed in the chest. "Ouch. Guess the honeymoon's over."

He leaned over and kissed my hair. "Love means being brutally honest sometimes. And I'm sure the other passengers on our twelve-hour flight will appreciate your hygiene."

"Good point."

When we got back to our rooms, we were greeted by a powerful, pungent smell. The containers from our last meal before leaving had been sitting out for several days now. It was a wonder the room wasn't filled with flies.

Donovan pulled out forty Euros from his wallet. He placed the bills on the nightstand. "This is the last cash I have on me. The maid who eventually has to clean our rooms deserves it."

Both of us took long showers in our rooms. Donovan spent a few minutes trimming his beard down so that he didn't look like a seventeenth-century pirate. Then we hastily gathered our belongings. It felt surreal to pack. Part of me had thought this day would never come.

"Molly?" Donovan called from the next room over. "Come here."

I found him on the balcony. He waved me over, and put his

298

arm around me.

"One final selfie before we go," he said, extending his phone and snapping a couple of photos.

"Wait," I said. "I have a better idea."

We ran up to the fifth floor and took the ladder to the roof. The view there was much better. Donovan wrapped an arm around me and took the photo. The sun was setting behind the Colosseum, casting long shadows across Rome.

"Our last Roman sunset," Donovan said, holding me close.

"Our last, *for now*," I said. "We'll come back someday. When everything's normal again."

"Forget that," Donovan said with a laugh. "The next time I come to Europe, I'm visiting Paris!"

We collected our suitcases and got into the elevator. Donovan laced his fingers into mine as the car began to move. Holding hands on the ride down, I felt sad to be leaving. It was an ending to something special.

But it was the beginning of something even better.

The door opened on the ground floor. We rolled our suitcases halfway across the lobby before we realized there was someone behind the front desk, bent over and rummaging through a drawer.

"Is that... The concierge?" Donovan asked.

The man suddenly stood up. He gasped when he saw us. "You two! You are still here? But we stopped the supply packages weeks ago!"

"We made do," Donovan said.

I handed him the key ring. "We had to use these to get in and out."

The concierge took the keys and scowled down at me. "You were instructed to remain in your rooms."

"Oh, we did," Donovan quickly said. "We only came out to do laundry, and to get food at the grocery store."

"That is all?" the concierge asked skeptically.

"That's it," I said. "We promise."

The door to the restaurant flew open and a man in a white apron stormed out. He aimed an accusatory finger at the two of us and spoke in passable English.

"WHAT HAVE YOU DONE TO MY BEAUTIFUL KITCHEN!"

51

Molly
The Day We Went Home

The flight home was only a quarter full, with the passengers spread out for safety. As soon as we reached our cruising altitude, Donovan got up from his seat and came over to sit next to me, and we spent the flight cuddling together.

Despite the nearly-empty plane, there was still a crying baby six rows behind us who made it impossible to sleep. Donovan didn't seem to mind, but it annoyed the heck out of me.

Then I remembered that I was pregnant. I was going to have one of those soon. The realization made me nervous, but excited, too. Especially since I was going to have it with Donovan.

We landed in O'Hare, collected our bags, and walked to where my car was parked. When I inserted my parking ticket into the machine at the exit, I almost had a heart attack.

"One thousand... Oh my God!"

Donovan leaned across me and squinted at the screen. "Fifty-one days times twenty bucks a day... Wow."

I opened my purse. "I'll go ahead and pay it now. Maybe we

301

can dispute it later by—"

Donovan opened the passenger door and ran in front of the car. He lifted the gate bar that was blocking our exit, pushing it up until it was vertical.

"What are you waiting for?" he said in a strained voice while holding the gate open.

I drove through, stopped so he could get back in, and then floored it. "Go go go!" Donovan shouted as we zoomed away.

"We're outlaws now," I said.

He nodded. "Quick, to the Indiana border!"

We laughed while racing away from the airport.

Donovan plugged the route into my GPS. "Two hours to Elkhart? Wow, you really do live in the middle of nowhere."

"Getting cold feet?" I teased.

"Yeah, I didn't really think this through. Pull over. I'll hitch-hike back to Boston."

He grinned widely as I shot him a glare.

"I don't have to become a Colts fan, do I?" he asked.

"We're about fifty percent Colts fans, fifty percent Bears. But you *do* have to root for Notre Dame."

He winced. "That might be a problem. My team is Boston College."

"We'll discuss this later," I said curtly. "Want to get dinner on the way home? There's an Italian place at the next exit."

Donovan rolled his eyes at me and said, "You know what? I'd kill for a cheeseburger."

"With fries," I agreed. "And a milkshake. Oh! What about *two* milkshakes?"

"You've got this whole pregnancy thing down," Donovan said.

"I could barely keep food down while I was sick with the

virus," I replied. "I'm eating to catch up, *and* eating for two!"

Elkhart was a quiet little town on the St. Joseph River, just east of South Bend. We drove straight to my apartment, carried our bags inside, and then crashed from exhaustion. I was *really* glad that I cleaned my apartment before leaving for Rome.

It was strange having someone else in my bed, but strange in a good way. Like the cold, empty apartment I'd been living in was finally a home.

The next morning Donovan woke me by kissing my neck. His lips moved down my chest, where he paused to appreciate my nipples for a few minutes, and then he eventually found his way between my legs. I closed my eyes and arched my back, savoring the way he worshipped me in bed.

After I came, he crawled back up to my lips and kissed me for awhile. Taking his time, like we had nowhere to be. Which I supposed was true. Then we made love slowly, carefully, *lovingly* while the sun gently rose in the window and filled my bedroom with sunshine and bliss.

We showered together, then drove to Elkhart's main street. Everything was shut down except the breakfast cafe on the corner, which was only open for to-go orders. It was a ghost town.

I parked in front of the store and got out. "This is it. *Nelly's Boutique*, the store my mom built herself."

"It's nice," Donovan said as we unlocked the door and went inside. "It has a lot more character than the big department stores. I can see why your mom loved it."

I sighed. "Yeah, me too."

He put an arm around my shoulder. "It'll be all right. As soon as the pandemic passes, you'll re-open and do fine. I promise."

I shook my head. "I had a lot of time to think while I was in the hospital. And on the flight home. This was my mom's store, not mine. I don't have any attachment to it, beyond guilt for my mom.

Now that she's gone I only have sad memories here. That won't change, no matter how hard I try to preserve the store. And it's just not successful without my mom's personal touch. I've decided to close the store."

Donovan pulled me into a hug, holding me tightly against his chest. I didn't understand why until I realized I was crying. He held me while I wept, rubbing my back while my tears soaked into his T-shirt.

"What are you going to do?" he asked.

I wiped my tears and gave him a brave smile. "Well, I own the building itself. The lockdown is the perfect time to renovate. And I have an idea of what I want to turn this place into."

He frowned. "What's that?"

When I told him, Donovan took me in his arms and spun me around the room.

52

Molly
The Day We Opened The Restaurant

We spent the summer renovating the store. Even after all the interest-free small-business loans, I had to take out a mortgage on the building to pay for everything. But it was worth it.

Knocking down interior walls was the fun part. Donovan was sexier than ever while wielding a sledgehammer, muscles bulging with every swing. He was only five minutes into the first wall knock-down before I jumped his bones and rode him there on the floor.

"Pregnancy hormones are a hell of a thing," I said afterward. "I keep bouncing between horny, worried, and hungry."

"I don't mind!" Donovan said while resting the sledgehammer against his shoulder. "When I'm done with this I'll pick up lunch from the cafe."

I swear, I could have made love to him again right then.

After all the internal walls were knocked down, we installed the kitchen. Donovan nervously instructed the delivery guys while they carried the industrial appliances through the building. When everything was installed, he rested his arms and head on the flat-top stove and smiled like he had never been happier. He spent the end of every day wiping down construction dust and dirt from the stainless-steel appliances with a micro-fiber cloth.

If he was half as caring for our child as he was for that kitchen, then he would be an amazing father.

We did most of the renovations ourselves, which took extra time but saved us money. We redid the floors and installed a fire-suppression system that was up to code. We painted the walls, and put up Italian landscape paintings. We bought tables and chairs from another restaurant that had gone out of business during the pandemic.

We made love on the floor, on the tables, and on every surface of the kitchen. Donovan made a joke about how we had to get it out of our system now, because we wouldn't want to get a health code violation once we opened.

For the Fourth of July, we took a road trip back to Boston to get Donovan's belongings and car. Sure enough, the diner he used to work at had permanently closed. Then we packed up his stuff into both cars.

"Thanks for not tossing all my stuff out on the curb," Donovan told his landlord. "Give me a few months and I'll pay back all the rent I missed."

"You don't owe me nothin'," the old man said. He was wearing a Red Sox mask. "Always paid your rent on time, and never complained when somethin' broke. Take care of yourselves. Send me a postcard."

The lockdown ended in July. Restaurants were allowed to open at half-capacity, and certain stores and bars could re-open.

But Donovan wasn't ready to open our restaurant. He spent all of August and September working on the menu. While I finished all the little details in the restaurant, he cooked food around the clock, tweaking recipes and throwing entire dishes out. He was like a composer working on his magnum opus.

I didn't mind because I got to be his taste tester. And now that I was nearing the end of my second trimester, I had a newfound appetite. Flatbread pizza, ground-lamb lasagna, veal osso bucco... I wolfed everything down and gave him my opinion.

I was also starting to show by this point. Every time I woke up and looked in the mirror it seemed like my belly was just a little more swollen than the night before.

"I still don't understand why you don't want to know," I told him one afternoon in the kitchen. He was coating two chicken breasts in breading while I sat and watched.

"It's more fun to wait," he said. "I want to find out when we're in the delivery room, and the doctor announces that it's a boy or girl."

"All right," I said. "But it just means that when he or she is born, you're going to have to re-paint the nursery."

"Green is a good neutral color." He gestured with the chicken breast. "There's going to be plenty of blue-or-pink clothes and toys in the baby's life. He or she won't need to have the walls of the nursery gendered too."

"It makes names difficult too," I pointed out.

"We'll come up with gender-neutral names." Donovan placed the chicken breast in a pan of oil, which immediately began sizzling. "Alex. Blake. Taylor. Jordan."

"I went to school with a guy named Jordan, and he was a huge asshole. Veto. And I don't like Blake because one of my exes had a *huge* crush on Blake Lively."

He glanced sideways at me. "Hmm. You wouldn't be saying that if the baby was a boy."

"Do you want to know the sex or not?"

"I don't! I just like analyzing your clues." He scratched his chin with the spatula. "It's totally a boy, isn't it?"

"If you keep pestering me I'm going to blurt it out," I warned.

By the end of September, Donovan had decided on a menu for opening night. My business degree helped me handle the logistics of supply delivery, and by the first week of October we were ready for our grand opening.

The two of us stood outside the restaurant. The name was written in cursive above the entranceway: *Solo Tu*. We took a selfie in front of it and then went inside.

"All the tables are prepped," I said, running down my checklist. "We have eight beers on tap, and sixteen different wines. You have all the food ingredients you need for tonight?"

"My sous-chefs are prepping them now," Donovan replied.

I nodded. In addition to Donovan himself, he had two station chefs and three sous-chefs working for him. We had one bartender, two bussers, and six servers working in the front-of-house. I didn't know what to do with myself tonight, so I was hostessing.

"You look dashing in your chef's uniform," I told him.

He gave a little bow. "And you look stunning in, uh, the front-of-house uniform."

"It's just black slacks and a blouse," I replied. "And I don't feel very sexy with this big bump."

Donovan laughed and kissed me on the forehead. "You've never been sexier. When we get home late tonight, I'm going to prove it in the bedroom."

"We'll see how much energy you have by then." I glanced at my watch. "Okay, it's time. Here we go!" I ceremonially flipped the sign by the front door from *CLOSED* to *OPEN*.

Donovan and I stood by the front door, gazing out at Elkhart's main street. There were eight street-parking spaces in front of the restaurant. All of them were empty.

Five minutes later, nothing had changed.

"It's fine," Donovan said. "It can take weeks to get up to normal speed. Especially with the pandemic happening. Lots of people aren't ready to eat indoors."

"That's why we have the outdoor patio," I replied. "And we've spent hundreds of dollars on ads in the local newspaper and on Facebook."

His hand rubbed my upper back. "It's opening night. We might not have many customers. Things might go wrong. That's okay. We'll go with the flow."

"We should have started with only five servers," I muttered. "Six is too many."

"Six is the right amount," he insisted. "Better to over-prepare."

Suddenly a car pulled into one of the spots in front of the restaurant. I slapped at Donovan's arm to get his attention. But when the people got out of the car, they weren't random customers. They were people I recognized.

"Andrea!" I said when the old manager for *Nelly's Boutique* came through the door. "You came!"

"Wouldn't miss it for the world! This is my boyfriend, Blake."

"Blake, nice name," Donovan said. He glanced sideways at me.

"Uh, thanks?" Blake replied.

Andrea approached me, then hesitated behind her mask and said, "Can I hug you? Is it safe?"

"We already had the virus, so hugs are safe." We embraced, and then I grabbed two menus from the hostess station. I cleared my throat and formally said, "Welcome to *Solo Tu!* Right this way to your table..."

By the time I returned to the front, there was another car parking. Before they could get out, four twenty-somethings walked by the restaurant, stopped, and then came inside.

"Better get to the back." Donovan gave me an eskimo kiss through our masks. "Good luck!"

"I don't need it—I've got the easy job. Good luck in the kitchen!"

I smiled as Donovan practically skipped back into the kitchen.

A steady trickle of customers arrived over the next hour. When the restaurant was a quarter full, I started to breathe easier. We could call that a successful first night.

Then one of my best friends came barging through the front door. "There she is, pregnant and glowing!" Sara exclaimed. Behind her followed Becky, Marisa, and Wanda. The four girls who were supposed to go to Rome with me.

We giggled and hugged. "You didn't have to come."

"Are you kidding? We weren't going to miss your big opening," Sara replied.

"I only came because I want to see this man I've been hearing so much about," Wanda said. "Where are you hiding him?"

"He's working in the kitchen."

"Tell him to get his cute butt out here," Sara insisted. "We want to see his *dumplings*."

The girls showered me with compliments about how wonderful I looked now that my baby bump was beginning to show. More customers were coming through the door so I led the girls to a table, then resumed my hostess duties.

Growing up, I had never felt like *Nelly's Boutique* was mine. It was mom's store, her pride and joy, and I was just a helper while I was there.

But this place, *Solo Tu?* Donovan and I had built it from the ground-up. We'd knocked out walls and painted and planned and fretted. The outer building may have been the same, but everything on the inside was different. And I had a strong desire to see it become successful. I welcomed every customer warmly and answered questions. I marked off tables on my hostess map with a highlighter to indicate which were occupied. Knowing this was *our* place made all the difference in the world.

And based on all the wine we were selling, I started feeling

310

hopeful about the profitability, too.

An hour after we opened, a middle-aged couple came through the door. The husband had the crew-cut look of a military man, and the wife had gorgeous dark hair and an olive-colored complexion that reminded me of the women I had seen in Italy.

The wife glanced down at my name tag. "Molly?"

"That's me!" I said cheerfully. "How many are in your party?"

The couple grinned at each other. "Just the two of us."

"Can we have a larger table?" the husband asked. He glanced at my belly and said, "We don't like to be cramped in those tiny booths."

"Not a problem." I gathered two menus and asked, "Is this a special occasion?"

The wife beamed at me behind her mask. "Just a happy night out. How far along are you, dear?"

"Six months," I said while leading them into the restaurant. "Just started my third trimester."

"Oh, that's so wonderful! I remember my pregnancy like it was yesterday. It was a delightful time."

"You hated it," the husband said. He smiled at me. "She hated it. Trust me."

"Oh shush." She smiled at me some more, eyes flicking down to my belly. "I'm sure your pregnancy is going just fine."

We reached their table and I placed their menus down. "Maggie will be your server. Tonight's special is steak pizzaiola, and..."

I trailed off as Donovan came out of the kitchen, weaving through the tables to reach me.

"Is something wrong?" I asked.

"Yeah, we have a huge problem," he said. "I haven't gotten to introduce you to my parents."

It took me a second to realize what he was saying.

I glanced down at the table. The lovely couple was grinning up at me with pride.

I gasped. "No."

"Mom, dad. This is her. This is Molly." He smiled warmly at me. "These are my parents, Herbert and Gloria."

"Come here, you!" Herbert—Donovan's dad—got up and wrapped his son in a big bear hug. I saw the resemblance now: the sharp nose, chiseled jawline, and the same dark hair but with a little salt sprinkled in.

"We're so happy to finally meet you," Gloria said while hugging me. "I can see why Donny fell in love."

"Donny?"

Donovan pointed at me. "Don't get any ideas."

I hugged Herbert and wiped tears from my eyes. That's why they kept glancing at my belly. Because their grandchild was inside. And to think I thought they were weirded out by a pregnant hostess.

"You don't need to order," Donovan told them, "because I know what I'm making both of you. Just sit down and enjoy the evening with Molly."

"I need to get back to the hostess station," I whispered.

"You will do no such thing," he replied. "That's why I insisted on *six* servers tonight. Zoey is handling the hostess duties now."

I glanced across the room and saw that Zoey was already behind the hostess podium, waving back at me happily.

"I've got to run," Donovan said. He kissed me, then kissed his mom on the cheek. "I'll sneak back out here when I get some free time."

I watched him rush back into the kitchen.

I smiled at the couple seated across from me. "I'm sorry, I'm just so overwhelmed," I said.

Gloria reached across the table and patted my hand. "It's not fair to be surprised like this. Meeting your boyfriend's parents for the first time. And you can't even drink to soothe your nerves!"

"I know!" I laughed.

"I needed a bottle of wine the first time I met Herb's parents," Gloria explained.

"My mother was a pill." Herbert leaned across the table. "I said we should come a week later, not on opening night. But Donovan insisted."

"I'm so happy you're here," I said. "Donovan said you might come visit for Christmas, but this is wonderful too."

They ordered a bottle of wine, and I sipped on water. Despite the pressure of the situation, the two of them were absolutely delightful. Sweet, and funny, and loving. I could feel how warm and welcoming they were towards me, a woman they barely knew. It was no wonder Donovan had turned out the way he had.

I kept glancing back at the hostess table, but Zoey had it covered. We were somewhere around half capacity now, too. Things were going well!

The server brought out our food some time later. Three bowls of angel hair pasta, with a creamy white sauce and slices of grilled chicken. Moments later Donovan came weaving through the restaurant toward us.

"Hot back there, son?" Herbert asked him.

Donovan wiped his forehead with a sleeve. "You know what they say about heat and kitchens."

I frowned down at my bowl. "What is this? I don't remember this being on the menu..."

"It's not on the menu," he said. "This was the very first meal I gave you. You said you were starving, and you traded me a bottle of wine for it."

"Oh! I remember now!" Memories flooded back to me and my heart swelled with love. "Donovan was cooking this in the room next to mine, and the smell drifted over to my room. It was the best meal I had ever eaten."

I saw motion to my left. Sara and the girls were two tables over, and Sara had pulled her phone out. She was discreetly taking a video of our table.

"You're embarrassing me," I told her. "Put that away. We don't need a video of our food coming out."

"She's not recording the food, Molly," Donovan said.

"What do you mean she's—"

When I turned around, Donovan's face was on my level. He was on the ground.

On one knee.

53

Donovan
The Day He Proposed

I had been a wreck all day. Talking to my parents and making sure their flight got in on time. Coordinating with Molly's friends behind her back. Mentally preparing myself for what I was going to do tonight in front of everyone.

Fortunately the grand opening gave me the cover I needed. Molly thought I was only nervous about that.

The ring burned a hole in my pocket all evening. I had to take it out of the box because otherwise a big, obvious bulge would stick out of my pocket, and I didn't feel like telling Molly that I was just happy to see her. While cooking in the kitchen, my hand kept drifting down to my hip to make sure it was still there. I was afraid it would fall out and end up in someone's carbonara.

Finally everything was in place. The special meal I had cooked them was picked up by one of the servers. I wiped my face with a cloth and walked out there, but I kept sweating. I had never been this nervous before in my life.

Sara was a good sport for offering to film the entire thing, and when I got to the table she flashed me a thumbs-up. Molly saw her do that though.

I guess there's no going back, I thought as I went to one knee. My mom clasped onto my dad's hand and they practically trembled with excitement.

Molly turned around. She must have been expecting me to still be standing, because she was gazing up into the air where my head had just been. Her eyes followed me down, confused. Then she looked at the ground and realized what was happening.

"Oh my God."

"Molly," I said in a shaky voice. Why was I so nervous? "The two months we spent together in Rome were the best of my life. Until we came back to Elkhart. *That* month was the best of my life. Then the month after that, and the month after that. Even this last month, with all the crazy preparations of opening the restaurant, was best of my life. *Every* month with you is better than the last. And I never want that to end."

The words were easy to say because they were true. They came from the heart. When I was in Rome I already loved Molly. But the past five months had convinced me that I wanted to spend the rest of my life with her.

"Oh my God," she whispered. "Oh my God, oh my God, oh my *God...*"

I reached into my pocket and pulled out the ring. "Through restaurant openings, and closings, and lake-effect snow, and even pandemics. I want to spend the rest of my life with you, Molly Carter. Only you."

My hands trembled as I held up the ring. "Will you marry—"

"YES I'LL MARRY YOU!" she shouted.

I slid the ring on her finger. One of her girlfriends at the other table cheered, and then the entire restaurant clapped along. Molly grabbed my face with both hands and kissed me while tears streamed down her face.

"It's not fair to propose to a pregnant woman!" she said while wiping her face. "This is the third time I've cried today and I'm running out of concealer!"

Our server opened a bottle of champagne—and a bottle of sparkling cider for Molly. I hugged my parents, and then they hugged my fiancée.

Fiancée. I liked the sound of that.

"We will never be able to replace your parents," mom said to Molly, holding her hands in hers. "But I hope you'll think of us as family, and I hope you'll be the daughter we never had."

The two of them hugged fiercely. "Look what you did, Gloria. She's crying again."

"So am I!" she snapped. "Why aren't you?"

Dad hugged me and said, "Proud of you, son. For her, and for all of this." He gestured around the room.

"Thanks, dad," I said. "It's been a weird year, and I've been luckier than most."

I went back to the kitchen, where the chefs were all waiting to clap me on the shoulder and congratulate me. I felt weightless as I worked through my orders, floating from station to station.

The next time I had a short break, everyone was eating Russo Pie at the table. "This is good," mom told me. "Almost as good as I make it."

"I don't know," Molly said with a smile. "Donovan's is pretty good."

"Molly told us the sex of our grandchild!" dad said. "I can't believe—"

"La la la!" I stuck my fingers in my ears. "I can't hear! I can't hear!"

Molly's friends had finished their meal and came over to hug her and say goodbye. "Sara, Becky, Wanda, Marisa, allow me to

317

introduce you to my fiancé: Donovan Russo."

"It's not fair," Wanda, the redhead, said. "We missed out on the trip, and Molly came home with a gorgeous hunk."

"Did you really carry her three miles to the hospital?" Sara asked.

"It was *six* miles," I said casually. "Uphill the entire way."

Molly rolled her eyes. "The distance gets longer every time you tell that story."

"It was storming too," I added. "The worst thunderstorm to hit Rome in a thousand years. There I was, carrying Molly in my arms while lightning crashed..."

I trailed off as I saw one of the other chefs waving at me from the kitchen.

"I'll tell you all the story another time. I have to get back to it."

"Can't you take tonight off, Donny?" mom asked me. "I hate to see you work so hard, especially when you should be celebrating..."

"I'm not working, mom," I said. "I'm doing what I love."

"It was only a kilometer away," I heard Molly say as I left. "But he was weak from the virus. He actually passed out the moment he handed me off to the nurses..."

I smiled with pride as I returned to the kitchen.

My kitchen.

Epilogue

Molly
The Day We Got Married

We went down to the courthouse the next day. With the pandemic still in full swing, we were happy to settle for saying our vows in a small group. Maybe when things were back to normal we could have a bigger gathering with friends. I'd be able to fit into a wedding dress then, too.

Herb and Gloria came down to the courthouse with us. We were happy to have them as our witnesses. Gloria was a sniffling mess before we even started, and she had to keep lowering her mask so she could blow her nose.

Donovan and I stood in front of the Justice of the Peace. He looked dashing in a black suit, with his hair combed back and his beard trimmed thin. The Justice was wearing a mask with the Indiana state flag on it, a gold torch surrounded by gold stars on a field of blue.

"You may remove your masks for the ceremony," The Justice said.

"Oh!" Donovan suddenly said. "I almost forgot. Be right back."

He ran out of the room.

"Did I just get left at the altar?" I asked.

"It happens more often than you would expect," the Justice of the Peace said.

"Stop scaring the bride," Herb growled at the man. "My son said he would be right back, which means he'll be *right back.*"

Donovan came running back into the room with something in his hand. He placed the object on the chair next to Gloria and Herb.

It was a framed photograph of my parents on their wedding day, with my mother's long white dress trailing behind her.

"Donovan..." I whispered.

"I grabbed it from your dining room," he told me. "Is that okay? I wanted them to be here for—"

I threw my arms around him. "It's perfect. *You're* perfect. Marry me, damnit."

He squeezed my hand and we turned to the Justice. "I don't want to live another minute without being married to this woman. We're ready."

The Justice cleared his throat. "Donovan, please repeat after me..."

The Justice said the words first, but I was totally focused on Donovan Russo, the man smiling down at me, the man who I was about to marry.

"I, Donovan Russo, in the presence of these witnesses, do take you, Molly Carter, to be my lawful wedded wife. To have and to hold, from this day forward, for better, for worse, for richer, for poorer, in sickness and in health, to love and to cherish, until death do us part."

He slid a wedding band onto my finger until it touched the engagement ring. I waggled my fingers, testing how it felt.

The Justice gestured to me. "Molly Carter, please repeat after me..."

I had imagined this day my entire life. I always thought I

320

would be a crying mess on my wedding day, but as I looked up at the man I loved, the father of the child growing inside of me, my voice was steady and confident.

"I, Molly Carter, in the presence of these witnesses, do take you, Donovan Russo, to be my lawful wedded husband. To have and to hold, from this day forward, for better, for worse, for richer, for poorer. In *pandemic* and in health, to love and to cherish, until death do us part."

Donovan chuckled at my word change while I slid his wedding band on.

"By joining hands," the Justice said, "you are consenting to be bound together as husband and wife. By the authority vested in me by the laws of the state of Indiana, I now pronounce you husband and wife."

Gloria let out a loud wail, and was promptly shushed by her husband.

Donovan took me in his arms and kissed me. It reminded me of that first kiss we shared on the balcony in Rome, when we were just two strangers looking to each other for support during a crisis. It reminded me of the first kiss we shared when I was released from the hospital. It was so much like the kiss Donovan surprised me with while we were renovating the store.

Every kiss had been different, but they had all contained the same amount of warmth, passion, and love. A love that I knew would never fade.

Donovan suddenly dipped me. It felt like I was falling until his strong hand held me a foot off the ground, with him leaning down at me, smiling.

"Careful with her!" Herb suddenly scolded. "She's carrying my grandchild!"

"I'll always be careful with you," he whispered, for my ears only. "Except for the times you want me to be rougher."

321

I beamed at him, and we kissed once more before he raised me back up.

"I have the tremendous honor," the Justice continued, "to introduce Mr. and Mrs..."

"Oh, not yet!" I said. "I'm not taking his name for a while. Not because I don't want to! It's because we own a business, and everything is in my name, and we *definitely* don't want to deal with the hassle of changing everything over right now. We'll wait until we're more settled."

"Don't care," Donovan said. "You're Mrs. Russo to me."

Mrs. Russo. I did like the sound of that.

"Okay, enough celebrating," I said. "Time to get back to the restaurant."

"Can't you take the day off?!" Gloria said. "You've been married for thirty seconds and you're already jumping back to work."

"We don't open until four," Donovan told me. "We can get brunch with my parents before we head back."

"Okay, we'll get a quick brunch," I allowed. "But then I want to head to the restaurant. Opening night was more packed than I expected, so I need to schedule the extra servers we talked about, and order more raw food supplies. Not to mention reevaluate the Cost of Goods Sold ratio on the wine, which I think we can tweak..."

"My feisty wife has a business degree," Donovan said, "and she never lets me forget it."

I grinned at him. "You just called me your wife."

"Get used to it, because I'm going to be calling you that a lot, *wife.*" He held out his finger. "I like how this feels."

"You'd better, *husband!*"

Donovan's parents stayed for a week. It was actually really helpful because while Donovan and I were at the restaurant constantly, they helped with other things around my apartment. Preparing the nursery, stocking up on diapers and wet-naps and other supplies, and even taking my car to get inspected before the sticker expired. Gloria and I spent a lot of time together, chatting about how fussy Donovan was as a baby, and the tips and tricks she used to get him to sleep.

"Oh, he *always* cheated at hide-and-seek," she revealed one morning. "He peeked through his fingers to watch where we would hide!"

"Don't believe a word that woman says," Donovan called from the kitchen. "I am, and have always been, a perfect little angel."

Gloria and I glanced at each other, then fell into a fit of giggles.

By the time they left, I was really sad to see them go. I realized I was one of the lucky women who actually *liked* her in-laws.

They could never replace my parents. No one could. But the way they welcomed me into their family, it did a pretty good job of filling the emotional hole in my heart.

The first week at *Solo Tu* was a resounding success, and it never slowed down. As the pandemic began to fade away and the lockdown restrictions were eased, people were eager to return to their normal lives. Going out, eating at restaurants, socializing with friends and family.

One of the first things I had learned in business school was that businesses were rarely profitable the first year they opened. But against all odds, *Solo Tu* turned a profit the first month—even with all the small-business loans we needed to pay back.

Neither of us could believe it. We felt like we were living in a dream, and we would wake up at any moment.

The days ran together and time flew by. We worked at the restaurant non-stop, but it was more fulfilling than any job I'd ever had. I had my check-ups at the doctor, and everything with the baby looked totally normal. The virus hadn't affected its growth at all in those first few weeks.

And pregnancy sex? *Way* better than I expected. Even though I felt about as sexy as a beach ball, Donovan couldn't keep his hands off me. We probably had just as much sex in my third trimester as we did when we were in Rome.

We hosted a Halloween party at the restaurant, and gave away bottles of wine to the customers with the best costumes. I dressed as a gumball machine, with my pregnant belly as the big glass gumball container. Donovan dressed like the Swedish Chef from The Muppets, with bushy red eyebrows and a thick red mustache, and ran around the restaurant while waving a rolling pin and shouting Swedish-sounding words at everyone.

We closed the restaurant on Thanksgiving, but not before preparing five hundred turkey dinners to deliver to the homeless shelters in Elkhart and South Bend. Donovan cooked a turkey in our apartment, and accidentally burned it to a crisp by hitting the *broil* button instead of *bake*.

"Don't you do this for a living?" I teased while he pulled the black bird out of the oven. "Or do you let the sous-chefs do all the work in the kitchen?"

"I don't like your kitchen," he grumbled. "I prefer the one at the restaurant. I can't believe I ruined Thanksgiving..."

I wrapped my arms around him and kissed his back. "You're allowed to screw up every now and then. I don't mind filling up on mashed potatoes and stuffing!"

Donovan's parents came to visit for Christmas. We closed the restaurant on Christmas Eve and Christmas Day, which gave us plenty of time to relax at home with them.

Donovan cooked another turkey. This one turned out perfect—crispy on the outside with juicy meat on the inside.

"I'm just saying, next year *you* should visit *us* for the holidays," Herb said over dinner. "We moved to Florida to get *away* from the snow. Not to chase it."

"They'll have the baby, Herb," Gloria scolded.

"We traveled with Donny when he was that age. He did fine."

"He cried on every single plane ride," she said dryly. "You didn't notice because you put earplugs in and went to sleep until we landed."

I gave Donovan a warning look.

"I promise to be *very* helpful with the baby," he said. "I'll be the dad walking his baby up and down the aisle to get it to go to sleep."

"We appreciate you visiting," I said. "With the restaurant and everything, it would have been tough to fly down to Florida. And the next time you visit, we'll have a larger place."

"Yeah? You're thinking of buying a house?" Herb asked.

"We've started looking," Donovan said. "The restaurant is booming, and the lease on this place expires in May. By then we'll want more room for the baby."

"I think it's *wonderful*," Gloria said, grinning at me. "How many bedrooms?"

"We want three beds, two baths," I said. "That gives us a nursery and a guest bedroom. So you can stay with us when you visit, rather than getting a hotel."

"I think it's a lot," Herb said while chewing on a piece of turkey. "The four most stressful events in my life were getting married, starting a new job, having a baby, and buying a house. You two are doing all four at once."

Donovan winked at me and said, "Marrying Molly was the easiest thing I've ever done. I'm sure the rest will be just as easy."

After dinner we gathered around our fake Christmas tree next to the fire. I played Christmas music out of my phone while we exchanged presents.

"These presents are for the baby," Gloria said while handing Donovan a big box.

"Mom, there's a dozen presents in here!"

"That's just to start," she said firmly. "It's my God-given right to spoil my first grandchild. Hold on. You can't open any of these until after the baby is born."

"Why not?" I asked.

"Because *somebody* insists on waiting until the baby is born to know the sex." Gloria rolled her eyes and handed her son a box. "This is the only baby gift you can open."

Donovan tore open the wrapping. "It's no fun giving us all these presents and making us wait until January to open them."

I leaned against him and rested my hand on my swollen belly. "Might not be that long. My due date is still ten days away but I feel like I'm ready to pop!"

Donovan finished unwrapping the gift and removed the lid on the box. "Baby clothes! What is this, a little chef outfit..."

Gloria gasped. "That's the wrong gift! You're not supposed to—"

Donovan held up the clothes. It was a onesie for a six-month-old, white like a chef uniform, with a hoodie that was shaped like a floppy chef hat. It was absolutely adorable, and my heart swelled with happiness at the sight.

And then I saw the words stitched onto the breast in blue thread:

CHEF'S SON

"Oh, for pete's sake," Herb mumbled. "I must have wrapped the wrong box..."

Donovan's grey eyes were wide as he stared at the onesie. He lowered it and looked at his parents. "Son? I'm going to have a son?" He turned to me. "It's a boy?"

I cringed and nodded slowly. "I'm so sorry the surprise was

326

spoiled..."

Tears welled in his eyes and he suddenly hugged me fiercely. "A boy! I'm having a boy!"

"*We're* having a boy," I said.

"You're not upset?" Gloria asked.

Donovan jumped up and hugged her. "Why would I be upset? I'm having a boy!" He hugged his dad next. "I'm going to have a son!"

"*We're* having a son," I corrected. "I guess now is a good time to tell you the name I settled on."

He froze. "What name?"

I stood up on unsteady legs. Being pregnant was murder on my back. "I know it's cliché to name children after the place they were conceived, but in this case I really like the idea of—"

"ROMAN!" Donovan suddenly blurted out. "I think that's the perfect name!"

"Really? You think so?" I asked.

He hugged me and gave me a long kiss. "I know so. Roman Russo."

I grinned. "I like the sound of that."

"And you know what the best part of all this is?" he asked. "Now we don't have to wait until the baby's born to open this huge pile of presents!"

Gloria rolled her eyes and stood. "Who wants Russo Pie?"

Donovan and I laughed while opening all the baby gifts in front of the Christmas tree, both of us happier than we ever thought we could be.

Bonus Scene

Still craving some quarantine love? Want to know what Molly and Donovan are up to a few years in the future? Click the link below (or type it into a browser) to receive a special bonus chapter that was cut from the original book. It's extra sappy and extra sweet!

www.ktquinn.com/bonus

K.T. Quinn is a romance writer living in Fort Worth, Texas with her husband and two German Shepherds. She also writes romance under the pen name Cassie Cole.

Books by
K.T. Quinn

Only You

Make You Mine

Yours Forever

Printed in Great Britain
by Amazon

66630162R00190